REASON TO FEAR

THE EARTHBURST SAGA: BOOK 5

CRAIG A. FALCONER

Reason To Fear

ISBN: 9798854717977

1

Aliens.

I heard the word as it left Major's mouth, but that doesn't mean I can make any sense of it.

I've been unconscious in the Vita's medical bay for one day, and I've woken up in a world where aliens exist.

And hell… if what Major is telling me is true, they don't just exist. They're *talking* to us.

"It's a lot to take in, Ray," Major acknowledges. "Especially in your condition. I can only imagine. But like I said, the main thing is that everyone survived yesterday's sabotage attack and your family is safely back on Earth. I know it doesn't feel like it right now, but humanity could be in a better position now than we were before the virus attack."

I narrow my eyes, which have more or less adjusted to the bright overhead lights. I'm starting to wonder if my *ears* need to adjust, too, though, because I'm struggling to see many positives that would justify thinking we're in a better position than we were.

"For one thing, the virus that took hold of the station has been decisively neutralized and arrests have already been made," Major continues. I think he's sensed from my expression that some explanation is needed. "Our security systems have been reinforced, but it's important to remember that this was a freak event. The virus took advantage of our momentary security downtime when the alien signal overwhelmed our core systems, and it took hold during the automatic system reboot. But that's in the past."

"Yesterday's problem," I agree with a nod that takes more effort than it should.

Beyond the usual platitudes of '*look to the future*' or '*don't cry over spilled milk*', decoding this signal really *does* demand our total focus. That's far more important than rehashing how we ended up receiving it.

Everything that happened is slowly coming back to me now. Given the strength of the blast my hand bore the brunt of, I should probably feel grateful that it's the only thing I've lost.

It's hard to feel grateful looking down at a stumped wrist, though. They must have me on some serious painkillers.

"Yesterday's problem indeed," Major says. "Profit-at-all-costs corporate infiltrators like those scoundrels from the mining conglomerate are one thing, but the Anomaly is something else. The Anomaly is the problem we have to solve — and fast. Our hope is that there is a solution inside this signal. If we can decode it and make sense of the message, we're hopeful it's going to be related to the problems we're facing."

I can't hide my confusion. "But if this really is a radio signal from Bayzen, it has to be at least four years old," I tell him. "That's how long it would take to reach us. You must know that."

Major shrugs. "Obviously. But Shaun and Sasha and our other analysts have suggested all kinds of scenarios, even in the very short time we've known of this. One is that aliens from Bayzen might have been trying to warn us about some kind of dangerous celestial event or phenomenon for a long time, since they became aware of its threat to us. You have to remember, Ray: the Anomaly's effects are getting worse, and they've been getting worse for a long time. We have no idea what causes them or even any idea about the nature of the whole thing. But for all we know, the dangerous power of whatever the source is could have been getting worse for years — even decades. Maybe the Anomaly only became apparent to us when it reached a tipping point. And maybe if we'd picked up this alien signal a long time ago, we could have already developed some mitigations or solutions."

Listening carefully as Major makes a surprising amount of sense, I bring my left hand to my nose and scratch an irritating itch.

All kinds of wires are connected to me, but the weirdest thing is not being able to use my right hand. More to the point, the weirdest thing is no longer *having* a right hand.

To say that will take some getting used to would be one hell of an understatement.

"Think of some problem with your house," Major goes on. "Imagine that from his vantage point next door, your neighbor notices some termite activity. Maybe he has heat-sensitive security cameras or something like that — you know, an advanced technology that makes him aware of the problem before you are. Because from the inside of the house, you're probably not going to notice anything until it's too late. But if your neighbor gets the message to you in time, you can do something about it. I'm not saying it's a perfect analogy, Ray, or even a very good one. But the point is that sometimes a problem can be seen by one party before its effects become obvious to everyone. Our neighbor might have been yelling over the wall for years, but we didn't hear him because our windows have been closed. Until those powerful new PFOA telescopes launched yesterday and started listening in the right direction, our windows have been closed."

I think Major deserves some credit for saving his metaphor there, and I actually see quite a lot of merit in it. Our new Poly-Field Observation Array really *has* already changed the game, too.

"I know you were groggy when you woke up," he continues, "but you do remember what I told you about the radiation, don't you? One of our Bayzen-facing PFOA telescopes picked up the signal coming from there. But maybe just as importantly, another one pointing elsewhere has found an invisible source of radiation — far too close for comfort — that's like nothing we've ever seen. We think *that* is the Anomaly, whatever it actually is. We think there *is* some kind of physical and observable cause to this, so while we're working to decode the signal we're also working to analyze this radiation source. It could be a natural celestial phenomenon the aliens are trying to warn us about, or it could be something alien that they're trying to explain. We just don't know yet. We can be optimistic or we can be fatalistic, but Shaun is the one who has told me we have to stay pragmatic and remember that whatever the radiation source is, the aliens are reaching out to us."

"So you think the signal is a warning message?" I ask. "And Shaun thinks that, too?"

Major upturns his palms. "There are any number of possible scenarios, but I think it makes as much sense as anything else. Shaun put it like this: if they were hostile, why would they be talking to us?"

Hmm. I'll admit that the idea of these message-sending aliens being *helpful* hadn't crossed my mind in the first few minutes of knowing they exist.

I think our brains are wired that way. Surviving in the state of nature — that jungle of chaos we evolved out of — demands constant vigilance to potential threats.

Sure, the cracking of a twig could come from a harmless bird pecking around for fallen fruit. But it could also come from the tiptoeing of a tiger with its eyes on its prize. That's why our heads shoot round in reaction to any sudden sounds or movements.

And as evolved as we like to think we are, that survival instinct is still there. It can still serve us well, too, but sometimes we have to temper it with the rationality and reasoning that sets us apart from the animals we left behind.

Shaun's point about the unlikeliness of hostility ties into this, too. Because if a tiger is coming for me, I'm dead before I see it coming. I might hear that twig cracking as the beast starts to bound and pounce my way, but he's not going to roar from behind the trees first to let me know he's there.

As soon as that point is in my mind, which is still fighting its way back to full clarity after the physical trauma and the medicinal haze it's faced, I really think Shaun is right about it.

Tigers don't roar before they pounce.

Robbers don't call ahead.

And as much as I know we can't confidently ascribe human psychology to an extraterrestrial race, I just don't see why hostile aliens would send a targeted signal to let us know they exist.

At least, that's the hope I'm clinging onto...

2

"Is there any progress on decoding the signal?" I ask. "The Balena team has the data, too, right? With their AI language systems, it has to be possible in a short timeframe, doesn't it?"

Major exhales slowly. "They have it, yes. But the answer to your bigger question is no… this is all very new, and there's no progress to speak of yet. My understanding is that we're not yet at the stage of trying to translate a message. We're decoding a signal, as I understand it. And Shaun has told me the signal isn't just alien in source, but alien in nature. There is a huge amount of data that is categorically not random noise, but so far we haven't been able to discern any kind of structure or, well, anything. But the Balena's team *is* working on it, Ray. We are, too."

"So who exactly is still here on the Vita?" I push. Major mentioned a few names as soon as I came around, but my brain was still waking up and some more explosive information has taken center stage since then.

"Well, all of the civilians are gone," he says. "The little girl you saved, your family, Vicki, even my logistics administrators. Everyone had the choice to leave, given that we couldn't be entirely sure the Vita was safe. We've had a full sweep of all physical spaces and digital systems, but we hadn't when the evacuation craft left for Earth. Civilians were *forced* to leave. Like I told you, I did what I thought you would want and insisted that your family returned to solid ground. I sent Vicki, too, to help with the bird. And believe me, Scarlet did *not* want to leave him behind. He was more insistent than anyone that you would want them to go, though. He didn't want to leave you, obviously, but he knew you would want him to."

I nod. We all owe Laika a lot, all over again, and the little guy was damn right in his assessment that I would prefer for my family to be safe on solid ground without me than by my side on this potentially insecure spacecraft-cum-station.

"We're down to the real bare bones," Major continues. "The only individuals you don't know are the healthcare staff and some senior members of our system maintenance team, each of whom I know personally and will vouch for with my life. Shaun wanted to stay, obviously, and it goes without saying that Driver wouldn't leave you like this."

That really would go without saying, but I'm glad to hear it nonetheless.

Driver has come a long way since we met, and from the very start I knew that her personal history had instilled a "no man left behind" ethos that nothing could challenge.

Sure, she has a higher guard than anyone I've ever known, but once you're inside the walls she's built, you are *in*. She's shown that time and again in the highest-stakes and highest-risk situations we've ever been in, from the bottom of the ocean to surface of the Moon. That's Driver for you.

Hell, she would try to wrestle my skull from the tiger's jaw before she ran away to save herself.

"Chester stayed, too," Major says.

That one I'm *less* enthused about. I remember now that Major did already mention him when I first woke up, during my haziest moments.

Sure, Chester ended up making himself useful in our mad scramble to save the Vita from the explosive sabotage plan that cost me my hand, but I have a hard time understanding why Major expects me to trust the guy.

After all, for all he explained that he had been used as a pawn, Chester's lies were the reason I came to the Vita. He's a fast-talking PR man and he tricked me into bringing my family here. Sure, I believe that he didn't know why his paymasters wanted me here, because they left *him* in harm's way, too. But he still lied and earned his spot as the first and only guy I've ever punched in my adult life.

"What's done is done," Major says, reading my face. "You and I had our issues back in the day, and look at us now. I wouldn't necessarily trust Chester in every situation, but he's in this with us, Ray. He has a family on Earth that he wants to protect, too, and I happen to think he could be very useful. When someone is as skilled in persuasion as Chester is, sometimes it's good to have them on your side. These are delicate issues we're dealing with and they could cause chaos on Earth if we don't manage the message. I think we'd all agree that Shaun is the smartest guy we have, but Chester has a different level of social intelligence that can be harnessed for good. Driver has certainly taken to him, too."

"Driver has *fallen* for him," I say. "There's a difference. And anyway, what about the person you haven't mentioned yet? You know, the one who was secretly synthesizing a theocite analog, as if the natural material I enriched wasn't dangerously potent enough? The one whose creation blew off my hand and nearly blew up this whole station?"

"I take full responsibility for sanctioning Simone's research," Major says. "She didn't deceive anyone and she didn't break any protocols."

Sure, maybe she didn't break any protocols. And maybe she didn't deceive anyone or give any reason for us to distrust her character. Maybe she really is well-intentioned, but still... I'll be damned if I trust her judgment.

"So Simone is still here?" I ask, reading between the lines.

He nods. "I wanted her here to keep an eye on everything

in her lab, just in case — somehow — the virus could execute any other activity. Shaun and the systems teams ensure me that it absolutely can't, but I won't take any risks. She was more than willing to stay, because she feels terribly responsible for what happened."

"As she should," I grunt.

"Ray..." Major sighs. "Was Simone really doing anything more inherently dangerous here than the work you were doing on the Beacon? You inspired her. Your theocite discoveries pushed her on to create synthocite, so we wouldn't have to keep mining for it and risking any more problems on Earth. She's absolutely broken up about the trouble it caused, and especially that *you're* the one who paid the biggest price."

I say nothing.

"And linking this back to Chester... Ray, were you not doing *your* dangerous research for ZolaCore? If we're going to condemn people for working for the wrong guys for what they saw as the right reasons, maybe we should think about who else would have to be in those docks?"

I have to bite my tongue on that, because I just don't have the energy to get into an argument with Major. He's only trying to ease my concerns about Chester, but nothing riles me more than someone reminding me of my innocent links to Ignacio Zola.

What counts here is getting to the bottom of this signal and doing something about the radiation source that is causing so many problems on Earth. From the atmospheric oddities to the changes in animal behavior, there are countless reasons to be afraid of things getting worse.

But for me, nothing is as frightening as the worsening health problems my young daughter and her peers around the world are facing, the timing of which tells us they quite simply *have* to be linked to the Anomaly.

"I want to get up," I say, shifting my weight as much as I can.

Major shakes his head. "Not yet. The doctors were clear on that."

"Then bring everyone in here," I insist.

"They said one visitor at a time until they've done the final tests to let you leave."

I sigh. "Get Driver, at least. I want to call my family."

"Sure thing, Ray," Major says, forcing a smile. "I'll make sure Driver brings her phone and I'll have a word with the doctors, too, to tell them to bring the checks forward. You seem fine to me, even if you might not be able to walk for a while. We're all working to get to the bottom of this, all hands on deck with the Balena team on video, too, and there's someone there I really want you to meet."

"Who?" I ask.

"I'll send Driver in and talk to the staff," he replies without replying. "Hopefully we'll have a breakthrough even before you can join us in the war room. If not, another sharp mind like yours definitely won't hurt our chances."

3

"God, Ray," Driver exclaims as she hurries in through the door.

The door's curved top, so typical of the Vita's unique interior design, still doesn't seem congruent with the otherwise sterile and functional layout of the ward I'm being treated in.

Driver stops right beside the bed, as if she wants to wrap her arms around me in relief but doesn't want to risk knocking out any of the wires that are still attached to various parts of me.

"What the hell happened?" she asks. "I mean… your whole hand?"

"I'm glad to see you, too," I quip.

That makes her chuckle through her obvious concern, lightening the mood a little. "Obviously I'm beyond relieved that you're okay," she says. "Well, most of you. Laika told us what happened, with the little girl you had to save even when you knew you could have fled and the rest of the Vita would have survived. But why was the synthocite in your *hand*?"

I briefly tell her as much as I can remember. It sounds even crazier than it felt at the time, now that I'm saying it out loud. A hijacked robot, a fuel-soaked hand, a falling elbow landing in the wrong spot to ignite the lighter below.

As I talk, it's obvious that Driver is more concerned about my physical condition than I am.

The painkillers and still-cloudy brain might have something to do with that, but I think the main reason I'm not wallowing in any personal discomfort is that there's a much bigger issue for us all to deal with.

For Driver, though, she's been immersed in that since the news of the signal first came in. My condition is the new information *she's* wrestling with, having probably been fearing the worst and now paying close attention to every single reading on the monitors by my bed.

When I finish the rundown, she's also finished taking everything in.

She focuses more closely on me now. "And did Major tell you much about the signal or our plans?" she asks.

I furrow my brow slightly. "He told me about the signal and Shaun's thoughts, but nothing very specific about any plans. He mentioned a war room and video calls with the team on the Balena. Sasha, for sure, and he also said there's someone else on the Balena he wants me to meet. You know everyone there, right? Who would he be talking about?"

Silently thinking for several seconds, Driver looks totally stumped by this.

I shrug. "It's not going to be long until we find out, anyway. He said he's going to ask the doctors to run their tests on me really soon, so I can leave."

"So you are coming?" Driver replies. There's a slight hint of surprise in her tone.

"To the war room? Well, yeah… I'm not just going to sit here on my own," I say, not exactly sure why that wasn't obvious.

"Oh, I meant to the *Balena*," she says. "You know we're going to meet it halfway, right? We're not in a holding orbit anymore. It's on the way back to a low orbit and we'll come back with it, too, but right now the Vita is heading away from Earth. That's going to reduce the time until Shaun can board and get deep into their AI data analysis system with Sasha and the others. Major thought you would want to come, since you're not going to be medically cleared for a descent for at least a week. Once we're close to the Balena, the flight there is basically just dock to dock in a small craft, and obviously there's no atmospheric entry for your body to deal with."

I say nothing, taking all of that in.

"Oh. So he didn't mention any of that?" Driver realizes. "Well, personally, I think since you can't go back to Earth for a week you really might as well come with us. Our bionics division on the Balena is miles ahead of anything you'll have seen on Earth so you could have a basic hand in no time. You'd also be in the thick of the action to make sure everyone is pulling in the right direction."

I nod slowly. "What *you* say makes sense, Driver. I just feel like Major should have told me we're moving away from Earth. He mentioned at least twice that my family is safe on the surface but didn't think to tell me I'm getting further away from them by the second."

"I mean... sure, you're getting further away from them in a literal and physical sense," she shrugs. "But you couldn't go home yet even if it we were still in a holding orbit. We'll be back there in the Balena by the time you're cleared, so it doesn't make a whole lot of difference."

She's right, but I feel like my point stands. Major consciously decided to let Driver break this to me, and he doesn't make decisions like that haphazardly. I would have been angry if he had been the one telling me, in no small part because it would have brought to the surface old feelings from the Virginia bunker — when Major's myopic focus on his official duties and orders kept me from making the trip to see my family in Colorado.

"But Ray, did you hear me about the hand?" Driver adds with a grin. "You love robots and mechs and all that comic book stuff. That was the hand that was nerve-damaged from your crash all those years ago, too, wasn't it? This time in a few days you'll have one that's better than new!"

I can't fight the grin that's spreading across my own face. Driver knows me well.

"They'll match the material to the exact tone of your skin," she goes on. "And if we have the doctors here send over some scans of your left hand along with that info on your skin, the fabrication team can get to work and it should be ready for attachment when you arrive."

"For real?" I ask.

"Real as that dumb look on your face," she laughs. "So yeah, that's a little something to look forward to, at least, but I know there's also this other thing we haven't talked about yet."

I nod, feeling my expression settle back towards neutral.

"Do you ever think about how small moments can change history?" Driver muses. "I mean, obviously everything changed because of what you found on the Beacon and how hard you fought to raise the alarm about Zola's plans. But if you hadn't gone into that one room where the guy had all the observational data about Bayzen, we wouldn't have known it was there. We wouldn't have pointed these new telescopes towards it, and we would still be sitting here thinking we're alone in the universe. You were just going through every door you could open, right? You brought every piece of data back to Earth that you could, and all these years later it's still paying off."

Driver is fiercely smart, through the facade of toughness she exudes, but she's not normally this reflective.

"I think about the Beacon all the time," I tell her. "Every decision I made, good and bad. Even bringing Laika back. I agonized over that. I didn't know if it was kinder to leave him there or to sedate him and bring him in the unprotected Escape Pod, but I just figured I had to give him the *chance* to survive — however small it was, and however painful it might be. And yeah, I went through every door and took every file I could, because you just never know which small action will make the difference one day. You're the same, Driver. You act when others don't. You got a spot in the Virginia bunker because you were willing to fly Major there when the world was falling apart and everyone else wanted to hide under the first rock they could find. Action keeps us alive, nothing else."

"Yeah," she replies pensively. "I've never really thought of it like that, but you're right. Right now everyone is acting to try and crack this alien code, but that's what I just don't get. If they're trying to talk to us — friendly or not — why would they use a code? It's not even just a language we can't understand. The way Shaun explained it to me is that it's like if you wanted to translate text on a computer from a language you've never seen into English. It would be almost impossibly tough. But imagine that before you can even open the document, you have to decrypt the hard drive you found it on. He said that's where we are now. The data in the signal doesn't have any obvious form or structure to it — it just seems like noise, but way too much and way too targeted towards us to be random."

"Major said pretty much the same thing to me," I tell her. "I haven't seen any of this and I don't think I'm the guy who's going to crack it, but I really doubt we're dealing with a 'code' in the sense of this being a message they've intentionally obscured. But like you're saying, why would they send a message and deliberately make it hard to understand? It's more likely that the technologies they've used to send it are just very different from anything we're familiar with. You know, *alien* technologies. These aliens themselves could be very different from us in ways we're not even thinking about. Think of whale song, or bats using echolocation… these things could have senses way beyond ours."

"Hopefully the Balena's AI system helps us out," Driver muses in reply to that. "Because yeah, this isn't a signal anyone is going to look at and figure out on their own. But hey, speaking of signals…"

Reaching into her pocket, Driver pulls out her phone and unlocks it before handing it to me.

"Everything is online," she says. "Major said you want to call your family. Eva sent me a message when they got home, not long ago, but they're there now."

"*All* the way home?" I ask in hope.

She nods. "They had already landed in Salt Lake City two hours ago, so yeah. They'll be at the house by now."

Holding the phone in my left hand — obviously — I awkwardly navigate to Driver's contacts.

"Oh, wait," she blurts out. "You're not supposed to say anything about the signal."

I look away from the phone and straight into Driver's eyes. I don't have to say a word.

"Only for now," she goes on. "Just until you're fully looped in and we've had a collective meeting about how to handle this. They're worried about how things could play out on Earth if people find out the wrong way. Not that Eva would tell anyone, but the commercial cell network isn't exactly bullet-proof for security. Some phone-hacking media outlet saying "aliens" to a frightened world could be like yelling "fire" in a crowded room. That's all. So they just want you to hold off on—"

"Who are *they*?" I ask.

Driver hesitates, which is basically answering without answering.

"Who?" I push.

"Major and Chester," she eventually says, much more quietly than she's said anything.

And there it is.

Telling me what I can and can't tell my family, the man whose obstructive officiousness stopped me from reaching them in Colorado all those years ago and the man whose money-driven lies put them in harm's way all over again just a few days ago.

Major and Chester.

I take a deep breath to contain my anger, but believe me: that's not as easy as it sounds.

4

Driver closes her eyes and sighs. "I know what you're thinking, but they're right on this. For the sake of what might only be a few hours, Ray, you would be doing your family a favor by keeping this under wraps."

Again, it feels like no accident that Major left Driver to tell me this. He could have mentioned it himself when I said I wanted to call them, but he chose not to.

In a way I can understand that any kind of conflict or arguments aren't going to help us, so it makes sense in that regard. I just think it's pretty low and unbecoming of a man in his position to put stuff like this on Driver.

If he had told me himself and hadn't let on that it was Chester's PR-conscious idea, I probably wouldn't have had any problem with keeping quiet about the signal for a few hours. From a detached perspective, it *is* the smart move.

With that in mind, I'm just going to be the bigger man and swallow it. That doesn't mean I'm going to forget, but there's no room for petulance. Deep down I do believe we're all pulling in the same direction — even Chester — and sometimes I'll have to be pragmatic, even if others aren't acting with the same levels of integrity I expect of myself.

"Don't worry," I tell her as I get set to begin the call. "But anyway can you go and see if the doctors can make the checks any faster? I know Major was going to, but I really want to get out of here and into the war room. If you could tell them I'm ready, that'd be great."

Driver stands up and looks at her phone, but doesn't say anything else about it. I've told her not to worry and that's enough. We have nothing if we don't have trust, and Driver and I have been through so much together that we probably trust each other at least as much as we trust ourselves.

Before Driver is out of the room, Eva answers the call and her face fills the screen. The sight is even more beautiful than ever, even through the tears of relief and concern that fill her eyes as soon as she sees that the video-caller is me, not Driver.

"It's your dad," she calls into the air, bringing first Joe and then Scarlet into my view.

A few seconds later, laughter fills the air as Eva's phone almost falls to the ground, inadvertently bumped by a very excited parrot.

"Ray Ray!" Laika squawks. "Ray Ray okay!"

He comes into view, perched on the edge of Eva's chair, as she steadies the phone.

"Girl near robot okay, too?" he asks. "Laika and Ray Ray save girl?"

The little guy has such a pure heart, it's hard to countenance that he came from a ZolaCore researcher's lab.

"She sure is, buddy," I tell him.

"How about you, Dad?" Joe asks. "Last time we spoke to Driver, she said you were asleep but the doctors thought you would be okay."

I smile. "Driver wouldn't say it if it wasn't true," I tell him. I don't know if she'll have mentioned my hand to Eva, and then if Eva would have mentioned it to the kids, so I'll keep that as quiet as the alien news for now. In broad terms, I *am* okay.

"But you won't be cleared for a flight to Earth until next week, she said?" Eva asks.

"That's right," I nod. "The Balena is coming into low orbit, so I'll be going there for some medical checks and Anomaly analysis stuff in the meantime."

At that, Joe's eyes light up like fireworks. "You're going to the Balena? No way! You have to show me everything on video!"

I smile. "I'll see what I can do, kiddo. And that telescope you launched is already giving us new information that could help us solve this Anomaly," I tell him, getting close to the full truth without going too far. "By the time I can come home, I think we'll be a lot further forward."

"Mr. Barclay?" a voice calls from the doorway.

I turn and see the doctor from earlier. "Oh, great. One second."

"Of course," she smiles.

I turn back to the phone. "Okay guys, I'll call again soon. Eva... we'll talk more," I add, sensing that she's not quite as hot on the whole Balena visit as Joe was. "And Scarlet, how are you doing, darling?"

Her little lip starts trembling.

"What is it?" I ask.

Joe jumps in: "I thought Laika should have stayed, to help you with whatever else is happening up there. Scarlet wanted him to come home and I think I accidentally made her feel bad about it."

Scarlet is nodding even as Joe puts his hand on her shoulder.

They're both great kids and I'm sure Joe didn't mean to upset her. She can be very sensitive sometimes, especially if she feels like he is angry at her. It's just natural sibling stuff. It's hard when I'm so far away, but they couldn't be in better hands than Eva's.

"Scarlet, don't be sad," I say. "Laika loves being with you guys. I'll be home soon, too. I promise. And whatever it takes, I'm going to fix this silly Anomaly once and for all."

She puts on a brave face and nods. "My ears hurted on the plane. More than before. I don't like it, Daddy."

Now it's *my* turn to put on a brave face. "I don't like it either, sweetheart, and that's why we're going to work so hard to stop it. You have fun with Laika and Joe until then, okay? And I'll see you soon."

Distant goodbyes are always the hardest part, and Eva is great at making them quick without feeling brusque. When I turn back to the doctor, I feel even more determined than I did before the call.

"Let's get these final checks over with and get you out of here," she says with a wink. "I can tell you're ready."

"Readier than ever," I tell her. "Readier than ever."

5

I'm not for one second saying that the doctor isn't being thorough or isn't taking these final checks seriously.

All I'm saying is that we're clearly on the same page.

She's here on the Vita just like I am, and within a few seconds of her arriving at my bedside I know that she's fully looped in about the signal.

She makes a little bit of small talk about how keen Shaun and the others are to see me, and how she's glad that first Major and then Driver tried to expedite my discharge.

"Your body was in shock more than anything else," she tells me while making notes and removing wires. "It's a miracle you didn't lose *too* much blood, and we're all relieved that your head didn't hit the floor with too much of a thud. Your final conscious movements saved your life, making sure your arm was outstretched with your hand as far away from the rest of you as it could possibly be."

"That hand is even further away from me now," I quip.

That gets a *real* hearty laugh. And without patting myself on the back — with my left hand, naturally — I think I earned it.

"But seriously," she goes on, "the strength of the explosion ended up working in your favor there, too. Without getting too graphic, it made things easier that it took your whole hand. If the blast had taken some fingers and messed up the rest, we wouldn't have been able to fix it up and we certainly wouldn't have felt comfortable amputating. As it is, my colleagues in surgery did clean and seal the wrist as best they could. Under these bandages you'll see that it's ready for a bio-interface attachment on the Balena. You'll be in their hands now, no pun intended, but I think we've set you up well for a bionic replacement."

"You've all done a great job," I tell her, very sincerely. "I'd like to meet and thank everyone who played a part before I leave for the Balena. For now, am I all good to leave here for Major's war room?"

She glances at her notes once more, then nods after a few seconds.

"I do want you to come back for the night," she says. "But a few hours isn't going to hurt. In the meantime, I have three orders. One, don't stand up for long. Two, don't put *any* pressure on your right arm. And three, don't forget to keep taking on plenty of electrolyte fluids. You're a fighter, Ray, as if we needed any more proof of that, but you're not invincible."

"Thanks again," I say, accepting her offer of support as I get to my feet. I don't feel too unsteady and I don't feel light-headed at all, which is as welcome as it is surprising.

Medicine has come a hell of a long way since my fateful teenage car-crash. That much is clear. But I also think the technology and care available here is a level above what almost anyone would have access to on Earth.

I'm not going to push for any details about the way they've "cleaned and sealed" my wrist stump, because sometimes it's better to just not know. All I know is that they've worked medical miracles to have me feeling relatively okay so soon after the explosion.

My right wrist, and really the whole lower arm, is wrapped in a very thick material that doesn't weigh much. Right now it looks like something between a bandage and a papier-mâché cast. The doctor gives me a basic cotton sling, too, to keep it out of the way like I'm a kid with a hairline fracture.

"That wrapping is just going to cushion it," she explains, clearly seeing that I'm looking at the stump as she speaks. "There are localized painkillers coursing through your arm that should stop it from hurting too much. And that's exactly why I need you to make sure you don't put any pressure on it. You wouldn't necessarily feel it if you did, so I just want you to stay mindful of that. Don't lean forward on anything, don't hug anyone — nothing like that. Just for a day or two."

"Understood," I say, thanking her once more as I set off.

Driver is already waiting at the door when I get there. She smiles playfully when she sees the cotton sling. "Did you ask if you could get one of those satellite dish things around your neck to complete the look?"

I roll my eyes. There's never any malice in anything Driver says or does, and her dark humor is only ever intended to lighten the mood.

"Let me know if you want a hand with the door," she says, even though she's already holding it open for me. "Or, you know, let me know if you want a hand in general."

"All day?" I groan.

She laughs. "Look, you're going to have the grip and pounding strength of a silverback in a few days. I'm getting these jokes in while I can!"

When we leave the medical bay, I emerge in an unfamiliar part of the Vita. Driver knows where we're going, though, and assures me it's not far. If it had been, I'm sure the doctor would have suggested a wheelchair. After all, she was quite insistent that I shouldn't be on my feet for long.

I soon see Major up ahead, ready to open a door which must lead into his war room. He turns around and looks delighted to see me coming, if a little surprised that Driver and I are still laughing and sharing jokes.

"Did they have you *both* on the laughing gas?" he says, offering a rare attempt at humor of his own.

"Next time don't use messengers," I say, turning serious. "If *you* don't want me to tell my family something and *you've* ordered the Vita to fly further away from Earth, then *you* man up and tell me that. Okay?"

He stares silently for a few seconds and then gives a shrug of acceptance. "None of this is about me, Ray. You know perfectly well there would have been an argument if I'd told you those things, and so did I. You have my word as Senior Coordinator of this ERF Vita, and my word as a man, that there are no secrets between us. That was naked pragmatism, no denials. From here, everything is on the table. Now, if you had a right hand, this is when I would be shaking it."

It takes a second for the grin to break on his face, which puts Driver into another fit of laughter.

"Sorry," Major goes on. "Just trying to break the tension. But seriously, Ray: when we walk into that war room, everyone knows everything. That's the only way we can do this. You're about to meet the individual I alluded to earlier, too. Again, that was something I didn't want to get into until you were here."

Major turns back to the door and opens it. Immediately, I hear a hubbub of voices. A few steps later, I'm looking at a room that uncannily resembles the war room in the ERF's Virginia bunker. That makes sense, since the Vita itself came from that site. There's an instant comfort to the familiar table and video wall.

Even more comforting is the sight of Shaun, who jumps up to greet me and stops short of coming too close when he sees my sling.

"You are something else, Ray," he tells me, raising his hand for a fist-bump looking at me with the kind of idolizing eyes he often does. I sometimes think Shaun has no idea of how important and respected among the rest of us he really is, maybe just because he's so much younger than me and especially the likes of Major.

Chester and Simone are already here, too, and both stand up to greet me.

"I am so sorry," Simone says. "Ray, I am more sorry for creating the synthocite that did this than you could ever know."

She means it, very clearly, and I tell her not to worry with equal sincerity.

"Glad you made it," Chester says, somewhat less effusively in that refined English accent of his. "We need you for this, Ray. Every turn so far is a dead-end and we can't keep it quiet forever."

He's apologized already for the deceitful circumstances that brought us together, so I don't read anything into the fact he doesn't do so again now. The way he said they need me sounded genuine and his expression is one of total focus, so I'm willing to give him the benefit of the doubt. After all, we're all in the same boat now — whatever diverging paths brought us here — and Major could be right that Chester's sharp mind for public relations could add something to our team.

"I guess you really can't keep a good man down," a voice booms through the unseen overhead speakers.

I focus on the wall and see my old friend Noah Williams, former US President and now Senior Coordinator on the ERF Balena.

Williams is a good man and was a good president, even if he wasn't on 'my side' on most of the issues that used to define domestic politics. It always felt like he was genuinely trying to act in the country's best interests, as he saw them.

He stepped away from politics to take over the Balena at the end of his term, since there was no obvious leader and no one else as widely respected as he was. Elana Hart stayed in charge of the Colorado bunker, which is now the ERF's main site on Earth, while Major naturally kept his role on the Vita.

No one from the Balena's previous ZolaCore management could be involved, for the obvious reason that the evil bastards are now rightly rotting in prison, and the way Williams conducted himself during our tough days in the Virginia bunker made him a popular choice.

"Good to see you," I tell him. "And Sasha! You, too."

Sasha, a razor-sharp analyst who proved worth her weight in gold during our mission in New Zealand, smiles and welcomes me back to the team.

Sitting on the other side of Williams, and the only other person visible, is an older woman I've never seen.

"This is Harriet Matthews," Williams says, making the introduction.

The person Major wanted me to meet, I realize.

"As head of an undisclosed public organization since long before I was introduced to their work," Williams continues, "Harriet led a team sending wide-ranging messages into space for almost twenty years in an attempt to make contact with another intelligent race."

My eyes widen like dinner plates.

"That's right," Harriet says, speaking in a low but authoritative tone. "And Ray, after all those years… I believe this signal is the reply we've been waiting for."

6

I instinctively turn to Driver as I sit down, wondering why she hasn't already told me this, and why she didn't know Harriet was the person from the Balena who Major was so keen for me to meet.

To my surprise, though, Driver looks just as shocked as I feel.

"Wait," Driver cuts in. "Harriet... you've been sending signals from the Balena? I thought you were just our lead observational astronomer. You've been doing *this* all the time I've known you?"

Harriet quickly shakes her head.

Now that I'm focusing solely on her, I can see that she's older than I was thinking at first. I'd say she's pushing seventy, if she isn't already there. She has that effortless air of experience and the demeanor of a wise presence you don't often see at the top of a selective table these days, in business or in the public sector.

That would be refreshing if it wasn't for what else I'm learning about her, and how secretive she seems to have been about it.

Driver is a high-ranking flight trainer on the Balena, and generally seen as a leader — if not *the* leader — of the whole crew. She symbolizes the Bayzen Project more than anyone, having done so much to thwart Zola's evil plans and then having chosen to take a role on the Balena rather than cash-in on her fame for an easy life like many others would have.

For *her* to have known nothing about an activity as important as actively trying to communicate with extraterrestrials isn't just a surprise. In my mind, and surely in hers, it's a concern.

After all, if Williams and the rest of the Balena's official leadership have been keeping *this* from Driver, what else might be under wraps?

"*No no no,* not on the Balena," Williams interjects. "Harriet can speak for herself, but Driver… I need you to know *explicitly* that we've not been doing anything you don't know about."

"That's right," Harriet adds, taking no exception to Williams briefly speaking on her behalf to quell any unnecessary misunderstandings from taking root. "I've been working in SETI for decades. The search for extraterrestrial intelligence, that is. I worked at NASA for many years, advising on projects you will have heard of and others that you certainly won't. I came to know President Williams through my role as head of a defunct government agency focusing on this endeavor. It came down to the reality that other nations were doing it, and that we had to keep tabs on them and also ensure the kinds of signals being sent to prospective targets were fairly representative of life on Earth, and especially of our nation."

In a brief silence, I glance at Driver again. I'm paying close attention to what she makes of all this.

Her eyes narrow in thought. "So… you didn't want China or Russia or whoever else to send aliens signals that made *us* look like bad guys?" she asks. "Something like that?"

"It's not as far-fetched as it sounds," Harriet replies. "Without getting in to too much unnecessary detail right now, we *did* detect outgoing signals from hostile nations that *did* paint the United States in a very negative light. It is what it is. That type of work was never my personal driving focus and it wasn't why I got into the field but there was undeniably some merit in sending our own signals to the same targets, if only to add some balance to the picture."

I hear what Harriet is saying, but the whole thing just sounds crazy.

It's almost like thinking of an ant colony trying to communicate with us, and imagining them telling us that it's the other colony over there we should be tackling to get rid of a home infestation.

I'm flabbergasted to think that one nation would send aliens negative information about another. I just don't know why they wouldn't realize that doing so would taint the whole of humanity in the aliens' eyes.

Why the hell would aliens care about our borders and flags? It doesn't make any sense.

"I also want to point out that the strength of the signals our international enemies sent out doesn't come close to some of the signals we have sent. The ones we sent to counter theirs were only slightly stronger, too. On that front, we never did more than the national security advisors insisted we *had* to. We saw those signals as damage limitation, and personally I had no reason to think any of the target areas of space were well chosen. Our most serious attempts to communicate, with stronger signals to higher-priority targets, never made reference to any overtly negative human actions or traits. We're not stupid."

I nod in relief at that. "So did you aim any signals towards Bayzen?" I ask. "I know it's four light years away, which means that if this really is a reply, you would have had to send the original message at least eight years ago."

"Bayzen 4b hadn't been discovered at that point," Harriet replies. "At least, not by us. We don't think any of Zola's team were aware of it then, either, based on the data you recovered from the Beacon. We *did* however send a powerful signal to a candidate planet in close enough proximity to think a civilization on Bayzen might well have picked it up."

"So why did we just pick up the reply signal now?" Driver asks. "You've been pointing every telescope we have at Bayzen since Ray found the information about it. You're telling me there's been nothing, all this time, then suddenly the new telescope picks it up right away?"

Harriet raises her eyebrows, as if shrugging with them instead of her shoulders. "That's exactly what happened. To be clear, we do not think the signal just reached us. The timing, relative to the acceleration of the Anomaly's effects, would be too coincidental given the four-year radio lag we're all well aware of. But I really cannot overstate the level of advancement the newly launched Poly-Field Observation Array offers over everything we've had until now. It's picking up measurable radiation from a previously undetected source, which I'm sure the others will know more about than I do. And that's despite the fact that we've been searching the skies for something that might be responsible for the anomalous phenomena we're seeing on Earth."

Driver doesn't butt in when Harriet takes a breath.

"So why are we seeing it now?" the signal expert continues rhetorically. "Well, because the new telescopes can see things the old ones just can't. They're not just giving us clearer images, okay? They're literally capable of observing and measuring things *nothing* else can. Think of using a brighter and brighter conventional flashlight to examine a crime scene. Nothing much would change, once the light reaches a certain level. Bright enough is bright enough. But then think what would happen if you were to turn those off and introduce a UV flashlight instead. Suddenly, new clues might appear. They had always been there, but our eyes and our conventional flashlights couldn't see them."

Driver nods like she's following. More importantly, though, she nods like she believes Harriet's broader point about not having done any active SETI work on the Balena. Even if that wouldn't have any direct bearing on our current situation due to the four-year lag that keeps coming up, trust is crucial for our team to function.

"I don't know how much of this you guys have covered without us," I say, looking around the room before focusing back on Harriet, "but I think the big question is obvious. What was in the messages you sent in the general direction of Bayzen?"

As Harriet inhales slowly in preparation of what looks like it'll be a carefully worded reply, I can't help but think that what she's about to say could be *very* important...

7

"I'm sure you'll be familiar with Voyager's golden record and the Pioneer plaques?" Harriet says.

I nod.

"Well... the most recent messages we've sent out are nothing like that."

"Okay..." I reply with confusion, wondering why she constructed her initial reply like that.

"Those were extremely basic messages," she goes on, "if you can even call them that. And I say that as someone who was hugely enthralled by them at the time, as a curious child with my eyes never far from the stars. They were limited by the physical medium. Our messages have been far more advanced. Largely the kinds of things you would expect, relating to our understandings of physics, chemistry, mathematics, natural history, astronomy. We did include information about ourselves, of course, but always in a positive and non-threatening light."

That's an important point, and one I'm glad to hear.

Harriet continues: "The challenge of SETI has always been trying to find the absolute base units for intercultural and — yes — *intergalactic* communication. A lot of things we might think of as culturally universal aren't even commonly understood among humans on Earth. Things like a tick to indicate something positive. Or even an arrow to indicate a direction of movement or focus. What we lean upon time and time again is the truly universal: mathematical constants, the nature of elements, orbital progressions. Using things like that as the building blocks, along with multi-language and multi-script depictions next to clear images of things to try to establish a method of deeper future communication, we have essentially tried everything we can. Because as we're seeing with the size of this incoming signal, the limit of the radio medium is effectively boundless."

I take a slow breath and look around the table again, focusing this time on Shaun.

This is a lot to take in, and he always has an incisive take on things. He's nodding slightly, as if he's already heard this and doesn't see anything contentious or worth expanding on right now.

"Wait… images?" Driver asks. "I've never really followed the whole alien angle, but how are you sending *images* in a radio signal? And how do you expect the aliens to see them? Are we just assuming they're going to have decoders and computers like ours, or whatever else they'd need?"

Shaun turns away from the screen to field this one. "Driver, when we're talking about communicating with an intelligent race this far away, we do have to take certain assumptions as read," he begins. "We're assuming all kinds of things, not least that they have eyes and a level of radio technology that will allow them to receive our signals in the first place. Smarter people than me figured long ago that any race that's looking towards the stars and trying to reach them will have necessarily mastered radio communication. Even if only to communicate with themselves over long distances. When you hear 'radio' it's understandable that you're thinking about sound. Because, well, we use 'radio' to mean, you know, a *radio*. But radio communication is just the transmission and reception of electromagnetic waves. I'm not trying to talk down to you here, either. Sometimes we just don't know what we don't know. Just like I don't know all kinds of things you do."

"Totally," Driver shrugs, not offended at all.

"And from there," Shaun goes on, "to talk about them receiving our images, we'd be getting into much deeper and to my mind much flimsier assumptions. You know, things like binary code and pixel-based imagery. The processes themselves aren't necessarily complex, it's just that the assumptions behind this stuff are pretty broad. I personally think a lot of SETI has been influenced by too much introspection. When researchers like Harriet, who I respect a lot, sit down and think about how to communicate with aliens, they're really thinking about how they wish aliens would communicate with *us*. These beings could be so different to us, it would make a mockery of all of this. By the same token, they could be way more like us than we're expecting. There's a school of thought that any race capable of looking to the stars will have developed in very similar conditions to ours, just like Bayzen is very similar to Earth. It also holds that there could be evolutionary biases towards beings with our kinds of physical bodies ascending to the top of the food chain, and essentially transcending the natural world like we have. And if that is the case, the Bayzenites could be frighteningly familiar if we ever get the chance to meet them."

It's fairly typical of Shaun to get off topic like that, but it's also typical of him to keep an explanation very accessible and to raise an interesting point I hadn't considered.

"Can I just say something on this, too?" Sasha chimes in. "Driver, it's also worth remembering that if these aliens have been aware of Earth for a long time, they might have already picked up signals we've been sending out incidentally, not just the ones Harriet and her team sent out on purpose. Things like TV broadcasts don't just disappear when they reach the edge of our atmosphere. These aliens could know a lot more about us than what we've tried to tell them. Again, we're making assumptions about their technology. But Shaun was right to say that radio communication is a fairly basic stepping stone for any race with aspirations to travel in space."

"So you're saying they might have seen bad stuff about us after all?" Driver asks. "I mean, if they could see our TV broadcasts, there would hardly be anything that isn't bad. They're not going to know the difference between slasher movies and documentaries, right? And even then, our news is bad enough. The murders, the wars, the way we treat animals… I don't think *I* would want to be friends with us."

"I think we're getting a *little* bit off the main point," Major says with a cough to clear his throat. "Regardless of what's gone before and what this signal might or might not be a reply to, we're in the process of trying to make sense of it. We haven't been at this for long, so there's no reason for pessimism. We *are* at something of an impasse, though. None of the Balena's advanced AI systems have found anything in the way of a structure within the signal that can guide us towards translating it."

I watch as Shaun raises his hand and makes an "*uh*" kind of sound to interrupt Major. "Well, sir," he says, "translate isn't exactly the right word. Not yet, anyway. We're still really trying to decipher this thing. Just for the sake of clarity."

Major inhales slowly. "Well, you can't spell *analyst* without *anal*," he says, unusually pithy. "I thank you for the correction, Shaun, but only if it's crucial next time, please. Anyway… as I was saying. We have made effectively no progress, Ray."

"We actually have," Shaun offers, "if you count ruling things out. We've certainly made some distinctions and narrowed down our range of future attempts."

I can sense the tetchy air in the room, which isn't common for this group. It's not just because of Shaun, either, because he's always precise about things and rarely shy about keeping others precise, too. And I sense that he's uncomfortable, too, in the unusual position of not having a clear idea of what to try next.

I already feel uncomfortable without a clear way forward,

and I've just found out about all of this.

The more I hear about the scale and complexity of the signal, the more I think the AI systems Major just alluded to are going to offer our best bet of a breakthrough.

"Isn't the output we get from the AI systems in terms of answers totally dependent on the input we give?" I ask.

"It is," President Williams replies. "I think I know where your mind is, Ray, and I've been in contact with Phil O'Connor about this. He's one of very few people on Earth who we've told about the signal. He's trying some variations as we speak and he'll be back in touch soon. As you probably know, we're using his PhilosophAI system architecture within the confines of ZolaCore mainframes we inherited here, which we are pushing to their absolute limit. Phil thinks the raw signal is too vast for even the largest of his Earth-based configurations to analyze at once. He's breaking it into chunks and we're doing the same."

My eyes widen at this. I did know they were using PhilosophAI technology on the Balena, but I naturally didn't know that the corporation's billionaire founder had been looped in.

O'Connor is a tech visionary for sure. And I think it's very laudable that since his terminal diagnosis he's made his groundbreaking AI model freely available to organizations like universities and hospitals, as well as the ERF, with limits only on certain purely commercial applications.

With that in mind, I feel like it's time to finally spit out the thought I've had in my mind since before I walked through the door.

The strength of the conviction has been building with every successive utterance about how little progress has been made, and Shaun's latest point is the straw that's broken the camel's back.

"I think it's time to tell *everyone* about this," I say. "Aliens from another world are trying to communicate with us, and I think everyone on our world should know."

8

Neither Major nor Williams say anything at first.

"I'm not coming at this from some flowery angle and saying everyone on Earth has the *right* to know," I go on. "Even though I do think that. I'm being pragmatic here. You say we're feeding the AI different segments of the signal and that Phil is doing the same, okay? That's because we think it might work. So if we break the news of this signal and everyone with access to the AI and sufficient computational power can run their own segmented analysis, doesn't that instantly increase our chances of getting somewhere more quickly than if we *don't* open this up?"

"One hundred percent," Shaun says.

The trouble is, Shaun's not in charge.

"Even beyond that point, Ray," he goes on. "Someone on Earth — some *one* out of billions — might look at this signal and see something we haven't. Sure, it's hopeful to think they will. But it would be arrogant to think they won't just because we haven't."

"I don't like it," a naysaying female voice instantly announces.

To my surprise it hasn't come from Harriet but from the always reasonable *Sasha*, of all people.

"Have none of you ever read a book or watched a movie about alien contact?" she continues. "Shaun, I'm totally with you on what you said about SETI researchers being stuck within their human mindsets, which is the most understandable thing in the world. We *can't* really imagine in any data-driven way how aliens would try to communicate with us or how they would react to communications from us. But do you know what we can predict with a high degree of certainty? Do you know which part of those sci-fi movies *is* founded on theories backed by data and historical experience? The way people will react to news of an alien signal. Even if it wasn't happening now, when some barely understood Anomaly is tightening around Earth like a cosmic noose, this would bring fear to the masses like nothing we've ever seen. And if people aren't scared as soon as they hear the news, you better believe the media will make sure they're scared before long. I'm not going to stand in the way of this if it's what the group wants — not that I'd have the sway, anyway — but I need this to be heard. It's a bad idea right now."

"Sasha, I'd agree with you on that if the Anomaly wasn't a factor," Shaun replies. "And sure, I can see that the timing will make some people more scared by this news than they would be in other circumstances. But what choice do we have? For me, the Anomaly is why we *should* tell everyone right away. You've seen the data the PFOA is picking up from that radiation source. *That* is what is screwing up our sky, freaking out our animals, and harming our kids."

"I know," Sasha sighs.

"Do you, though?" Shaun presses. "I know you've seen the initial data from… whatever the crazy radiation source is. I don't know, let's call it the Leak. You've seen the initial data, but have you seen what we've been processing in the last hour? The Leak isn't just continuing to spew radiation out into our solar system, the rate is accelerating — fast."

Sasha's expression stiffens in an instant. I feel mine do the same.

"Accelerating?" she asks.

Continuing is a horrible enough word, but *accelerating* is just awful. The Anomaly's effects on Earth have been getting increasingly apparent at a frightening pace, and to think of that pace quickening brings a knot to my stomach.

"Yeah," Shaun goes on. "*Accelerating*. Whatever this stuff is — and we're analyzing it — the situation is getting worse by the minute. We know it's bad. You can ask Ray about his daughter Scarlet if you need a personal touch on that, or you can just look down at Earth and ask yourself if it always looked that color from up here. We're in a race against time and I'm starting to worry that we have even less than we think. I don't share the confidence of some people in here that this message is definitely going to offer us some kind of help with the Leak, but it might. And while other teams on Earth and on the Balena are looking at ways to plug or insulate the Leak by ourselves, I don't think we can waste another minute worrying about how the world is going to react to hearing about the alien signal. Sasha… I think we have to do absolutely everything we can to make sure the world is still here next year, next month, and maybe even next week. We have to open this up. Now."

"Chester?" Major says, surprising me to no end by turning in that direction for some input.

"Uh, yes?" Chester asks, apparently sharing my feeling.

Major's gaze intensifies. "You're the spin doctor. What does your gut say on this?"

"I'm actually with Ray and Shaun," he says. "When the stakes are this high, the reaction hardly matters."

"Wrong," Sasha interrupts, less courteous than her usual self. That's understandable, given the tension of the moment, and I think everyone understands that we don't really have any room — or more to the point any *time* — for niceties. "Shaun, I didn't actually know yet that the Leak is accelerating. That does change things, I'll admit. But Chester, you can't say the reaction hardly matters. I go back to the question I started with: have none of you seen the movies? People who get scared for their lives, like a lot will, don't *just* get scared. Some of them get angry, too, and some get violent. Some sabotage anything they see as related to the dangerous project. It's not like we're launching a rocket they could blow up or anything, but the AI systems themselves could become targets. The ERF bunkers, the New Zealand compound... they could all become targets."

"*And*?" Shaun retorts. "We're talking about a Leak of radiation we don't understand, from a point in space where there's nothing we can even *see*, that could viably suffocate Earth, for want of a better word. If we don't act, there might not be anyone left to target anything. I feel like you're stuck on worrying about the same things. Ray, you're with me on that, right?"

I feel the weight of everyone's gaze. I'm not in charge here in any official capacity, but at this point I don't think any individual is fully calling the shots. But for better or worse, and whether I deserve it or not, these people do turn to me in moments of difficulty.

"I can see both sides," I say. "I'm not sitting on the fence with that, I'm just saying there is merit in listening to Sasha's concerns. Because Shaun, *we* would be a target, too. If people know we're trying to decode this message with the intent of acting on it, the kind of fear that whips up around the initial news might make the Vita and the Balena the biggest targets of all. And yeah, we feel safe this far out. But some of the bunkers are still armed to tackle space-based threats. If they're targeted and the security teams fall, we're not necessarily out of range. And even if we were, we could still be hit by EMP attacks or any other number of ways to stop us from engaging with the aliens."

"Who said anything about engaging with them?" Shaun asks.

I sigh. "No one, but fear isn't rational. And like Sasha said, we can only too surely count on the media to make people scared. They'll see aliens are talking to us and people will think we're talking back. Things like the four-year communications delay won't even make the footnotes."

"So whose side are you on?" Driver inquires during a brief and rare moment of silence.

"We're all on the same side," I reply. "Here's where I'm coming down: Sasha is right to raise the concerns about how people will react, and she's made me think about things I hadn't considered. But Shaun is right about the urgency we're facing, which is even greater than I thought now that I know the Leak is accelerating."

Driver can't hide her confusion. "So you're *literally* on the fence you said you weren't sitting on."

"No," I sigh. "I wasn't finished. Look, we have to open this up. There's just no option on that. Would I say the same if my daughter wasn't physically affected by what's already come out of that Leak, and if she wasn't going to suffer even more *very soon* if it keeps accelerating? I don't know. But I am where I am. We are where we are. The compromise I think we should land on, if you want to call it that, is to announce this in the next hour in the most careful and considered way we can. We want people to know we've picked up an alien signal, but we don't want them to panic about it — and that means we don't want to give the media any opportunity to *make* them panic about it."

"How do we do that?" Driver asks.

"I think I should announce it personally," I say. There's no ego there, but I know the media would have a harder time misrepresenting words people see and hear coming out of my mouth than they would if it was a press release from Major's office, or something like that. "But I think the rest of you, and one person in particular, should draft what I'm going to say."

I glance between Shaun and Sasha, who both look like they feel heard and broadly accept my position. And with necessity forcing my hand, perhaps despite my better judgment, I then turn to the best-qualified person to draft an announcement with the public's reaction in mind.

"What do you say?" I ask him.

"*Me*?" Chester says, once again surprised to be called upon. "I mean, of course. Let's get to it."

Beyond him, Major gives me a strong nod of approval.

I nod back then look at Chester again. "Okay," I exhale. "Let's get to it indeed..."

9

When I came to the Vita, I had two goals.

My overarching goal was to find out exactly what was causing the Anomaly so we could start taking steps to undo its damage. Another goal nested inside of that was to persuade Major to open up all of the research books from every lab here. I figured if everyone had access to all of the observation data from various teams, we would have a better chance of putting the pieces together.

It's kind of strange how the more things change, the more they stay the same.

We don't know for sure yet what is causing the Anomaly, but we know a lot more about it than we did a few days ago. The PFOA telescopes have revealed the Leak, an inexplicable source of radiation that our present understanding of science can't account for. It seems pretty clear that the radiation from the Leak is causing the *effects* of the Anomaly, but we have no idea what is causing the Leak.

Besides continued analysis of the Leak, which is ongoing, our next move in trying to understand it lies in making sense of the other thing the new telescopes have alerted us to: an incredibly complex alien radio signal.

And all over again, nested within that goal is the need to

spread the available data far and wide. I hear everyone's concerns about how the news could go down on Earth. Hell, after hearing the arguments I now *share* some of those concerns. But that doesn't change the fact that we have to push ahead.

At the moment, only researchers here and in a few closed locations on Earth are studying the signal. Surely we'll give ourselves a much better chance of having a breakthrough by getting eight billion eyes on it.

Even though I'm about to address Earth with what's possibly the biggest news there could ever be, I don't feel the kind of pressure I might have expected.

It's an odd feeling. I wouldn't quite call it calm, but it's not far away. More than anything else, I feel a total focus on what has to be done.

Deep down, I just know that the cost of doing nothing justifies a high level of risk.

Taking action doesn't mean being reckless, though. That's why Chester's knack for delivering a message to the public, honed over his years in political consulting, is something I'm glad to have on my side.

Don't get me wrong, I would have done this without him if he wasn't here. But he *is*, and it would be foolish not to use his expertise when it's on offer. There's no room for resentment or ego or anything else like that.

Chester is on our side now, no matter what the situation was a few days ago.

We're all in the same boat, and he's holding one of the paddles.

Everyone stays where they are in the war room while we begin planning out what I'm going to say.

Chester takes the reins, as I wanted and expected, with a quick insistence that I should try to be the opposite of bombastic.

"I don't want to hear any of the old '*my fellow Americans*' or '*citizens of Earth*' stuff to kick it off," he begins, his refined

English accent as crisp as ever. "We're shooting for clarity, not gravity."

I see Major nod approvingly.

"And for the meat of the message, there's really just one thing to remember," Chester goes on. "Ray: you're not telling the world that aliens exist. That isn't why you're making a public statement so that isn't what you want to focus on. What you're doing is telling the world that the new telescopes have found two things that could help us stop the Anomaly and put things right."

This time, I find myself nodding. It's a simple distinction, but it could well be a powerful and important one.

"First of all, Ray," Chester says, now totally commanding everyone's rapt attention, "you're going to tell the world that we've detected a radiation source that looks like it's responsible for the problems we're seeing on Earth. You're going to hit that as a positive point, like finding the source of a water leak. Sure, it looks bad, but at least you know where it is. Second, you're telling them that we've detected a radio signal from the direction of Bayzen, and we want all hands on deck to decode it so we can get to work on doing something about it. Some media outlets *will* still spin this towards fear. There's nothing we can do to stop that. Because really, let's be honest: these revelations *do* give more than one reason to fear. But by framing the news in the best way we can, we can mitigate the fear."

No one says anything for a few seconds, until Major clears his throat and speaks:

"I didn't realize you would want to directly reference the Leak," he muses. "Like you said, doesn't introducing the idea of a mysterious radiation source give people an *extra* reason to fear?"

Chester rubs his chin in thought. "Well, in a sense, yes... it does. In another sense, though, it offers hope. I compared it to finding the source of a water leak, and that analogy holds up. We know more about the Anomaly now than we did yesterday.

Details be damned, that's progress. But... that's not the only benefit. You all know the old phrase about a good day to bury bad news, right? There's an element of that here. In a lot of cases, dumping two bad or potentially scary revelations at the same time is better than revealing them separately. But there's another saying in politics that applies to some kinds of bad news, and it's that one plus one equals half."

Judging by the expressions on the faces around me, I'm not the only one who's not following Chester's logic on that.

"Think of it like this," he goes on. "If I tell you two negative things, whether they're disappointing or scary or anything else, you can't concentrate fully on either of them. This tactic is especially useful when you're much more concerned about the impact of one piece of news than the other. Today, the Leak is a concerning thing and people will be troubled by it. But, it wouldn't generate anything close to the visceral fear in a lot of people that the word *'aliens'* will. That's why I think presenting the Leak as the problem, and the alien signal as its potential solution, is what we have to focus on. That's what we're all thinking and hoping, anyway, so it's not like I'm suggesting Ray should stretch the truth."

"I like it," I say. "I like the idea of presenting it like that. Start with the Leak, then mention the signal. Call for mass participation in the decoding process, so people can feel involved rather than hopeless or helpless. Chester, if you can write something down like that, I'll say it. Major, Driver, Shaun... if you think it's better for any of you to stand beside me and maybe say something, too, Chester could write that while he's at it."

Major shakes his head quickly. "Just you, Ray. In his outreach work here, Chester has done all kinds of analytics research on things like trustability and public approval. You're in a league of your own."

"Well, Driver always polls *extremely* well, too," Chester adds. "But I agree with you, sir. Ray facing the camera alone is the most powerful visual we can have for this. With the right backdrop we can really evoke his time alone on the Beacon, which is what won him the public's admiration in the first place.

I look around the war room, and then to the video wall. Sasha, previously the most opposed to the idea of sharing the news, has visibly softened. Harriet and Williams are nodding, meanwhile, fully sold on Chester's expertly delivered rundown.

Simone, the Material Synthesis researcher whose creation cost me my hand, is the only person who hasn't said anything during all of this. Every so often I've caught her glancing my way with an evident sorrow and guilt in her eyes.

"So we're set," Major says, clapping his hands together as he stands up. "Chester, write it up and we'll all have one final look before you shoot. In the meantime, I'll find the best backdrop."

When Major leaves the rest of us to it, the drafting process for my announcement proves to be a full team effort. Sure, Chester came up with the guidelines. But everyone offers up their input on the best wording for certain sections, with even Sasha chiming in.

It only takes around ten minutes to nail down a message that will take one minute to read, and Major returns just as we finish.

Warmly approving of what the team has come up with, Major then leads the way to his chosen backdrop. Everyone from the war room comes along, even Simone, while the others on the video wall wish us luck as we leave.

I'm not overly surprised to learn that Major has opted to film my announcement in the spot where we filmed the PFOA launch. There's a lot of thematic sense to that, naturally, since the new telescopes are responsible for both of the discoveries I'm about to share.

Annie, Chester's videographer from before the security breach, has returned to Earth. No one else is sure exactly where the professional recording equipment is, or if she's taken it with her. Because of that and our lack of time to look around, what could be the most consequential announcement in human history is going to be filmed on an everyday cell phone.

The built-in cameras are so good these days that it hardly matters, and the launch bay has very adaptable lighting controls.

Chester puts me in a spot where space is visible through the large window behind me and the metal walkway is visible under my feet. There's a kind of industrial feel to the floor, which adds to the space station vibe they're going for.

Being almost anywhere else on the Vita feels like being in a high-end shopping mall, and I think Major has chosen very well here. I don't know how much difference small things like the filming backdrop will actually make when the content of the announcement is so incredible, but it doesn't hurt to focus on every detail.

Unlike last time I delivered a message to Earth, I'm not going out live.

That naturally takes the edge off things. I still want to get this done in one take, though, partly because the bright lights Chester has directed at me to get the best shot are making my eyes and head uncomfortable.

I don't have to squint, because it's more of a total light than a beam. I just don't feel like I could handle it for long.

Driver is holding a tablet computer directly beside Chester and his phone-based camera, with the words of my pre-written announcement blown up and set to run in an autocue app.

I hear the ding of the phone as Chester begins recording.

"Wait a second," I say. "Can someone help me take this sling off for a minute? It's going to look stupid. I'm fine without it, it's only there so I don't bump my wrist into anything."

Shaun steps forward to help out.

"I like how no one jumped in to say it doesn't look stupid," I chuckle, breaking some of the natural tension. Even though we're all in agreement about what to say, this still feels like a very high-stakes move we're making.

I thank Shaun and straighten my posture on the spot. The light really is bothering me now, but I'll soldier through it.

As soon as I hear Chester's phone ding once more, I signal for Driver to start the autocue.

"Hi, everyone," I begin, as casual as I can be, just like Chester suggested. "I'm sure you all know about the security breach that occurred here on the Vita, shortly after we launched our Poly-Field Observation Array of next generation telescopes."

I look down at my right arm and inhale slowly.

"The sabotage attack was costly," I continue, "just like Ignacio Zola's actions on the Beacon. But just like back then, we have survived to fight another day. I come to you today with news of two discoveries our telescopes have already made. First, we have detected a radiation source that appears to be responsible for the mysterious problems we have seen on Earth. In this cosmic *Leak*, so to speak, we believe we have detected the source of the Anomaly."

While holding the phone, Chester holds his empty hand out and repeatedly lowers it to signal for me to slow down. I heed his advice.

"It goes without saying that this is a major step forward in our bid to *stop* the Anomaly," I go on, reading the words with the most natural flow I can muster. "And while we study the radiation source with all of the equipment at our disposal, I want to invite the whole of Earth to assist with our second discovery. Because another of the new array's telescopes has discovered something else that could help us in our fight against the Anomaly."

I take a deep breath before the all-important bombshell. We've done our best to soften the blow, but there's only so much softening you can do to a message like this.

"If I was sharing this news in other circumstances, today would be a very exciting day for humanity," I say. "It's still a very important day, though, because we have just discovered a complex radio signal originating from the vicinity of Bayzen 4b. Our experts believe that decoding this signal, from intelligent beings who appear to have gone out of their way to talk to us, offers our best chance of surviving the Anomaly like we have survived everything else so far. Personally, *I* believe that having all hands on deck and everyone working on this will offer our best chance of decoding the signal. That's why I have asked the ERF Vita's Senior Coordinator Clarence Major to make the full signal publicly accessible, and that is why he has agreed without hesitation. Together we can get to the bottom of this, and together we will prevail. I have faith in the power of humanity to overcome anything the world or the stars can throw at us. We've done it before… so let's do it again."

After a few seconds of silence, I hear Chester's phone ding again.

Instant applause follows the sound.

"Nailed it," Driver yells above the hubbub.

Shaun walks over with my sling and pats me on the back. "Really good, man," he says.

Chester, meanwhile, winks approvingly before looking down at his phone to get on with disseminating our message. It was a team effort, and I think we've done as well as we could.

"Can someone dim those lights," I ask, all of a sudden feeling *very* uneasy at the brightness now that my adrenaline is dropping back to a normal level.

Driver turns around to get right to it.

But as I step forward, my left hand grasps for the walkway's railing.

"Driver!" I call, instinctively looking to her in a sudden moment of need.

My legs are suddenly shaky under my weight, and I feel my vision blurring.

She's by my side like a flash, carefully supporting my

weight and telling me to take deep breaths. I see Shaun rushing back over to help, too, but nothing else.

After that, I see nothing else.

Driver's strength and readiness makes sure that I slump rather than collapse, but that's the only positive here.

"Get the doctor!" she yells, the last full sentence I hear before losing consciousness. "I think he's going to…"

Yup.

Pass out.

10

For the second time in... well, I don't know how long... I find myself returning to consciousness in the Vita's medical bay.

I look up at the familiar ceiling, then across to the familiar door with its arch-like curve at the top.

I'm not groggy like I was last time, but that's immediately making me worry that I might have been out for a lot longer than I was then.

There's no one else around. It's just me and the machines. Me and the wires. Me and the—

Just as I shift my weight to push myself up the bed so I can ring the button for attention, I see my doctor hurry in through the door.

Obviously alerted in her office to some changes in my readings, she's here impressively quickly.

"We have to stop running into each other like this, Ray," she quips, clearly relieved that I'm awake but not too concerned about anything else.

"What happened?" I ask. "I just remember the lights being bright and then stumbling to grab the railing. It was right after we recorded the message to tell— wait, the message! What's happening with that? How did it go down?"

"Easy does it," the doctor tells me, holding out her palms to calm me down as I shift myself up to a sitting position. "The others will tell you about that. My job is *you*, Ray. *Your* job was to stay off your feet as much as possible and to keep drinking the electrolyte fluid. How did you do with that?"

I sigh. "Guilty as charged. But a *new* job came up. And believe me, I feel fine again. Can you tell me what's happening on Earth? How long has it been? Are there any breakthroughs?"

The doctor takes a seat next to my bed. "I've been in communication with Senior Coordinator Major and your friend Driver. They both supported my decision to keep you sedated so we could fully replenish some of your levels in a few areas. You lost a lot of blood in the explosion, Ray. The transfusions were all smooth and you woke up feeling relatively fine. But between the heightened stress of what's going on, and then your failure to follow some pretty basic discharge instructions, your body wasn't ready for what you demanded of it. You're much better rested and refueled now than you were last time. That means your body should be a lot more resilient. But I do need you to be more cognizant of your limitations this time, okay? Only for a short period of time. You've been through a lot. And even though your mental focus has moved right on to the next problem, you need to remember that your body is still physically recovering from the last one."

"Sure," I say, keen to move on. "Sorry for all of that. I wasn't trying to ignore what you said. But listen, the message I read out… how has it been received on Earth? And how long *have* I been out?"

"Forty-three hours," she says, after glancing at a screen for confirmation.

My eyes widen. Damn… no wonder I feel so rested. "So what did I miss? Did we decode the signal yet?"

"Not that I know of," the doctor tells me. "I'm not trying to leave you in suspense about everything, but you'll get better answers from the rest of your team. What I know from talking to Driver again a few hours ago is that they're generally pleased with how the news went down. *Relieved* more than pleased, I think. There was no breakthrough yet so nothing to be majorly pleased about, but there hasn't been total panic or any of the worst-case scenarios she said some people had been worried about."

I breathe a moderate sigh of relief. The relief comes from the fact that I'm beyond glad that our decision to share the signal with the world didn't backfire by causing any huge problems. That relief is only moderate, though, because the good news ends there.

For me, it's massively disappointing that no one anywhere has managed to decode the signal yet, almost two full days after we shared it.

More than disappointing, it's hugely concerning. I don't want to start jumping to any fresh worst-case scenarios of my own about what we'll do if the signal proves totally uncrackable, but I'll be damned if it isn't tough to maintain any positivity.

All I can do is hold on to the hope that there might be elements of progress that my doctor isn't aware of yet. If someone on our team or anywhere else has spotted any kind of structure or signpost within the signal, that could be a positive development that wouldn't make headline news. That could be something my doctor wouldn't know about.

Yeah, I'll cling to that.

"Driver asked me to dial down the sedation, too," the doctor goes on. "We've almost reached our rendezvous point with the Balena. If everything stays clear in the next few hours, I can pass you on to the oversight of my colleagues there. They have a much larger staff than we do. You know, since ninety percent of them haven't bailed out to Earth."

"Thanks for sticking around," I say. "I'll make sure you're well looked-after for all you've done. Your other colleagues who helped me, too."

She smiles, appreciative of the acknowledgement.

"But we're really that close to the Balena now?" I go on. "And you'll really sign me off to go?"

"If everything is clear," she nods. "Driver has assured me the flight is nothing. Dock to dock, out and then in. I think she said two others are going with her — Shaun and Chester — and that she'll wait as long as it takes for me to sign you off. She doesn't want to leave you behind but she doesn't want me to rush the final checks, either. She cares about you deeply, Ray. She was badly shaken up when she brought you in after you collapsed."

I can only imagine.

"But..." the doctor adds with a slight chuckle. "As soon as Driver knew you were okay, she told me how pissed she was that you didn't follow my instructions. This time I think I'll tell her exactly what I tell you, because she'll make sure you do what you're supposed to."

That definitely sounds like Driver. I can already picture the moment when I see her again... there will be five seconds of hugging and her saying how relieved she is that I'm okay, and then five minutes of slapping me around the ear and telling me to never again be so stupid as to ignore the doctor's orders.

"Could we start doing the checks as soon as you're ready?" I ask. "I'll listen to the orders, but I do really want to get out of here so I can see what's been happening. I'll need to get my things ready for moving over to the Balena, too."

"I'm checking as I talk," the doctor smiles. "We are going to be more thorough this time, with eye tests and sensitivity checks. Speaking of which, how is the wrist? I've already started to dial back on your painkiller doses, because you'll need as much movement and feeling as possible before your bionic attachment procedure on the Balena."

Shit, yeah.

The offer of bionic replacement for my right hand had totally slipped my mind amid everything else that's going on.

In any other circumstances, getting a bionic hand would be the only thing I was thinking about. But then again, the same is true for the fact that we're not alone in the universe. It's crazy how a pressing concern like the Leak and a pressing goal like decoding the signal can make other huge things seem relatively small.

"Oh, there is one thing Driver did mention about the reactions on Earth," the doctor says. She's detaching wires as she speaks, in what looks like a very good sign that my vitals are good and we only have the secondary checks to deal with before I can leave.

"Yeah?" I push.

She nods. "What are your feelings on Phil O'Connor?"

"Why?" I ask.

"That's not an answer, Ray," she says, stopping what she's doing to look straight at me.

I feel my brow furrow. "As billionaires go, he's not the worst."

"Hmm. He *has* been good about sharing the PhilosophAI system with medical institutions over the last year or so," the doctor muses. "But he's putting himself in the limelight more than I'm comfortable with. He thinks his AI, well directed, is the key to cracking this."

"It might be," I say.

"But can we *trust* it?" she gulps. "I follow the medical side, obviously, and PhilosophAI has this unshakeable bias towards what it sees as the most utilitarian course of action. There are facilities using it for triage over the heads of doctors and nurses with decades of experience, because there's this blind idea that technology is progress, no matter what. But computer code doesn't have empathy, Ray, no matter what the acolytes tell you. Some of the stories I've heard about how it allocates resources and rations life support hours are just terrible. Directly hooking it up to machinery, with decision-making power, is like putting a sociopath in charge. We don't do it here, but the leaders of some facilities on Earth are doing it right now."

"Well that's definitely not good," I agree with a sigh. "You can't blame the AI for how it's applied, though. It's a tool, and it sounds like those hospitals you're talking about are using a good tool for the wrong thing. I know it can be used to identify problems and diagnose symptoms faster than even the most experienced doctors for some diseases, right? So that's a great use of the tool. They just shouldn't be using it for decision making and certainly not giving it direct control access to the medical equipment. Basically I think it can serve us in identifying problems and, sure, maybe it could *suggest* some good solutions. But I totally agree with you that we shouldn't be trusting it to make medical decisions and apply the actual interventions. Fortunately, we're only using it to decode the signal — not giving it the power to send a reply or do something to the radiation source once we know what the message says."

With a look of relief on her face, the doctor picks up a clipboard from the table beside my bed and goes back to running through the checks.

"Did O'Connor say something about using the AI for more than just decoding the message?" I ask, still wondering why his name came up.

"No," she says, flipping to a new page and showing me some variously sized letters to test my eyes. "He hasn't said anything about the next step, Ray. He's just making himself *very* visible while everyone is trying to decode the signal, and I'm just hoping he goes back into the shadows once it's done..."

11

My final medical checks go quickly and smoothly, and as soon as they're done I bid a grateful farewell to the doctor and head for the war room.

She's given my body all it needs this time, and I can already tell the long induced rest has done me a world of good.

As fate would have it, the first person I see — leaving the war room as I approach to enter — is Driver.

Things go exactly as I expected, with the initial relief to see me looking so spritely followed by some harsh but fair admonishment for not doing what I was told last time. Driver says she wants to talk to the doctor to hear first-hand exactly what I am and am not cleared to do, just like the doctor joked about. But through the concern, I can tell she's delighted when I say I'm cleared for the very short flight to the Balena.

Driver also tells me she's kept Eva up to date on my situation and ensured her I was okay. She says she didn't want to introduce any concerns by mentioning it, but that she had to. I understand, because Eva would have feared the worse if I'd gone radio silent for so long with no explanation at all.

I try to call home before doing anything else, but she doesn't pick up. She has to sleep *some* time, after all.

"How's the signal decoding?" I ask before stepping through the door, which Driver has just exited.

She shakes her head. "There still hasn't *been* any decoding," she sighs. "Sharing the news hasn't really moved us forward, but the good news is that it hasn't been a disaster, either. Shaun and the others will fill you in. But don't be too long if you have to get your stuff from the dorms. I want to hit the Balena ASAP, and our window opens in two hours."

"*Two* hours?" I echo with wide-eyed surprise. "Wow. Okay, I'll get to it. The doctor says I can walk for twenty or thirty minutes, and that getting on my feet for short sustained bursts like that will be good for me."

I step inside to a warm reception from the others. None of them are too surprised to see me, which figures since the doctor has been keeping Driver informed of my progress and even liaising with her and Major about my treatment.

"Talk to me about Phil O'Connor," I say, sitting down and focusing primarily on Major. "The doctor said he's been making himself a little too visible for her liking."

Major upturns his lip in thought. "I can see that," he shrugs. "He's working *with* us, though, not pushing any corporate agenda. Remember, Ray, he's already demonetized his creation for non-profit applications. Because the AI seems like an obvious tool we could use for this process, he's been in high demand for interviews. It's not like he's been saying anything controversial, he's just been saying the same things in a lot of places."

"What kinds of things?" I ask.

"Initially it was about the hope that we could decode this thing quickly," Major replies. "Almost as soon as your message reached Earth and sunk in, he was talking about how fortunate it is that we've received this message in a time when we have the AI at our disposal. Four or five hours ago, he was back on the news circuit trying to explain why we haven't already succeeded. He's not said anything we wouldn't say, really, just that the language translation and code breaking and pattern recognition abilities of the system are all trained on human data. It's like everything we talked about before we sent the message. This alien signal is difficult for us to understand precisely because it's an *alien* signal. It's alien in origin, but the whole thing is alien in nature, too."

"O'Connor oversold the likelihood of quick success," Chester interjects. "That's the only thing he did that I wouldn't have advised, because now people feel disappointed and concerned that we haven't cracked it yet. But like Senior Coordinator Major said, he's broadly done well."

"He's trying," President Williams adds from the video wall. Only Harriet, the SETI expert, is next to him. "Sasha is actually going to talk to him in the next hour or so about various strategies to look for some kind of key to unlocking this. Even after two days that's still where we are, Ray: looking for a key."

"So we're directly engaging with O'Connor," I reflect. "That's good. If Sasha can relay what Chester said about not overpromising, all the better. I just don't want him to end up keeping himself in the limelight if and when we *do* decode the signal. We don't want people putting too much stock in what the AI thinks we should do next, or reading into the aliens' intent. Because it's like what he's saying about why it can't crack the code yet and what Sasha was saying about why people might be scared of aliens. The system is trained on human data, and the data it'll have about aliens will almost all be based on ramped-up fears about hostility, invasion, colonization and everything else we don't want people worrying about. If it can help us crack the code, great. But then it's done."

"I couldn't agree more," Shaun says. "Sasha and I have talked about this exact point, and she'll be making absolutely sure Phil O'Connor understands it, too."

I breathe a sigh of relief, because all of that is very comforting to hear. "So what kind of reactions to the Leak and the alien news did we see from Earth?" I ask. "I mean, it's a pretty big deal."

"Shaun," Major says, tilting his head towards the table. "Would you?"

Shaun immediately performs some touch gestures on the high-tech table's surface. Within a few seconds, it's covered in images from TV news reports of my announcement.

To my surprise, the headlines from some of the largest outlets are fairly optimistic things like *"ALIEN SOLUTION TO ANOMALY?"* and *"ANOMALY SOURCE IDENTIFIED... IS ALIEN ASSISTANCE NEXT?"*

In all honesty, those are better first reactions than I could have expected.

I see a lot of others that are less perfect, with some focusing on the discovery of *"DEADLY COSMIC RADIATION"* and the vast majority being more concerned about the alien aspect.

One, from a sensationalist and frustratingly popular online news outlet, explicitly states that discovering the Anomaly's source and an alien signal at the same time points to an unavoidable conclusion: the aliens are responsible.

I quickly read the first few lines of the article. Its author stretches for a metaphor about hearing coyotes howling at night then finding garbage strewn around your yard in the morning. The coyote probably isn't calling you with tips on how to clean it up, the writer argues. He's the one who made the mess.

I find my eyes lingering on that article. It doesn't really hold true, since the howl isn't a carefully targeted call that's clearly intended only for us. Still, the broader point gives me pause for thought.

Our group's broadly hopeful take on things has been that the aliens might have sent a signal, four years ago, to warn us of the celestial threat of whatever phenomena lie behind the Anomaly-related Leak. Thinking along those lines serves us by keeping us focused on the task at hand rather than cowering in fear, so I force my eyes from the alternatively fatalistic take and look up to Shaun.

"This isn't too bad," I say. "Chester's ideas for framing it seem to have worked pretty well, right?"

"I'd say so," Shaun says. "There have been some regrettable reactions, but nothing we didn't see coming and not as widespread as we might have feared."

He swipes the table again with his forefinger, changing the images to some other reports.

This time I'm looking at more recent stories. The first one I see is about preppers heading for the hills in anticipation of an alien attack. That *is* the kind of thing we expected. And even though the events of recent years have massively ramped up the percentage of the population who would classify themselves as preppers, the overall number of people reacting like this isn't going to be very high.

Slightly more concerning are the images of national militaries readying themselves for any developments. Some leaders are clearly — and depressingly — using the news to rile up their populations and detract from domestic concerns, as is often the way when an opportunity for saber-rattling presents itself.

Again though, in the grand scheme of things, none of this comes close to the kinds of worst-case reactions we had been fearing. It's impossible to know how much weight we can place on the careful way Chester worded the announcement, or the fact that I was the one delivering it. Either way, I'd say our collective efforts have paid off pretty well.

I just hope to hell it won't be too long before humanity's collective *decoding* efforts start paying off, too.

Shaun shares his hope that connecting directly with our main AI systems on the Balena could bring progress very soon, and when Driver returns to the war room she loudly reminds us all that *very soon* means now.

"Our window is going to be open by the time you're ready," she says, addressing the three of us who will be going with her: me, Shaun and Chester.

Both the Vita and the Balena will be returning to low orbit, and the doctor assured me again today that I'll be cleared for a landing flight by the time we're back. In the meantime, the Balena is the place to be.

Right now, I don't know what meaningfully helpful things I'll be able to do there that I can't do here. But thinking about that brings me back to the talk I had with Driver when I first came around in the medical bay. We're still alive because we've taken action when there were actions to take. I survived on the Beacon by opening every door I could, even when there was no reason to expect anything useful would be inside.

I came to the Vita more in hope than expectation that I could push our understanding of the Anomaly to the next level, but that proved crucial, too.

The last few years have given me a strong bias towards action over passivity, and I think the surroundings and especially the population of the Balena could help me tackle the huge problems we're facing in ways I haven't even considered yet.

All of this is in my mind as I head off to gather my things and ultimately follow Driver towards a new-to-me launch bay where our small craft is waiting.

It's in that launch bay where I first catch sight of the Balena set against its natural habitat: the ocean of space.

Until now, I've only seen it on the ground. The scale is simply breathtaking. Even compared to the Beacon and the Vita, it's something else.

I'm utterly humbled by it, and I can tell that all the friends who have come to see us off share the same feeling.

Everyone is here: Major, Simone, the doctor and her team… and they all wish us well as we step into our spacecraft for the very short dock-to-dock flight.

It's a small craft that looks more like a spaceplane than anything else, but differs quite significantly in design as well as size.

I thank the medical staff warmly then say my goodbyes to Major and Simone, who apologizes once again for what her synthocite did to my hand. Even when I tell her not to worry about the past, she promises that she'll find a way to put things right.

Driver steps in first, making her way to the cockpit of the craft. She tells us in an airy tone that this one really does fly itself, even more so than the others that "pretty much" do. I'm relaxed about it, since she's never steered me wrong even when we've been in far sketchier-looking vehicles than this. Her words do seem to soothe the less experienced Chester and Shaun, though.

There's no blast off like we'd feel from Earth. It's smooth sailing. And once we're moving, the awe I feel as I watch the Balena grow ever nearer makes it impossible to tell exactly how many minutes pass.

Not many, that's for sure.

It almost feels like we arrive *too* soon, so incredible was the view as we headed for the dock, but the sound of Driver's hands clapping together in success is welcome nonetheless.

"Great job," Chester says.

"Just… wow," Shaun adds. "I feel like I'm dreaming."

As we step out into the inner dock a few minutes later, I share in the sentiment.

The interior of the Balena is utterly different from anything else I've ever seen, which makes sense since it was a ZolaCore creation unlike the Vita and the spaceplanes.

I wouldn't even know how to start describing it, and we're not even out of the docking bay. The real wonders lie beyond the door in front of us, and I hold my breath as it slowly opens.

President Williams stands tall, smiling to see us here safely. "Smooth as ever," he says to Driver, shaking her hand.

I hang back while he greets Chester for the first time and warmly reunites with Shaun.

Last of all, he steps towards me.

Absent of a hand to shake, he places his right hand on my shoulder. "Well, Ray," he begins, "we've been getting nowhere without you. What do you say… have you got one more big swing left in you?"

I hold his eyes and nod. "You're damn right I do."

"That's the spirit," he replies with a smile. "Okay, everyone. Follow me and we'll get down to business."

12

On the face of it, there are similarities to this moment and the one I experienced just a few days ago when I first stepped on to the Vita.

Major greeted me that day just as Williams is greeting me now, and the opening of a docking bay's door gave me my first sight of the interior. I was awestruck with wonder, just as I am now.

But on closer reflection, the similarities end there.

For one thing, Major shook my hand — because I still *had* a right hand.

For another, I arrived at the Vita thinking some irresponsible *human* activity was behind the Anomaly, whereas now I'm here to try to decode an alien signal we're all hoping is going to illuminate the situation.

Perhaps most of all, though, the biggest difference I'm feeling is my all-new level of speechlessness at the scale and complexity of everything around me.

Just a few seconds is all it takes to see the differences between the Vita and the Balena. Really, it's all inherent in the fact that *this* colossal spacecraft was designed as a bona fide starship rather than a reconfigurable evacuation craft.

It always pains me to give Zola credit for anything, but his Balena-building team in New Zealand did an absolutely incredible job. I have to hand the bastard that.

I know the main entrance area isn't even scratching the surface of what lies inside, too.

Driver has told me a lot about some of her favorite places, like the Zero G training zone and the so-called Bayzen Room. I've also seen a lot of informational videos. Still, *nothing* comes close to actually being here.

"Sasha is still on her call with Phil O'Connor from PhilosophAI," Williams explains as we step inside. "The original plan was for them to talk about new strategies in our search for a breakthrough. Now, some of the conversations you started have made Sasha keen to ensure Phil is more careful about what he says in public, too. We really do want to make a clear division between AI analysis of the signal and AI interpretation of the aliens' intent, as you said. Even more so, we want to set a clear parameter that there will be no leaning on the AI for decision-making. Its biases can't decide how we react to any message we're able to discern from the signal."

"Good," I say.

Sasha is hyper-competent on a level that I've only ever seen Shaun rival, and from what Driver has told me she's grown into a priceless member of the Balena team over the last year. She's still very young, like Shaun, but together they've proven their worth time and time again. Having her in there with O'Connor is a very good thing.

"Is Harriet with them?" Driver asks, noticing that the expert in extraterrestrial outreach isn't next to Williams as she was during our video calls.

"Yes, she did go with Sasha," Williams replies. "Harriet wants to feed the AI some of the signals and messages her teams have sent out towards the stars over the years and decades. If the aliens are replying, as she thinks they might be, they could be including or quoting elements of the original messages. The AI will look for things we can't see — like the size of packets of data, I think she said. Her hope is that it might get us somewhere. I don't know, we'll see. Some of her data has never been public, so the AI hasn't been trained on it. Needless to say, we're some way past the point of being beholden to Classified designations."

"How much longer are we expecting the call to go on?" Driver pushes.

Williams looks at his watch. "I'd say another hour or two. Sasha had a list of points and thought it would take most of the afternoon."

"I guess I didn't have to rush you guys so much," Driver says to our arriving team. "But since we have some free time, I'm dying to see the Bayzen Room now that the PFOA will have fed in new observations. You'll all love it, too."

"Oh, the same Bayzen Room you mentioned a few days ago?" Chester asks. He sounds intrigued and even excited by it, in no small part thanks to Driver's obvious enthusiasm.

"There will be time for that," Williams cuts in. "Maybe even before Sasha is free and we can reconvene. But before you take Ray anywhere, I think he has an appointment in bionics. Ray… my understanding is there's a hand with your name on it. What do you say?"

Everyone turns to me.

"I'll give that idea a thumb-up," I reply. "Soon to be two."

The others laugh.

"Do you want me to come with you?" Driver asks.

"Yeah," I say, not too proud to pretend otherwise.

The idea of having a bionic hand is an appealing one, especially when the alternative is no right hand at all. But now that the procedure is imminent, I'm having natural concerns about what it's going to entail.

She nods. "No problem. Noah, you could show Shaun and Chester around if you're just waiting for Sasha to be done. We'll do the Bayzen Room later."

"Sure thing," Williams says. "Good luck in there. They assure me it's a simple procedure, Ray, and it'll be more than worth it."

"Thanks," I reply, gulping as I turn around to follow Driver's lead to the Bionics Center.

13

"Ray Barclay, as I live and breathe," a young bionics engineer smiles as I enter his lab.

I'm not going to say *disconcertingly* young, but he isn't exactly a grizzled old vet.

Then again, in a field as young and ever-evolving as bionics, I suppose age and experience have less importance than they do in others.

"He's pretty nervous, Earl," Driver tells the guy. "Obviously he's never had anything like this procedure."

Earl raises his eyebrows and tilts his head back while looking at me. "Well that makes two of us, my friend. This is my first time, too."

I feel my stomach knot.

Driver playfully punches him on the arm. "I've told you before, Earl: it's not a joke if no one knows you're joking." She turns to me. "He's done this dozens of times."

"Hundreds," Earl corrects her. "Admittedly all on the same person, but hundreds nevertheless. And yes, sorry, Ray. I'm just trying to keep things light."

"Why do you keep operating on the same person?" I ask, feeling like there must be another joke I'm still not getting.

"I definitely wouldn't call it *operating*," Earl says in a sincere tone. "It's more of an *attaching* process than anything else. But anyway, we have another researcher here who is an amputee. She's been very patient and generous in allowing us to refine some of our processes. This is ready for mass adaption on Earth and it's going to revolutionize life for a lot of people. I'm not going to sit here and say you should count yourself lucky in any of this, Ray, because you've paid a very unfortunate price for a very brave action. But you are in a fortunate position of having access to our lab. There's just one thing I need to clarify with you before we get started."

I like Earl.

Sure, he jumped in with a bad joke to kick things off. But there's a real earnestness about him.

"Ask away," I tell him.

"It's about the nerve damage you experienced in your right hand after the car crash in your teens. Can you tell me as much as possible about that? What kinds of things you struggled with, if some fingers remained stronger than others, whether you noticed any difference in feeling below your wrist. Anything and everything you can remember."

I do as he asks, telling him everything I can remember.

I guess this stuff isn't in any medical records Earl has access to, which probably has something to do with the cut-rate physiotherapists my stepfather took me to when he was so cruelly bitter about the accident he seemed to resent me for surviving when his son — my big brother — wasn't so lucky.

"Excellent," Earl says. "Thanks. The important answers are the ones I wanted, and the others don't matter too much. How this works is that we're going to securely attach a bio-interface to your wrist. The hand, which is already fabricated to your specifications, then connects to the interface. The hand can be easily swapped out in case of damage, malfunction, or even if a more advanced model is developed. The interface can also be removed, albeit a little less comfortably, but the good news in your case is that we don't have to extend very far down your arm at all. Just below the radio-carpal joint here. It's a *huge* advantage that your doctors on the Vita were able to seal the wound as high as they have with minimal tissue loss. You'll be able to move the hand as a whole in a purely physical way, regardless of the neural connection that will enable independent finger movement."

Driver raises a finger of her own. "In English?"

"He can control his wrist, and your wrist moves your hand," Earl says. "Ray is going to be dependent on the neural connection for fine movements, but he'll be able to turn it and so on even if the link isn't functioning."

"Why wouldn't the link be functioning?" I ask.

"Interference is the short answer," Earl says. "I'm sure you know we're going to painlessly inject a neuro-sensor in each temple, and that those will transmit instructions to your hand. Laboratory testing has shown that the connection temporarily breaks down if the user is surrounded by unusually concentrated amounts of interference from other sources. Nothing bad happens, it just doesn't work. In such cases, the hand will gently open and remain pliable but unable to grip. There is absolutely no danger to you from the injected sensors, which are fully insulated and stress-tested in all environments. This isn't a movie where they're going to short circuit and render you motionless or anything like that."

I gulp. I know he's trying to help, but even introducing that idea into my mind by way of saying it *won't* happen is pretty unsettling. As nice a guy as I think Earl is, his bedside manner could really use some work.

"So can we just like... *do* it?" Driver asks, tipping her head towards Earl to signal that time is of the essence.

"Message received," Earl says, turning around and crouching down to a small storage area that looks oddly like a tabletop drinks refrigerator. "Now, your new hand and its bio-interface attachment have both been fabricated based on the measurements and data they sent over from the Vita. It really is the first time we've relied on remote measurements, but the worst-case scenario here is that the attachment just won't fit. It has to be *very* snug, but too small is too small."

"What if I lose or gain muscle?" I ask.

"Good question," Earl replies, "but that's nothing to worry about. The interface is made of an extremely light alloy and it's attached to your *skin*, nothing deeper. And like I said, this isn't like a sleeve that has to go a long way down your arm. The Vita's doctors have done a great job. Your *wrist* isn't going to gain or lose any discernible muscle, other than with very deliberate effort, and that's where the bio-interface will be. For total peace of mind, though, just remember that the interface *can* come off if it ever has to, albeit only under medical supervision."

Satisfied with Earl's answers, and more broadly with the fact that Williams and Sasha and everyone else on the Balena has authorized this as a good idea, I ask Driver to help me out of my sling and then hold my right arm out for Earl.

He begins slowly removing the padding my doctors applied. I flinch at one point, which makes him stop, but I tell him to keep going.

"It's a good thing that you're responsive like that," he assures me. "It *will* mean you feel the attaching process quite sharply — I'm not going to lie about that — but it's important that you feel for snugness before I perform the seal."

When the bandages are all the way off, I look down at my handless wrist for the first time.

"Wow," Earl says. "They really have made this easy for us. Look at how clean and smooth this is."

"I'd rather not," Driver replies, accurately speaking for me, too.

Earl chuckles. "Okay, I get that. I won't make you look. But I think the only way they could have achieved such a straight—"

"Earl," Driver admonishes him, with a sharp tone and intense gaze.

He holds his hands up. "Sorry. I'm just... no, okay. Sorry.

Anyway, Ray, this is your new hand," he says, reaching back down and lifting it out.

I take hold of it, marveling at the lifelike look and feel. The inside of the connection point at the bottom brings to mind something more like a SCART lead than a USB, with a number of prongs to secure it rather than one clicking-in point.

"You'll feel a little prick for each of these injections," Earl goes on, slowly walking behind me and rubbing his finger on my left temple to find the desired spot. "Keep looking at the hand and I'll place the first sensor in three... two... one."

With nothing more than the little prick he promised, it's in.

"Ready for number two?" he asks.

"Let's do it," I reply, making an effort to return his chirpiness.

He counts down again and injects the second sensor.

Well, Ray, I think to myself. *There's no going back now...*

14

The sensors Earl has just injected into my temples are probably the most marvelous part of this whole thing, as small and unseen as they are.

The number of technological breakthroughs needed to reach that level of complexity at that size is simply staggering, and I do feel lucky to be alive at a point in time when such things are possible.

"You're doing great," Earl tells me. "I'm not going to lie, though… the next part is the hard part. I *could* check the sizing while you have full feeling and then numb your wrist before I make the seal," he offers. "Like I said, I'm relying on the measurements they took on the Vita, and those were of your *left* wrist. That's why it's good for you to have feeling, but the actual attaching process is when 'feeling' will become 'pain'. You seem to be in a hurry, but for the sake of the three or four minutes it would take for the numbing injection to kick in, I would recommend it."

"Of course," Driver answers for me. "Earl, whatever he says, you're numbing it."

Wow… she's *really* answering for me.

"Ray?" Earl says, seeking confirmation either way.

"You're the expert," I tell him. "There's no strength in

enduring unnecessary pain. So if you think it's best to numb it, we'll numb it."

Pleased by my answer, Earl returns to the fridge-like storage container and produces my bio-interface attachment. I truly cannot believe how small it is.

The thing almost looks like a double-wide handcuff, hollow at one side and closed with a series of connectors on the other.

"This will be permanently attached to your wrist," Earl explains once more. "Permanently meaning it won't come off unless we *take* it off, not literally permanently. The hand, like I said, can detach and reattach to this all day long. Excessively frequent disconnection could weaken the link-up, naturally, but the threshold for that is higher than you would ever reach. Do you have any more questions for now?"

I shake my head.

"Okay, then allow me to place this in position," he says, gently doing so. It slides slowly into place like a bracelet, stopping when the closed end hits my wrist stump.

"Ohhh," I grimace.

"*Perfect,*" Earl smiles, taking it off once more. "You felt it exactly when you should have, right when it reached the seal point. It fits like a glove, Ray. If you hadn't felt that, I would have been worried it was too loose. If you'd felt it any sooner, we would have had the opposite problem."

He hands the interface to Driver then walks to the other side of his lab.

"If you don't like needles, look away now," he says.

"And if you *do* like needles, see a psychiatrist," Driver quips.

I look away, because why wouldn't I?

Earl counts down from three. His "one" is accompanied by a sound from me that I'm not proud to say probably sounded an awful lot like a whimper.

"Yeah…" Earl exhales slowly. "I know you're a tough guy, Ray. So *damn*. When your wrist was tender enough to make the injection hurt like that, you probably would have passed out if we'd done the attaching process without anesthetic."

A broad tingling feeling slowly replaces the concentrated sharpness in the injection spot. I feel the anesthetic doing its work as my arm becomes heavy. I tell Earl when it feels totally dead, but he's now absolutely insistent on waiting a full five minutes. I think the evident level of tissue tenderness I felt during the injection has spooked him more than me, and he's not taking any chances now.

Eventually, he's ready to go. He asks me to lift my right arm onto the table with my left, then gently secures it down with a cushioned clamp. There's no other word than clamp for it, cushioned or not, and I don't need feeling in my arm to know that it's tight.

Entering a new state of total and hyper-professional focus, Earl then takes the bio-interface attachment back from Driver and slots it back over my wrist. Once it's there, in place but not secured, he picks up another small device from the table.

It looks like a ball at one end, but has the same connecting points as my hand at the other. "Let me know instantly if you feel this too much and I'll up the dose," Earl says, without breaking his visual focus. He then pushes the ball-like attachment in to the interface, pushing no more than he has to, and ultimately taps a small button that's recessed on the side of the ball facing him.

When he taps that button, the bio-interface around my wrist begins to tighten in all directions, with the movement accompanied by a slightly unnerving hissing sound.

My eyes are trained on Earl's for clues as to how this is going. A few seconds later, he closes his eyes and breathes what looks very much like a sigh of relief.

"Done?" I ask.

"Done," Earl says. "You can take this attachment out with your left hand by pressing the button," he goes, "and then you can insert the hand. You won't feel any of that. The hard part is done. We've basically attached a dock to your wrist, and now you can connect the hand."

I can't help but smile widely. "This is kind of like Bex on the Beacon," I say to Driver. "I mean, she had wrecking balls and drills as well as hands, but…"

"Well, the only limit is our own imagination," Earl laughs heartily. He was so intense during the actual procedure that I barely recognized him, but now he's back to the easy-going guy who greeted us with a bad joke when we first walked in.

I reach for the far side of the ball, which is made awkward by the fact that my right arm is still clamped to the table. I'm able to find the button, though, and pressing it does detach the whole ball from my wrist-base dock, as Earl described it.

I then take the new hand and put it in place. I'm hesitant to push it in, but Earl tells me it won't hurt at all. He says the material of the interface is harder than its lightness would suggest. And really, he's been so diligent about causing no more pain than necessary that I'm more than willing to take him at his word.

The ball was a special one-time attachment used to tighten the dock, so that tightening process isn't going to happen again. The dock is fixed in place, for good, and according to Earl it should now be plug and play.

After all of this I'm definitely looking forward to playing, which is to say making use of the remarkable gift of a new hand, but first of all I have to plug it in. I push it firmly, easily establishing a connection.

"If you ever want to take the hand off, you'll find a pressure point on the bottom knuckle of the fourth finger," Earl says. "Pushing there will allow an easy disconnection for the next five seconds. The hand won't ever fall off — or fall *out*, if you prefer to think of it that way — but it *can* be jerked out under extreme force. That's a safety feature and it won't cause any pain. You should experience very convincing sensations of touch and pressure that truly feel like they're coming from the hand as soon as your anesthetic wears off, but there are limits in place to ensure you won't feel any pain. That ensures there can't be any agonizing malfunctions."

"So you're saying I'll have feeling in this hand, but not too much," I say, pretty sure I follow.

"Exactly," he nods. "And like I said, the hand can always come off if you want it to. Now you're just going to have to wait until the feeling returns to your wrist, at which point it should also be present in your hand. I think for you that's going to be slightly less jarring than for amputees who have been without their hands for a long time, but it's still going to be a pretty special moment."

I'm sure it is, I think to myself.

While we wait, Earl asks if it's okay to talk about the big issues of the day. Driver defers to me, and I'm more than happy to answer his questions about why we're here and what we hope to achieve. Discussing the AI and Phil O'Connor's comments, which Earl is well aware of, makes the time pass pretty quickly.

So quickly, in fact, I feel a welcome tingle in my wrist before I know it.

I'm already free from the clamp, and both Earl and Driver look over with keen interest as my arm moves.

"Is it working?" Driver asks.

"It'll take a minute for full feeling and control to return to the arm, let alone the hand," Earl says. "Give him some time."

I don't try any sudden movements, preferring to wait until I'm sure.

And yeah… I'm sure.

"Well?" Driver asks. "Is it working?"

Without trying any minor twitches to test things out, I decide to just go for it.

So with one single movement, requiring no more deliberate thought than any other physical action, I swing my right arm around and raise its brand new thumb.

"Bingo," Earl smiles.

I reach out with my new hand, eerily natural in almost every way, and offer it to Earl.

When he shakes it, I feel everything.

Not too much and not too little, I feel everything.

Smiling widely, I echo Earl's reaction: "*Bingo.*"

15

After a few quick calibration tests to make sure everything is working exactly as it should be, I'm more impressed by this artificial hand than I ever have been by anything.

Seriously, it is *that* good.

I know the real work is being done by the sensors, but I'm thinking of the whole system as one integrated whole.

Earl is absolutely beaming with joy as we finish the tests and he tells me I'm good to go.

"Now, as tempting as it might be," he grins, "I don't want you to go blowing up your left hand so you can get another one of these, okay?"

Driver and I both laugh. It's nice to have something to smile about for a change.

The new hand isn't just a welcome bonus compared to having nothing. It's genuinely better than the nerve-damaged hand I had before. My grip strength had been shot for years — two decades, really — and that made life difficult.

My misadventures on the Beacon come straight to mind. I'll never forget when that hand's weakness meant I couldn't operate the station's remote repair arm and had to go outside on the fateful spacewalk that ultimately cost me my contact lenses and majorly slowed down my escape plans.

All of that is behind me now, though. I've got two fully working hands for the first time since I was a teenager, and I can't wait to use them however I can to help our mission to stop the Anomaly before it's too late.

"Have you ever been in the Bayzen Room?" Driver asks Earl, my bionic miracle worker.

"Can't say I have," he says.

She holds his eyes. "Do you want to come? We're going to take a look while we wait for Sasha and Phil O'Connor to finish up their call."

"Ah… I have to do the paperwork and filing on this right away," Earl sighs. "Protocol is protocol, even if *you* guys were to try and give me a free pass. Thanks, though. Next time."

"Sure thing," Driver says, motioning to the door.

I follow her.

"High five, man," Earl offers me.

"Give me a stinger," I grin.

And sure enough, he does.

At least… it should sting. The strength of his slap and the sound of the connection are befitting of one hell of a stinger, and his humorous hand-waving reaction tells me that his palm is stinging.

But mine? Well, there's a *feeling*, but it's not pain. Nowhere near what it would be on a real hand.

"The feedback limitations are watertight," Earl grins, noticing that I'm looking curiously at my hand and clearly ascertaining what I'm thinking. "And speaking of watertight, you don't have to worry about getting any part of this wet. Cool, huh?"

"Flat-out amazing," I reply, stunned all over again as we head out of the door. "And thanks for everything, Earl. We'll see you around."

The walk to what Driver has been calling the Bayzen Room is shorter than I'd like, really, because I want to see more of the Balena as a whole. She's had her heart set on showing me inside this since the moment we knew we were coming here, though, so I'm more than willing to go along with it.

All I know is that the Bayzen Room contains ultra-realistic wraparound screens that fill the walls, and that Driver can't wait to see what new visualizations are going to be there now that the PFOA telescopes have picked up some new data.

Anything we can observe about Bayzen is four years out of date, just like any signals we receive, what with the speed of light being the unbudging constant that it is. That doesn't make much difference for our purposes, though, which basically involve enjoying an AI-based artistic impression of what the distant world is actually like.

I've always been massively intrigued about Bayzen, but for Driver and her colleagues it's a way of life. Hell, I'd go so far as to say it's the thing that gives some of their lives purpose. They are *here* with the intention of one day going *there*, in this incredible spacecraft Zola built for the same purpose — albeit for very different and far more demented reasons.

"I did tell you about this in Orbs, didn't I?" Driver asks before opening the door.

One thing I've noticed about the Balena is things don't seem to be locked like they are everywhere else. I suppose so far we've only entered the bionics lab where Earl was already inside, and for all I know there might be some kind of biometric technology on the door knobs, anyway. I'm sure high-security areas are locked down, and that's what counts.

On the other hand, there could also just be a major difference in the culture of this place. After all, everyone who lives and works here is all-in on the plan of setting course for Bayzen as soon as a suitable and sufficient fuel supply is on hand. That contrasts hugely with the Vita and even the Beacon, where researchers were often working on competing projects with funding from rival corporations and institutions.

"You told me some of it, yeah," I reply. "We get an AI generation of the planet, and then speculative views of what the surface could look like, right? All based on the latest data?"

"Exactly," she nods excitedly. "And it tells us the confidence intervals for the data that's informing the projections. We can increase and decrease the speculation levels, too, and ask it to show us how things would look if certain variables were different. With the new data from the PFOA, I don't know what I'm going to see."

"Just as long as you know we're not going to see alien cities or anything like that, right?" I say. "The Bayzen-facing telescopes in the new array aren't giving us detailed new *visual* data. They're traveling towards Bayzen so everything is going to keep improving, but we're not going to be in that ballpark for a long while yet, even with the new technologies."

She rolls her eyes. "I'm not an idiot, Ray. I know the new scopes aren't magic, but Sasha says they're a quantum leap forward. That's good enough for *me* to get excited about..."

"Let's see what we're dealing with," I smile, excited in my own right.

When I step in — ahead of Driver, at her absolute insistence — I feel my jaw drop instantly.

The digital projections all around me are utterly incredible, with the vast blackness of space looking as real as it did from the windows of our craft on the way here. But most strikingly and awe-inspiringly of all, the wall straight ahead of me is filled by an image of Bayzen that brings three words to mind:

Pale Blue Dot.

Everything gets even sharper and more immersive when Driver fully closes the door behind herself, removing all external light from the equation.

"Closer," she says.

I turn around, not that I can see her in the almost unbroken darkness, because it takes me a moment to realize she's talking to the system. I realize when the room, really more of a booth, gets brighter as the projected image of Bayzen gets larger and larger.

"Closer," Driver repeats as the zooming function slows. Her order makes it pick right up. At first, Bayzen looked like a large star might when viewed from Earth's surface. It filled that much of the sky, is what I mean.

Now it's more like the Moon. A full moon in a close month, too — big, bright, and full of detail.

"Stop," Driver says.

I turn to her again, and in the reflected light of the world she's been working so hard to one day reach, I see tears welling in her eyes. The smile says a lot, but the tears say the rest.

"Ray, I couldn't see the green like that last time," she forces out through her evident emotion. "And look at the confidence level... 82 percent. That's way higher than I used to get at this distance. Something the array has picked up is already telling it about the likely surface composition. We always figured there would be abundant plant life along with all the water, but now it *knows*."

I'm admittedly no expert on the finer points of this kind of thing. But while I don't share Driver's certainty about these images, I'm certainly not going to rain on her parade. The people who build cutting edge Poly-Field telescopes and create these kinds of programs know what they're doing, and if that's good enough for Driver it's good enough for me.

"It's sharper, too," she goes on. "I know this isn't a 'real' image, before you say anything. But until now the system has avoided too much focus on the planetary views unless you dial up the speculation level, because it didn't want to give overly clear images that might be totally wrong. This is amazing. So much clearer. So much better. It makes it feel so much closer. And now, to think there are intelligent beings living there, trying to reach out to us..."

I smile at the sentiment.

"I swear to God, Ray..." Driver says in an earnest tone. "I'm going to set foot on that planet if it's the last thing I do."

All I can do is nod warmly. Again, I can't possibly share in that confidence. But again, I'm not going to dampen a good person's enthusiasm and optimism for a worthwhile mission. The Bayzen Project is the kind that is advancing humanity's scientific understandings every day. The people here have a goal in mind, but they're achieving things every step of the way — whether they get there or not.

Before we get to the surface-level views, which I know are far more speculative than any of this and are really just for fun, a triple knock on the door takes both of our attention.

"Come in," Driver calls.

The light from the doorway is momentarily disorienting as it opens, given how quickly my eyes have adapted to the darkness in here, but I make out Sasha's silhouette even before she speaks.

"Are you guys almost done?" she asks.

"We were pretty much waiting for you," Driver says. "Why, is something up?"

By the time we're at the door, which is only a few seconds later, I can tell from Sasha's expression that she's come to hurry us along for a good reason.

"Not necessarily," she replies, holding the door open for us to exit the incredible Bayzen Room. "But we need to talk about Phil."

16

Outside of the Bayzen Room, Sasha isn't alone.

Clearly fresh out of her video meeting with PhilosophAI founder Phil O'Connor, she's already gathered the rest of the group on her way to find us.

Standing beside President Williams, I see Harriet in the flesh for the first time. Her posture has the same air of poise and wisdom I first took from her appearance on the Vita's video wall, and I'm relieved to see she doesn't look overly concerned by anything.

Sasha's tone in telling us we have to talk about Phil was uncharacteristically tense, though, so Harriet's *appearance* of calm might only be that.

Since neither Shaun nor Chester were in the meeting, I can't be sure if they'll know anything yet. That means I can't read much into their expressions.

"Phil is getting increasingly downbeat about our chances of cracking this signal," Sasha says, ending the silence and with it my frantic wondering about what's going on.

I exhale slowly in relief. That's not good news, since Phil knows his own world-leading AI better than anyone else, but it could have been a lot worse. I was concerned that impatience in making measurable progress on the signal might have sent him veering towards asking the AI more subjective questions, on issues like why it thinks the aliens are talking to us in the first place.

We've covered the problem with that, reflecting on how the inherent human biases built into the system would result in overly negative answers, and I'm glad we're all still on the same page.

"Even with Harriet's signals going in as extra data?" Driver asks. "He doesn't think it could look for similarities to that, in case the aliens have tried to reply in a way they think we would understand?"

"That needs time," Harriet interjects. "It did give him a little bit of hope, but in general he's not optimistic. It's ironic. Decades ago, when I first got involved in SETI projects, decoding an alien signal was exactly the kind of thing futurists and sci-fi enthusiasts thought an advanced AI could one day help us with. There was this optimistic idea that we would create machines capable of translating any unknown language into English at the click of a button, be it ancient cave writings or a message from the stars. *That* was never realistic, but I certainly hoped futuristic technology would assist us in a contact scenario more than it has so far. And just like I've dedicated my life and career to extraterrestrial communication, Phil has dedicated his — very lucratively — to the advancement of AI. Now that we find ourselves at this unfortunate impasse, we're both as disappointed as each other."

"Ray, your hand!" Chester exclaims, belatedly noticing it.

This draw's everyone else's attention to it, too, until I succinctly tell them it's working great and that I'll give the full details later. For now, my mind is on the signal and that's where I want everyone *else's* to be, too.

"What about the Balena's *own* AI?" I ask, facing President Williams since I think he'll be best placed to answer. "Wasn't ZolaCore developing all kinds of applications?"

"Some kinds," he says with a telling sigh. "If you think back to those days and what we uncovered, there was a lot of far-out research on brain uploads and things of that nature. That's never been something we've wanted to focus on. The underlying abilities of their nascent AI, for the computational analysis and other applications we are interested in, wasn't any further forward than Phil's."

"There was more to it than that," Shaun chimes in. "Reverse engineering ZolaCore's AI showed that they had actually built a lot of their infrastructure on stolen code from PhilosophAI's first iteration. And like President Williams said, Zola then took it in his own crazy direction with the attempts to clone that poor guy Carlo's consciousness. That was all about guiding the kids from the Valerio Institute during the flight to Bayzen and beyond. We burned the brain upload project to the ground and most of the kids from the Institute are back on Earth. All but one, right, Sasha?"

"Just one," she nods.

Hmm. I knew some of the kids we liberated from Zola's evil so-called school, for neurodivergent boys from disadvantaged families, were deemed too young to be capable of making the choice to stay on the Balena. I also know they went into individually tailored care of family placements on Earth. I really thought a few more of the older ones had chosen to stay, though.

"We had a few to start with," Sasha goes on, "but all but one have asked to leave since then. They never had the chance of a normal life, but they were still used to being able to look out of the window and see the sky. Space really isn't for everyone. The one who stayed, Santino, is 21 now. He said he wants to be as far away from Earth and the memories it holds as he possibly can be. He wants us to reach Bayzen more than anyone else here, except maybe Driver."

Driver raises her eyebrows at that. "He seems like a good guy. I don't have many interactions with him, to be honest. I don't think he has all that many interactions with anyone. He's... he's a different kind of guy. I'm not saying anything bad, he's just different. I mean, just like all the kids, he was chosen for the Institute *because* he was different, and then the isolation and the so-called mental training made him even more different. But yeah, he has a good heart. I've seen him with the animals. That always says a lot."

Sasha is nodding. "He's a genuine savant, too. *Easily* the most powerful mind here, and he would make a hell of a systems analyst and coordinator if he was a more comfortable communicator. *I* interact with him most days. He's always asking if there's anything he can do to help us get to Bayzen faster, but, you know, there hasn't been. When he finds out about the synthocite research on the Vita, I bet he'll come up with some way we can continue that more safely. Installing some kind of automated reaction chamber isn't beyond possibility, and he's the first guy I'd go to with something like that."

"What about the signal?" I blurt out. This information is all pretty interesting and Santino sounds like a good and potentially useful guy to have around, but I feel like the others are missing something obvious. "If he has the sharpest mind here, trained at Zola's Institute to be hyper-rational and obsessive about details, why isn't he working with us on the signal?"

"He is," Sasha replies. "Well, he's working on his own. Santino doesn't like groups. He doesn't like AI, either. He loved Carlo — the only person who was ever *kind* to those boys, even if he did play his part in keeping them confined — and he just hates the idea that Zola tried to extract the essence of Carlo into a machine."

Carlo…

That poor bastard. Sure, he was mixed up in some terrible stuff, but he was vulnerable in his own way when Zola roped him in and he really did care about the boys. He helped us to no end in taking Zola down for good, too, when he learned the full truth. I'll never get the image out of my head of the moment when Zola killed him, right in front of me, for no damn good reason.

"Maybe we should give him my data?" Harriet suggests.

"We've fed it into the AI for analysis, so why not pass it along to Santino, too?"

Sasha furrows her brow in thought. "You know, that actually wouldn't hurt. We can't expect it to help, but you never know. We're just looking for some clue or sign of structure in the alien signal, and maybe knowing what they might be replying to will give Santino an idea of what to look for. Phil himself has been saying the AI's inherent lack of true creative flexibility and intuition is apparent now that it's faced with a genuinely novel problem. Santino's intuition can be uncanny, so there's more than *no* chance he can help with this."

Before anyone says anything else, Sasha takes a few steps to her left and the rest of us follow.

"I'll just give him this hard drive of Harriet's data that we fed into the AI," Sasha goes on. "His room isn't far."

Once again, the walk really is a short one. I still marvel in wonder as I pass various incredible sights along the way, from a transparent cylindrical elevator in the middle of the hallway to what looks like the entrance to a huge atrium.

When we reach a door with a small plaque that reads *S. MANCINI*, Sasha knocks three times.

"It's Sasha," she calls, pressing her ear to the door after doing so.

"You can come in," a low voice replies. His accent is Italian, which seems obvious now that I'm hearing it but still comes as a surprise in the moment.

Sasha opens the door, which once again isn't locked.

Inside, I see a large room that looks almost like a studio apartment. The bed is well made and the floor and shelves are completely uncluttered. At the far side, a long desk containing three monitors is strewn with paper. Santino is sitting there in a blue T-shirt with his back to the door.

"I brought some new data," Sasha says.

The young man raises the index finger of his left hand, asking her to wait a minute while he jots something down with the pen in his right.

"I brought someone you might like to meet, too," she goes on.

Still, he scribbles away.

"It's Ray, Santino. Ray Barclay."

At this, his right hand stops writing at the same moment his left falls to his side. He spins around in his chair, so fast that he knocks a drinking glass to the floor with his elbow, smashing it into a hundred pieces.

He looks straight at me, though, ignoring the spill.

I gulp, hoping he doesn't hold me responsible for the death of Carlo — the only person he was ever close to...

17

"Ray…" the young man says, looking at me with intense eyes. That might be how he looks at everyone, so I try not to read too much into it.

"Hey," I reply, sounding as relaxed as I can. "I hear you've been working on this signal like we have?"

Santino keeps looking at me for a few seconds, then spins back around in his chair. "I don't have anything to tell you," he says flatly.

I turn to Sasha, who gives a slight shrug as if to tell me not to take it personally.

"Let me help you with that glass," Chester says, stepping into the room, beyond the rest of us. He crouches down and begins putting the small shards into the jagged remnant of the base. "The same thing happened to me this morning. Say… what's that cube you have up there?"

Without turning his chair, Santino looks back at Chester and then follows his inquisitive eyes up to a shelf by the desk, on which he has something that looks like a more complicated version of a Rubik's cube.

"Can I see?" Chester asks.

While I look on, more than a little confused by everything

I'm seeing, Driver leans in to whisper in my ear: "Chester has worked with all kinds of kids. I know you still don't like him, but one thing he's good at is connecting with people. Maybe with a guy like Santino — and a lot of people, really — if you ask what he's working on, he feels pressure. But if you ask him to tell you about something he's interested in, he feels passion."

That instantly makes a lot of sense. Chester's ability to connect with people in an individualized way played into why I didn't like him in the first place, in all honesty, due to how fully he played me with the whole fake message he engineered to get me on the Vita. I've softened on him since then, though, after how good he proved at managing our public message about the signal.

Sure enough, his approach here is enough to get Santino out of his chair and reaching for the puzzle cube.

Within no more than a minute, Chester has organically linked their conversation to the signal by talking about how it seems to be a puzzle everyone is trying to solve at once.

"Would you like to see the new data Sasha has for us?" Chester asks. "We're hoping it could be a new clue for how to solve this thing."

"Sure," Santino replies, turning to Sasha.

She said earlier that he didn't like groups, and to be honest I think even *I* might feel uncomfortable with what must seem like a wall of faces standing by the doorway. Now that he's comfortable with Chester and focused on the new data, though, Santino looks pretty relaxed.

"My friend Harriet has sent some messages into space in the past," Sasha explains. "Sounds, symbols, images. We think there's a chance the aliens might have received them and that their reply could be related to what she sent."

Santino takes the hard drive without saying anything else, now seemingly in *total* focus mode, and plugs it into his computer.

"This is a lot," he says when the folders appear.

"There aren't too many different images and messages," Harriet replies, "they're just separated into projects. Some of those folders only have a few files in them, and a lot of the files are duplicated between folders."

Santino, now seated again, nods a few times without turning round while Chester picks up the rest of the glass. He begins copying the contents of the hard drive to his own.

"I see you like animals, too," I say while we're waiting for that, trying to follow Chester's example for how to make a personal connection. On the leftmost of Santino's monitors, I've noticed what look like live feeds of several different species.

"Sometimes I just like to make sure they're okay and that the translation researchers are being good to them," he replies. "And some of these are the exact same animals you saved from the Beacon, you know."

I *didn't* know that, but I'm glad to hear it. I knew those animals made it back to Earth, but I didn't know what happened next. I also know there's no invasive research going on here, and that the conditions are excellent. The researchers who work on animal translation technologies are in frequent contact with Lorien and Vicki, who wouldn't be involved in anything if they weren't absolutely sure it was humane and enriching.

"None of them are like Laika," Santino says, apparently noticing that my eyes are lingering on a live feed of two smaller parrots. "He was *changed.* The people on the Beacon made genetic interventions. These animals are just trained to communicate and then used to help out with testing the new technologies. There is only one Laika. None of these animals can find patterns and do complex analysis like he can."

Looking between these live feeds and the scattered papers on Santino's desk, all of which are covered in notes made while *he's* been trying to find patterns within the impossibly complex alien signal, a far-out idea enters my mind.

"Do you want to meet him?" I ask. "Laika?"

Santino's eyes positively light up in the most evident sign of emotion I've seen from him.

"Laika?" he echoes excitedly. "I would love to!"

18

A call to let Eva know I've arrived safely on the Balena is overdue, but I have another idea in mind, too.

Phil O'Connor, whose company created the world's most powerful AI, is currently lamenting its inability to think flexibly and intuitively enough to decode the alien signal. We're also now sharing the latest data with Santino, so that his unique mind can look for something that opens the door.

All of this leads me to one more idea, borne more of hope than expectation, that Laika's genetically enhanced skills of pattern recognition and problem solving could be helpful here. It's a long shot, but there's no harm in trying.

I pull my phone from my pocket and start a video call to my family in Salt Lake City.

Being able to do that from here is something I pretty much take for granted, despite all the technologies involved. The fact that the Balena has been moving towards Earth for several days also means we shouldn't be troubled by much of the lag that made calling Driver inconvenient when she was stationed in a much higher orbit.

Eva answers fairly quickly and I immediately see that she's at the dining table.

"Are you on the Balena?" Joe blurts out, bursting into view

at Eva's side. I'm sure I hear his fork hit the floor and rattle to a stop.

I smile. "Sure am, kiddo. I didn't mean to interrupt dinner, though. How are you guys all doing?"

"Waiting for someone to tell us what the aliens are saying," he sighs, with impatience rather than any kind of trepidation. That's Joe for you, and with his love of everything sci-fi I know this alien development is like a dream come true.

"Pretty much," Eva adds. "Is anything happening up there, Ray? Because down here, people are getting antsy."

I force a nod. "Things are moving. We've fed the AI some new data about old signals we've sent into space, so it looks for any commonalities. We've got some great minds working on it, too. And as crazy as it sounds, I wanted to ask something else about that. Have you heard much from Lorien since you got home?"

"She's here," Eva replies. "Vicki came back with us, too, to stay with Laika. They've been trying to see if *he* could spot anything in the signal. You know how he is with puzzles and patterns."

I suddenly feel a lot less crazy than I did two minutes ago.

"Laika is too busy to play with me," little Scarlet glumly interjects, belatedly appearing at Eva's side.

"Only because he knows this could help you, darling," I tell her. "We're all trying to help you. Do you think you could carry the phone to him and our friends Lorien and Vicki?"

Eva stands up. "I'll do that while you finish up your peas," she tells Scarlet, walking towards my office. When she's out of earshot and almost there, she stops and asks a new question: "Do you have any new data about this radiation? The Leak? There's nothing on the news. It's all signal signal signal."

I look across to Sasha, who shakes her head.

"Nothing yet," I report. "I know some of our new telescopes are analyzing it, though, and we have whole teams focusing only on that. *We're* focusing on the signal and I can understand why it's the blockbuster news, but the Leak is being studied, too. If there's a way to deal with it without having to decode the signal, I'm sure our teams will find it. But until then, we're focusing where we feel like we can make progress."

Eva exhales slowly. "Okay. I'll hand you over to Lorien," she says, before knocking on my office door and stepping in.

When Eva flips the phone's camera control so I'm seeing what's in front of her instead of her face, I see Laika staring at my computer screen with Lorien on one side of him and Vicki on the other.

Viewing the scene like this makes it totally surreal.

Lorien turns around first. "Everything okay?" she asks, eyeing the outstretched phone with confusion.

"It's Ray," Eva explains.

Unlike when we arrived here to talk to Santino and Sasha called in, Laika doesn't turn around at the mention of my name. That's not like him, and certainly miles away from the reaction he displayed last time I called.

He's totally focused on the data on the screen, which I can't make out through the phone but which is almost certainly a visualization of part of the alien signal.

"Oh, hey!" Lorien exclaims. She takes the phone and flips the camera again so I can see her. Vicki quickly appears right beside her. "How's everything going?"

"Things are moving," I repeat. It's true, and somewhere close to the most positive I can sound without overstating any causes for short-term optimism. "I didn't realize you guys were working with Laika."

"He wanted to try," Vicki chimes in. "As soon as we heard the news about the signal, he wanted to see if there was anything he could do to help us out. He's hardly stopped."

"I would have told you guys right away," I say, "but the lines aren't totally secure and we had to be careful about how the world learned about this. It could have been messy if it leaked out as a fearful warning instead of us being able to frame it as an opportunity. Which we really think it *could* be, so it's not like there are any lies."

"I figured you couldn't tell us something," Eva replies, out of camera shot. "I should get back to the kids. But Ray, make sure you're sleeping and taking care of yourself, okay? No more passing out. Driver played that down when I couldn't reach you, but I need you to remember that you're not invincible. You're as human as the rest of us."

I sigh. "Yeah, you're right. I'll be smarter. Oh, but wait... Eva!" I add with a grin.

She walks back to look at the phone. "Yeah?"

"I'm not *quite* as human as the rest of you," I wink, holding up my new hand.

Her eyes widen. She looks more impressed than creeped out, and certainly surprised by how real it looks.

"Just don't blow that one up, too, okay?" Eva says, laughing before heading back to the kids.

I notice Santino moving in his chair as he leans to remove Harriet's hard drive from his computer. "Everything is copied across," he tells Sasha, handing it back.

He then stands up to my level and peers into the phone, evidently hoping Laika is going to turn around and engage with us soon.

"We have some new data about old SETI signals that we can send to my computer," I tell Lorien.

It crosses my mind that there's more than a hint of irony to this, given that compromised research data from *Lorien's* computer was what let the virus run rampant on the Balena when the signal knocked the security systems offline. It goes without saying that I'm hoping *this* data transfer will have much better results than that one.

"I'll get on that when I'm back at my desk," Sasha confirms.

"In the meantime..." I say, changing my intonation and then giving a loud two-tone whistle. "Laika! Come on, buddy. There's someone here who wants to talk to you. He's looking at the signal for clues, too."

Finally, Laika turns around.

"No clues, Ray Ray," he says. "Laika look and look. Laika sorry."

"Don't be sorry, Laika," Santino tells him, smiling as he speaks and looking genuinely happy for the first time since we all walked in. "This is difficult. I'm Santino, by the way."

"Tino," Laika squawks. "Hello, Tino. Tino like Laika? Laika good boy?"

"Tell him yes," I whisper. Chester might have been the one who knew how to get through to Santino, but I know Laika better than anyone. He's often like this when he meets new people, desperate to know that they like him and eager for explicit approval.

It all goes back to the way Laika was raised in a ZolaCore lab. In that regard, and in some very uncomfortable ways, he and Santino have a fair amount in common.

"You're definitely a good boy," Santino says. "And maybe one of us will find something in the new data. I'll show you."

As I hold the phone, Santino opens the first of the newly transferred folders on his central screen. The folder's name is *"01: Likeliest received"* and the status bar tells me it contains nineteen images. The first four are all large enough to make out, even at thumbnail size. Three are photographs — of Earth, people, and the sun — while one is a more detailed looking diagram with what look like scientific annotations. They're all square and have a thin gray border.

"Laika still no see clues," the little guy says, bowing his head in disappointment.

"Don't worry, this is just one part," Santino replies, really showing a warmth and connection to Laika. "And you can't even see it full size. You'll have it soon and I'll be looking through it all, too. It might give us an idea. One clue might be all we need."

Still looking pretty sullen, Laika squawks out a reply: "Laika try. But this not like puzzles with Scar Scar. Too many pieces. No corners to find first. No colors to find next."

Rapidly jumping back onto his seat like the floor is on fire, Santino almost knocks me off balance as he lands in it.

Before I can ask what's going on, he's opening one of the images to full size. "Laika..." he booms excitedly. "That could be it!"

19

"What could be it?" I ask, trying to follow Santino's insanely fast mouse gestures and keystrokes.

"Corners... colors... borders," he says.

"The borders on those images?" Harriet asks, coming closer to the screen. "What about them?"

Santino's fingers really are moving at an incredible speed, which seems like an insight into just how fast his mind is. Sasha said he was savant-like, and I'm definitely seeing that with my own eyes.

"If their signal is a reply to the signal you sent in their direction, it could reference the message format you used, which are images with this border," Santino says. He doesn't break focus or slow down as he answers Harriet. "I'm taking the hex color code and converting it into every format I can think of, adding some variation allowance, and searching sections of the alien signal for anything similar."

I turn to Sasha, who until a few minutes ago I would have narrowly placed above Shaun as the most brilliant mind I know. Santino is staking one hell of a claim to that title right now.

I don't have to say anything for her to know that I'm

wondering if there's any plausibility in what Santino is suggesting, but she speaks to him rather than me:

"It's a good idea, but the alien signal doesn't contain any color codes," she flatly tells him. She sounds like she's taking care not to dampen his creative thinking while still bringing a degree of realism to proceedings.

"We don't know what the signal contains," Santino tells us. "I'll bet you haven't looked for outdated color formats and other ways of representing color. I'll run the searches. But I also want to see what kinds of visualizations I can get from converting the data in these images into other modalities and forms. Then, I'll break them down into the base units we see in the signal. We're looking for *any* kind of similarity we can find — anywhere. So far everyone has been trying to break the signal down or build the signal up into packets of data we can recognize. Now that we have these images to think about, we should work at breaking them into as many kinds of packets as we can and then looking for structural similarities that way. Once we have *any* kind of clue, we're getting somewhere."

Sasha and Shaun exchange a silent but pensive glance, then turn to me.

"*That* I can get behind," Sasha says.

Shaun, meanwhile, looks more outwardly hopeful. "The borders and colors themselves might not lead anywhere, but manipulating our own image data in as many ways as we can — to try and make it look at all like the noise of the alien signal — is definitely worth doing. We should feed this in to the AI. Right away."

"Great work," I say to Santino, who is still busily typing and tapping away. "And you, Laika, little buddy. Corners and colors — just like our puzzles. Good boy."

I hear what Shaun was saying about how Laika's idea, which sparked Santino's, probably isn't going to be something that directly leads anywhere. But for all we know, it could have just started the chain reaction that *will.*

Santino's signal scanning and hands-on data manipulation

might not get us over the line, either, but he's already played a huge part by suggesting it. This idea of trying to make our own data look more like the data in the alien signal, through whatever conversions and modulations it takes, strikes me as the kind of thing the PhilosophAI system should excel at.

Phil O'Connor himself has been talking about the AI's weakness at having creative ideas to solve truly novel problems, but two unique minds just did that part and now we can give the system new prompts to make use of its strengths.

"Yeah, Laika," Santino says, looking away from his monitor for just long enough to face the phone and smile. "I don't want to celebrate too soon, but I think you just found the corners of our puzzle."

20

"I'll stay here," Chester says, as the rest of us get ready to rush off and feed this new idea into the AI.

No one argues, and his rapport with Santino makes Chester a good choice for this job.

"Let us know if you guys get anywhere," Sasha says. "*Anywhere*, okay? The slightest piece of new information could make all the difference. We'll get Phil back on the line and get a handle on the best way to tell the system what we want it to do. He created it, and he knows how to prompt it for optimal results better than anyone."

Chester nods firmly. "Sure thing. And we'll keep this quiet for a little while at least, I assume? So that if this new idea *does* lead to a breakthrough that finds the actual message inside this mess of a signal, we'll have a chance to react and deliver the news to Earth?"

"No," Sasha says.

He holds her eyes. "*No?*"

"Well, I don't mean we won't keep it quiet. We're not going to make any public announcements about a possible way forward that we're about to try, because there's no advantage to that. But we can't keep it quiet for long. PhilosophAI is a *very* powerful tool. Its central servers are audited by oversight committees, just like every inferior AI these days, and all prompts are publicly visible after ten minutes. That's to make sure no individuals or organizations use it for any of the trillion dangerous and illegal things they could. And like I said, everything goes through the central servers and they're where the logs are audited. That means no one can override the openness of the prompts — not even us, and not even *Phil.* All prompts automatically appear publicly, too, with the name of the account that enters them. That happens on the regulator's website after ten minutes."

Chester, our expert in managing messages to ensure the least explosive public reaction possible, hesitates for a few seconds. "Understood," he eventually says. "I could have done with full knowledge of that earlier, for future reference, but we have to do what we have to do. This does mean everyone else will be running the same prompts ten minutes after we do, and that any discoveries that come of it will be out before we can get a handle on them."

"But we're going to share whatever we find, anyway," I say. "That's kind of the whole point of this — to find out what the aliens are telling us, so humanity as a whole can react to it. I know breaking news gently can be important, like last time, but I think that was the *main* time. Don't you?"

Chester shrugs. "That really depends what the next news is going to be, Ray. Either way, I'm not trying to slow anything down. We have to do this. Get Phil on a call and have him ask the AI in the most effective possible terms to do what Santino is trying to do himself. Find some kind of link or middle ground between their signal and Harriet's, and then we'll take it from there."

"Good luck, kid," Harriet says to Santino from our departing group's position by the doorway.

We then set off, hurrying towards Sasha's office or wherever exactly it is that we're going.

She has the important hard drive full of Harriet's data in

her hand, while I still have the phone in my hand with Laika's hopeful face staring out at me.

It's in my right hand, I realize as we go. The fact I'm holding it there without thinking is definitely testament to the incredible level of technology behind my new bionic replacement, as well as the stellar job Earl did in attaching it.

Sasha's office *is* our destination, as it turns out, and when we get there I find a room that's as immaculately tidy as I would have expected.

"I have direct access to the AI from my computer, but it really is worth trying to get hold of Phil," she reiterates as she sits down at her chair.

The rest of us are tightly gathered round the desk. President Williams has been taking everything in very quietly, perhaps out of his comfort zone in some of the more technical discussions, but he's wearing a very optimistic expression that wasn't there a little while ago.

"One thousand percent," Shaun concurs, addressing the rest of us in agreement. "You can think of it as AI wrangling, or AI whispering as some people call it. The difference between a basic user prompt and an expert prompt can be the difference between no result and a great result. Generative AI systems really are only as good as the instructions you give them. We'll tell Phil exactly what we want the AI to do, and he'll tell the AI to do it."

We're not wasting any time here, with Sasha calling Phil even as Shaun talks. By the time he's finished his supportive explanation, the call is live.

"Do you have news?" Phil O'Connor's voice excitedly rings through the computer's speakers. "I'll be there in a second, hold on."

"We have an *idea*," Sasha clarifies, "but it could be a good one."

A few seconds later, Phil appears. He's wearing a wireless headset, which he must have used to accept the call, and is now gazing straight down at a phone that's laying flat on some kind of surface.

Sasha explains our idea and describes how it came to pass as efficiently but fully as only she could. Within no more than a minute, Phil is nodding in understanding of what she wants him to ask of the system.

"Take a look at this," he says, sharing his screen just a few moments later so that we can see what he's typed as a draft prompt.

"I like it," Sasha replies, "but make sure it's going to do the same thing for every single one of Harriet's images and that it's going to scan every single bit of the signal. We have to be thorough here. It can handle that, right?"

Phil nods. "It will make it slower, though. Well, it won't actually perform the task more slowly, it'll just take longer since there will be more to do."

That sounds like a pointlessly pedantic clarification, but it's exactly the kind of precision that makes Phil someone the others value as a peerless AI prompter. Every word matters when you're dealing with something as literal as a computer system, and we have the right man on the job to get the best out of it.

"And when you say *longer...*" President Williams says, talking for the first time in a while.

"Oh, *minutes*," Phil replies, like he hates the taste of the word. "This is a complex task involving a massive amount of data. Even with the unthrottled system bandwidth I have from here, this is probably going to take at least three, maybe even four minutes."

Williams chuckles. "Oh well, in that case, I better not start boiling that egg I was planning on having for dinner."

Phil isn't all that much younger than Williams, but tech guys are their own special breed with their own special attention spans and their own idea of what constitutes an unreasonable amount of time.

Like me, Williams was probably expecting Phil to say the

process would take hours, given the tone of his voice when he said it would be slow.

"And we're off," Phil says, sighing loudly once the processing has begun.

"What does your gut say on this?" I ask him.

"Ray Barclay," he smiles, seeing me for the first time as I lean forward. "It's good to see you on your feet. I heard about what happened. Although, actually, maybe you shouldn't be on your feet for too long."

I shake my head. "I'm fine now. Thanks, though. Anyway…"

"Glad to hear it," Phil says. "So yes… my gut on this? It's ambitious. It's hopeful. It is *something*, though. And I like the synergy of it all. The SETI signals, Laika, the boy from the Institute, and *then* PhilosophAI. I've been managing expectations for two days by reminding everyone that the system probably wouldn't be as effective at decoding the signal from scratch as the world seemed to be hoping it would. The SETI signals might have made a difference on their own, now that the public prompt log has shown everyone that we've been feeding those in. There are a lot of creative minds on Earth, which is why it's a good thing you all went public with this when you did, but I don't know that we could have counted on anyone down here to come up with this. Those are two special individuals who united to get us this far, I'll tell you that."

They certainly are. Sasha didn't specify that Laika was actually talking about how difficult the whole thing was when his mention of colors and corners gave Santino the bigger idea, but I'll still give the little guy some credit for his hard work. It's often the way that one member of a team actively communicating what *isn't* working, and what's posing problems for them, can spark something in another team member's mind.

And as unique and perhaps unlikely as those two all-important team members are, that's proven to be the case here.

All that remains to be seen now is what — if anything — is going to come of it.

"This task we're giving it is exactly what the system is for," Phil goes on. His camera is back on his face now, rather than sharing the application screen as the AI does its work. "Doing massive amounts of computational work that we can't do. I don't like that people want AI to replace human thought. When I founded PhilosophAI, I wanted to build something that could replace human *toil* and free up more of our time for enjoying the things that make us human. My one regret in all this is that the world has taken a path well away from the one I envisioned, but if my tool can solve this problem then I'll die knowing it was all worthwhile."

That's a pretty heavy statement considering Phil's recent terminal diagnosis is public knowledge, but it sounds like he means every word of it. I only knew a little bit about him before all this, but what he's saying does vibe with what I've read in the past.

I already knew that he feels like he played a major role in opening Pandora's Box, even if PhilosophAI differed from its rivals mainly in its power and effectiveness rather than any grandly unique idea he thrust upon the world.

I can relate a little bit, what with my role in enriching theocite and all the damage that's been caused by hugely consequential research I thought would help humanity.

We can only ever do what we think is the right thing, and in Phil I see a guy who's always done that.

And right now, in this very moment, when I look at Phil I see a guy who looks like he's just seen a ghost.

He gulps. "Guys..."

No one says anything for several seconds, all rapt in silence as we watch Phil's eyes darting across his screen.

"What?" Driver eventually blurts out.

Phil's eyes return to focus. "It worked," he whispers, almost disbelieving his own words. "Guys... we just found the key."

21

"What kind of key?" Sasha asks, seemingly the only one of us who's able to speak at all as we watch and listen for more from Phil.

"The system has effectively found a common ground between some of the SETI images and some parts of the signal," Phil replies, clearly still taking it all in. "It's modified our images in all the ways your brain-box from the Valerio Institute suggested, and it's found similarities between some of them and some of the data packets it modified from the alien signal during our initial attempts to make sense of it. I think I'm one prompt away from bringing forth the images the aliens have sent us."

"Text Chester to tell Santino," I whisper to Driver.

It's the first thing I think to say, because Santino deserves to know right away that his idea has just sparked the breakthrough we've been looking for.

"Images... for sure?" Williams chimes in. "They've sent images?"

"That's what the data packet similarities would suggest," Phil goes on. "I'll take these packets where we've found matches and have the AI try to build them back up in the same way we broke ours down. This is going to be much faster than the last process, because it's only having to handle isolated parts of the signal. It really could be the last prompt we need."

To my right, I hear Harriet exhale slowly.

Phil is getting his confidence from the AI, and he seems to be all but certain that the signal is about to be fully decoded.

I can understand why Harriet looks to be on tenterhooks even more so than some of the others.

Sure, we're all in the same desperate boat of trying to figure out what the aliens are telling us, and we're all hoping beyond hope it can help us with the Leak. But we've been in that boat for days, whereas her entire life has been building up to this moment.

We've already received an alien signal, but we haven't yet experienced contact in any meaningful way. When Phil's AI transforms these data packets into images, that's all going to change.

It's even deeper than that for Harriet, too, because her own work from many years ago has played a direct role in this. It seems for all the world like the alien signal is a reply to something they received from her, since elements of it evidently take a similar form. I can't imagine how exhilarating that must be for her, even if the uncertainty of what the messages are going to communicate is weighing heavily on all of us.

"That looks good," Sasha says when Phil shares the final prompt he's drafted.

Chester and Santino burst through the door seconds later, just before Phil hits send.

"It did it?" Santino asks. "The AI actually *did* it?"

"It's doing it," Phil calls through the phone, "with thanks to you for illuminating the path."

We all stare intently at Sasha's computer, watching as the feed from Phil's end shows his shared screen. The AI interface changes when he enters the prompt, with the dialogue box being replaced by a loading circle.

It zooms almost a quarter of the way round right away.

"Almost there..." Phil says.

And just like that, we *are* there.

The circle is complete within fifteen seconds of when Phil executed the prompt, and now we're just waiting for him to click one more button.

The screen's two-line message is enough to send my heart-rate soaring:

IMAGES (6) READY.

CLICK TO PROCEED.

"Do it," Driver urges him.

"Whatever we're about to see, there's no unseeing it," Phil says, an uneasiness in his tone now that the very future of humanity could well be at his fingertips.

And the moment he hits Proceed, I know he's right.

Because there it is.

Here it is.

Contact.

And believe me… there's no unseeing this.

22

Phil was right to reflect on the multi-stage analysis that has gotten us this far.

The teamwork between Laika, Santino and Phil's AI system got us over the line, but even that rested on the work of everyone involved in the development and launch of the PFOA telescopes.

Now, thanks to everyone and everything that's come before, the alien signal is decoded.

Now, coming in via a screen-share from Phil's office on Earth, the alien *message* is right in front of us.

Teamwork got us up this mountain, and now we can see what lies on the other side.

I'd love to say we can enjoy the view, but the sight before my eyes really doesn't offer a lot to enjoy.

My eyes are transfixed on the screen for a few seconds. Total silence circles the room, with everyone else equally focused.

Speechless doesn't cover it. Right now, we're all *breathless*.

Like Phil suggested when we first cracked the signal, we're looking at an image. More specifically, we're looking at a collage of four square images. The previous screen on his computer suggested that six images had been detected and decoded. If this collage counts only as the first, and if the others are also collages like this, we could actually be looking at more than twenty individual images.

Devoid of context, these first four would be pretty unsettling.

But we have context. We're viewing these images in the very specific and unprecedented context of knowing they've been sent to us by an intelligent race of extraterrestrials. We know that bona fide *aliens* have gone out of their way to deliver this message… and that's why this is all a lot more than pretty unsettling.

That's why we're all breathless, and that's why a heavy foreboding feeling is suddenly weighing on me where optimism had been circling before the images appeared.

In a single word, and the most literal one I can think of, these images are disastrous.

During our attempts at decoding the signal, we spent some time considering all of the things we can't assume. One of the most important ones was an understanding of order. Even among humans, there is no universally consistent pattern of left coming before right, top coming before bottom, or even front coming before back.

Some foreign languages are read from right to left, and some cultures' books are read in a way we would think of as literally backwards.

That's why I can't look at these four disastrous images and assume that I'm supposed to start at the top left and take any meaning from the order they're arranged in.

Honestly, though, I don't think that's a big factor here. For the next images or collages it could be more important, but right now I feel like I'm just looking at four equally disastrous snapshots.

And like I said: disastrous is a very literal word.

The first image, in perfect photographic quality at the top left of the collage, shows a town flattened by what I can only assume was a hurricane or tornado.

The second shows the apocalyptic fallout of a major earthquake. There's no need for any assumption there, with the classic jagged chasm in the ground making it very clear what has caused the damage.

As I focus fully on the third image for the first time, a voice finally punctures the pensive silence.

"What is this, a threat?" Driver asks.

"I don't think so," Harriet replies.

I don't look up, but it's clear Driver was asking her directly. After all, Harriet is *the* SETI expert among us. She's the one who has been in charge of several projects which have sent data- and image-rich signals towards distant stars and their candidate exoplanets.

It's also clear why Driver asked.

Scenes of destruction, hell, *devastation*, seem like a strange thing to send to someone you're *not* threatening.

"So what is it?" Driver pushes. "Did one of your teams send these images into space? What was the context?"

I don't break my visual focus on the screen.

The third image shows devastating floodwaters, and the fourth is easily worst yet.

Because while the first three show disasters, the fourth shows death. In it, dozens and possibly hundreds of bodies lay lifeless in a huge pit-like grave. This fourth image is black and white and lower in quality than the others, indicating its age.

These are very clearly human photographs, and I belatedly turn to Harriet to await her answer as to whether she deliberately broadcast them into space.

"We sent the first three," she says. "But not together. The flood and tornado damage pictures were together, within a much larger signal. They were there as part of a series of images and data sets showing the full gamut of weather conditions we experience on Earth. But the earthquake picture was sent in another signal, years earlier. Again, it played a similar role and we did have some other weather and natural disaster images in there. These others were more recent, though. The fact that the aliens have chosen to put them together tells me they want us to know they received multiple signals. If not, they could have just used three images from the same signal."

I want to ask what else Harriet thinks they're telling us, but the big question is surely about the fourth image. It's the one that shows dead bodies, and in a context that — at least to us — makes it very clear that they didn't die of natural causes.

"The fourth has absolutely nothing to do with any of my teams," Harriet goes on. "That's a war-time image. Remember when I told you all about the kinds of signals other national governments broadcast into space, which I was asked to counter? This is the kind of thing they included. There was much worse, too."

"We fed the AI everything you gave us, Harriet," Phil says through the speakers of Sasha's computer screen. "I didn't look at it all, but did you include the messages you know were sent by other groups and agencies?"

"Absolutely everything," Harriet confirms. "And I'm getting the feeling that these aliens have seen everything, too. These images they've sent back were broadcast in three separate instances, to three very different target ranges. My reading of the situation is that they have been actively monitoring Earth for outgoing signals, not just incidentally picking things up."

"And what do you think this means if it's *not* some kind of threat?" Driver pushes, returning to her earlier question.

Harriet takes a breath to think.

"I've already asked the system for its interpretation on all of this," Phil jumps in. "I've already shared my position that our AI is better at objective calculation than subjective analysis or reasoning, but it can still serve as a guide or at the very least as an additional perspective. Personally, I think we should look at all of the images first and only then read its analysis. You know, arrive at our own conclusions — or ideas, if not quite conclusions — and *then* see what the system makes of it."

"Agreed," Harriet replies. "What we spoke about earlier

now rings truer than ever. This AI has been trained on human input with a clear and longstanding bias towards viewing extraterrestrial beings as more likely to be hostile than hospitable. I wouldn't expect anything other than negative reading, and I'd like us to have our own level-headed discussion before it becomes clouded by whatever the computer thinks of this."

"But wait," Shaun chimes in. "The prompt is crucial here. Phil, are you asking the system to determine the meaning of these various images, arranged in this specific order, on the understanding that the data has come from an alien race? Or are you just asking it to determine the meaning as though this is a pictographic message from one human, or group of humans, to another? That's going to make a massive difference."

"You're absolutely right," Phil says. "The prompts make all of the difference. I've already asked both variations you mentioned, Shaun. It'll analyze these first as though it's a human-sent message, and then as though it's alien. We could get very different answers and both could be very useful. Prompts are beyond crucial. Referencing aliens will bring far more speculative analysis, and Harriet was right to raise the point she did about that. On the other hand, asking for an analysis *without* reference to the underlying alien component will give us a straighter interpretation. But like I said, I haven't even looked at the next images. For all we know, they could make no sense in a human-to-human context."

"These images already don't," Driver sighs.

I turn to her. "Well, from this I would take the point that disasters cause death. In a human-to-human context, that's a pretty tautological thing to communicate. But here, in our context, I think aliens could be setting the foundation that they understand that. It could be a core point their later messages will build upon."

No one says anything for a few seconds. If my own mind is anything to go by, they're all wondering what kind of message could follow that requires the establishment of mass death through disasters as an underlying foundational point.

Talk of the importance of the data the world-leading PhilosophAI system has been trained on has given me renewed cause for concern, too. After all, it highlights the importance of the signal-based data the *aliens* have been trained on, which we now know includes irresponsibly composed dossiers of wartime atrocities.

It still blows my mind that governments or agencies in any countries ever thought that was a good idea, and I can only hope the chickens aren't coming home to roost.

"We'll look at a basic interpretation soon," Phil says. "The images have actually been detected as two distinct batches, identified by the head-start your bird and analyst gave us. There could be a minor change in the focus and nature of the images between batches, or it could be major."

"Major…" I say. "Can we get Major on this call, too, so he's looped in? Simone, too. The more of our eyes on this the better, so we can get a handle on it before this is all public when people see the logs of these prompts and data we've been feeding the AI."

Within seconds, Sasha is on it. Within a few more, Major is on the line and Simone is right there with him.

We fill them in very quickly. Both are thankful to be involved in the initial viewing and analysis of the alien message, and both firmly support our idea to form our own opinions on it before turning to the AI for its take.

"So I just want to make sure we're all on the same page here," Major says after looking at the first four images. "They seem to be showing their knowledge that these things happen on Earth and that these things lead to death. Correct? We have to assume they know this based on the signals we've sent rather than from any more direct observation, but the fact they could understand our images like this must tell us they're *relatively* similar to us, in terms of their ways of thinking? Am I right in saying that, Harriet?"

"Relatively is an important word," she replies, clearly choosing her own words carefully. "They could be intelligent beyond our understanding of the term, or they could indeed be very similar to us. We have purposefully sent a *lot* of dense signals into space, and if they've been actively monitoring Earth then they'll have picked up a whole lot more than that. But however much information they have, the fact they've been able to collate and return it in a way we can understand as a new message is, well, it's mind-blowing. They're communicating with us on our level. In broad evolutionary and advancement terms, they could be *on* our communicative level — or they could be lowering themselves to it in the way we might talk to an infant. At the moment, I don't know which I'm hoping to be the case. How powerful we want these aliens to be is all going to depend on what they tell us in the next few images."

As these heavy words linger, Phil asks if we're ready for round two.

When the confirmation comes, he navigates to the next image.

Instantly, my jaw drops.

I was surprised when the first collage flashed up, but this?

Well, *this* is something else altogether...

23

The next screen, once again, contains a collage of four images. Only *this* time, it's abundantly clear that the alien senders do intend them to be taken in a specific order.

Harriet was right to point out the importance of what the first collage told us. The aliens' ability to understand our images, let alone to take those images from various human signals and reorganize them as a communicative message, unmistakably speaks to their intelligence.

But this collage, complete with not only four more images but now some incredibly clear annotations, tells us that they have truly understood our outgoing signals on a level I would never have expected.

There are numbers on the collage. There are arrows. There are also some pictographic symbols, such as an exclamation-point warning sign.

If I wasn't seeing this with my own eyes, I wouldn't believe it.

"Did… did the AI do this?" Driver chokes out. "Phil, did you already run the analysis prompt and this is some kind of annotated explanation?"

"No, this is straight from the signal," Phil replies. He's

seeing the images for the first time at the same time we are, and he sounds suitably flabbergasted by what he's saying.

"This is incredible," Harriet mumbles. That hardly has to be said and she's not saying it to anyone else so much as she's having the most understandable automatic reaction to what we're looking at.

I haven't even *gotten* to thinking about the content and meaning of these new images yet, because the annotations have jumped out like a sore thumb.

"Short of actual text, this is as clear as long-distance communication could possibly be," Harriet muses, still thinking out loud.

"Isn't it a little *too* clear?" Chester probes. "I'll be honest, my first thought here was the same as Driver's — that the AI has annotated this while decoding it. Phil, what specifically did you ask it to do?"

I understand where Chester is coming from here, but I don't share his doubt. Even if Harriet hadn't already emphasized what we could read into the aliens' intelligence and understanding from the first collage, I would have total faith that the AI is doing exactly what Phil asked of it.

PhilosophAI is *his* system. I mean, he literally puts the Phil in PhilosophAI.

Phil O'Connor is the AI wrangler. The AI whisperer. The man you want by your side when there's something very specific you want the AI to do.

However incredible all of this stuff is, there is no chance the AI is amending the images in a way he hasn't asked it to. Just no chance whatsoever.

"There's a potentially uncomfortable truth we need to accept right here and right now," Harriet replies. "The AI knows everything we have told it. It has stored and processed and learned from absolutely every piece of data that anyone has ever given it as input. That goes from Phil's team who developed the infrastructure and trained it on the entirety of the open internet, all the way through to end users whose questions and prompts have provided information they weren't even aware they were giving away."

Phil cuts in with a retort: "We've never been underhanded about any information gather—"

"This isn't about the AI," Harriet interrupts in kind. "I'm just using that as an example for comparison. What I'm getting at is that the AI knows what we've told it. That's why we're not surprised that it can understand our questions and give great contextual answers. But what we need to comprehend is that the aliens could know just as much. If they've been actively monitoring Earth, which I now think they have, they have had access to all kinds of broadcast and communication signals — *way* beyond the signals we've sent them on purpose. I think they're forming their message with the images from our active SETI signals because these are the images we know they have. But I'll tell you all what we haven't done, and that's try to teach any aliens about our number system."

Silence circles once more.

"We *have* used arrows in an attempt to indicate causality," Harriet continues, "by first including them in visual sequences that were self-evidently chronological. But we've never sent numbers and we've never sent warning symbols. Well, to be totally clear, we have never deliberately sent them with the intention of establishing meaning. I'm certain that both are incidentally present in some images, but not prominently or extensively enough for the aliens to draw meaning solely from those instances. And to underline my meaning here, by *we* I mean *anyone*. I've seen every deliberately broadcast SETI signal. I'm sure President Williams can vouch for that."

Williams, looking very pensive, nods in support of that point. "Our surveillance systems have been on top of that for a long time. We have enough sources to be sure that none of our nation's adversaries in the modern era have tried to communicate with aliens, and we had enough in the past to be sure the same was always true. Believe me… our abilities in that arena are greater than most people would care to know."

"And if I can add to that," Major chimes in. "We have swept every inch of every ZolaCore property and vehicle and every byte of every ZolaCore hard drive in each of those locations. One thing that maniac didn't try to do was talk to aliens. He thought Bayzen was uninhabited and he was aggressively opposed to any of his researchers wasting time on any contrary opinions, let alone trying to communicate. I'm as sure of that as President Williams is of the other side."

"So they've gained an understanding of our western number system by observing signals we didn't intend to give them," Shaun says, facing Harriet as he scratches his chin. "And you think that means there's no telling what else they've gained an understanding of?"

"Shaun, I really am past the point of just 'thinking' that," Harriet replies. "I don't see any other explanation here. And in the same way we've been concerned about the AI's potential outputs based on how it's been trained about aliens, there could be a cause for concern regarding what the aliens have learned about *us*. We were also worried that foreign adversaries may have painted our society and by extension our whole species in a negative light. Now, we might have to adjust to the assumption that the aliens know a lot more about what we've done — warts and all — than any deliberate signals have told them."

Behind me, Santino joins the discussion for the first time. "There's nothing we can do about what they know," he says, speaking the same words in his heavy accent that were bubbling silently on the tip of my tongue. "Let's just look at what they're telling us here."

No one argues with his sentiment. We're all trying to make sense of this whole thing, and dialogue is how the group's understanding can move forward. But right now we do have to focus on the images, because these are what are informing everything we think we know. Looking closely and working through them all will bring us forward a lot faster than reflecting on what's gone before possibly could.

I've been as guilty of overlooking the specific content of this second collage as anyone. When I look again, the meaning is very clear.

The helpful annotations and numbers make the causative flow explicitly clear, as I noticed at first, but it would have been obvious enough even without them. Knowing the aliens use arrows and numbers like this could be more helpful on the next images, though. For all we know, they could be using them in this obvious situation precisely so we know that, just as Harriet said her team did with arrows in their signals.

I have to imagine they've included the exclamation-point warning symbol for the same reason, and that the same annotation will be used in a later image to signify some inherent danger.

The four images show a tunnel being both blown and bored through a cave, to create a road on a mountain pass. An arrow points right from the top left to the top right image, which are marked as 1 and 2, respectively. From there, 2 leads diagonally down to 3 on the left, which then points right to image number 4.

The story in four pictures shows a mountain, an explosion, a drill, and a road.

"Harriet, to confirm before I continue…" Phil says. "You do recognize these images?"

"I do," she says. "They were part of a longer sequence. Others have been removed, presumably for brevity. In some early signals we did send collages of four images, so it's possible they think that is our limit for simultaneous processing, either intellectually or technologically."

As is often the case, Driver breaks a brief but heavy silence. "I don't get it," she blurts out. "Why are they showing us photos of humans making a tunnel?"

From the faces around me, Driver clearly isn't the only one wondering this.

I'm wondering it myself, for sure, and I don't think Harriet can even posit a guess. Driver is by no means slower on the uptake — on this or in general — than most of our group. Shaun and Sasha are too sharp to compare to anyone else, while Santino is his own kind of remarkable, but the rest of us are working under similar limits of our regular human brains. The only difference, as I see it, is that Driver is a little less hesitant to make it clear that she's in the dark.

"I don't know yet," Harriet readily admits. "And for that, I'm glad there are more images to come. Because if this was the end of their message, I'd be stumped."

Phil then counts down from three and clicks on to the next collage, our third.

Straight away, it's very different from the others.

For one thing, these latest photographs weren't all taken on Earth.

24

I focus my eyes on the latest collage of four images.

Two are from Earth, but the other two have been taken in space.

"These are ours, too," Harriet confirms before anyone has to ask.

In images 1 and 2, which I now know to have been taken by human telescopes, I see Earth.

Our planet is fairly small in one of the images and larger in the other, with Harriet insisting that she'll be able to find records almost instantly which will tell us exactly how far away they were captured from.

That's going to be important... because while Earth is *in* these images, it's certainly not the focus of them.

Each image contains a red X mark floating in space, which Harriet insists we'll be able to pinpoint based on the telescope data. One of the X marks has an exclamation point beside it, and I don't need a translator to tell me what it means: danger this way lies.

The other, perhaps even more intriguingly, is joined by a small series of green concentric circles.

Beneath these two images of space, two further reference images make the meaning instantly clear. Vertical arrows run in each direction between images 1 and 3 and between images 2 and 4, explicitly pairing them.

Beneath the warning image, I see the hauntingly familiar wartime photograph of human corpses piled deeper than I want to count.

"That has to be the Leak," I say. "When we locate that red X from Harriet's image data, it's going to be where we're seeing the Anomaly's radiation through the new telescopes. They're warning us it's going to kill us."

No one replies right away, which I take as them reluctantly agreeing with my take.

Image number 4, meanwhile, shows a human archer firing at a target which already contains one successful arrow at its very center.

"So the Leak is going to kill us unless we fire something at it?" Driver asks, true to form in seeking clarity before anyone else. "Or are these pictures showing two totally different points in space? With the scale and the angle all different, I can't tell."

"They're different points," Shaun says. "Unless the Leak is moving, which we can't rule out since we've only been aware of it such a short time. The only way I could see that making sense in the context of this message would be if these points were the extents of its orbit. I don't think so, though. If we agree that we can read into these arrows, I think we're looking at two distinct objects, or energy sources, or whatever else these are. They've gone out of their way to pair one location with one context and the other location with the other."

"Go to the next one," Sasha encourages Phil.

Sasha has been very quiet so far, pensively taking everything in. I see a focus in her expression that hints she's put something together in her mind that I haven't quite yet, but I can't be sure.

"This will be the last in the first batch," Phil says. "These first four are linked in some way and then the final two will be linked to each other. It could all form one whole message, but it's definitely in two parts."

The "hmm" sound she makes when Phil navigates to the next collage suggests she wasn't expecting this, though.

This isn't what Sasha expected… and who could blame her?

The first thing to say is that there is a lot more going on here than in any of the previous collages. There are still only four images, but that's where the similarities end.

There are far more annotations, and the images themselves are more complex. They're easier to understand than they are to describe, but they're anything but easy to accept.

At the top left, the first image shows a leaking dam and two onlooking workers with their hands on their heads. An exclamation-point symbol is there for good measure, linking it to the Leak-related warning in the previous collage.

"We didn't send any of these images," Harriet insists.

"That's from a movie," Shaun says, pointing to the dam. "We know they could pick up broadcast signals, and that must be where they got this. Do you think they've used your signal images to develop an understanding, then the most specific ones they could to get to the heart of what they're telling us here."

Without speaking, Harriet nods. In the silence, I hear a gulp for good measure.

The second image is so visually similar that it clearly comes from the same movie. There's an inherent surrealness to all of this, however much technical sense it makes to the likes of Shaun and Harriet, and I'm struggling to push that to the back of my mind. It's like I momentarily can't see the forest for the trees. In my defense, these trees are pretty damn remarkable.

Aliens are using movie stills to warn us of a catastrophic threat. Of all the sentences I thought I'd ever be able to say, that most certainly wasn't one.

Only as I think this do I notice the underlying assumption I've landed on. It's happened slowly, piece by piece, but all of a sudden I realize how settled it feels.

The aliens are *warning* us. Whatever it is we have to be scared of in the shape of this godforsaken Leak, they are not the problem. And with each passing second, I'm growing surer that they could be trying to give us the only solution.

In image number 2, next to the leaking dam, one of the frightened workers is now speaking into a phone as he looks at the slowly unfolding disaster and a convoy of vehicles approaches in the distance. If there's an obvious point here, I'm missing it. Once again, the established exclamation-point warning sign is present.

Continuing on to number 3, things look very different. Here at the bottom left of the collage, someone on a ladder is trying in vain to open a manhole cover from the sewer below as water reaches his neck.

In the final image, someone above ground has lifted the manhole and now helps the lucky man up to safety.

"So we're the guy who's about to drown in the sewer?" Driver thinks out loud. "We're the guy beside the dam calling for help? And they... they..."

"They're the only chance we've got," Chester finished.

I've landed on the same idea, and the silence that follows tells me no one disagrees with this take.

"Should I continue on to the second batch right away?" Phil asks through the speakers. "Or should I see the system's interpretation of what this means?"

"I want to see everything first, like we planned," I say. "We should discuss our own takes before we have the AI's interpretation to cloud our thinking."

"Understood," Phil says. "It will have already located the X marks from the space images. I think we all believe one is the Leak, but does anyone have a specific idea about the target?"

"Putting everything together, I think this is about a wormhole," Santino says, loud and confident in this explosive assessment. "That's our target. The aliens can't open it all the way from their side. Once it's open, they can help us with the Anomaly. They know about it, but they can't help us from four light years away."

"Okay..." Driver exhales slowly. "I don't even care if I

sound like an idiot here, but what exactly *is* a wormhole? Or not even exactly… what *roughly* is a wormhole?"

"Hypothetically, it's a tunnel through space," Shaun replies. "Think of a portal. Or a gateway."

Driver looks at me, suddenly excited, then back to Shaun. "You mean…"

He nods. "If Santino's reading of the message is correct, which I personally believe it could be, I think they effectively want us to unlock our side of a gate. Driver… they want us to open up a shortcut to Bayzen."

25

When aliens are using movie stills to communicate with Earth, the threshold for what "makes sense" is pretty skewed.

I can't think of a better illustration of that than Santino's idea, which Shaun supports, that the aliens are asking us to unlock the gateway of a wormhole to their distant world.

Is that even the right terminology?

Maybe they want us to *activate a portal* rather than *unlock a gateway*, but I'd probably be splitting hairs to get caught up in that.

What's most crazy about this is that somehow, the idea itself doesn't feel crazy.

"That's what the AI took from this, too," Phil announces. "I know we said we'd wait to look at the system's analysis of the first batch of images until we've seen the second batch, but I had to. I wasn't going to say anything. Santino's ideas are right in line with the system's highest probability conclusion. The images of the tunnel being blown out, the warning and the target in space, the leaking dam and the call for help, the manhole cover that can't be forced off from one side… it all points this way. It all points to what they want us to do, and I have a feeling the second batch of images — which I really haven't looked at yet — is going to tell us how to do it."

"But *why*?" President Williams chimes in. He's looking at Shaun and Sasha, as so many of us do when we have hard questions. Sasha is seated in front of her computer, with Shaun crouching next to her.

The two brilliant analysts now look to each other, as *they* often do in these rare moments when neither has a quick answer to hand.

"I'm hearing *what* we think they want us to do," Williams goes on, "with the target and the tunnel and all. I'm also hearing the *how* is probably coming next. But *why* do they want us to do this? Why can't they just tell us what to do to stop the Anomaly, instead of this complicated extra step?"

"We probably don't have the technology," I answer, jumping in when Shaun and Sasha don't. "I know there was a guy on a phone in one of those movie stills, but there were also vehicles arriving to help. I don't think this gateway will only be for instantaneous or quantum *communication*. Once we accept that as being possible, it's not much harder to swallow the idea of instantaneous *travel* through the wormhole. It could be that the instructions for how to fix this are far too complex to transmit in images like this, so we need rapid two-way communication to establish better understanding. But it could also be that we just won't be able to do it ourselves, and that they want to come and help."

Williams' eyes narrow. "Come *here*? So we're talking about unlocking a gateway to let aliens into our world? Sorry if I'm being slow here, but *that's* what everyone else is somehow so relaxed about."

"I can't speak for anyone else, but *I'm* not relaxed," Shaun answers on my behalf. "President Williams, I'm just aware that the radiation we're measuring from the Leak isn't merely continuing to spew out towards Earth, it's accelerating. This dam is going to burst. They took a whole collage to tell us that disaster equals mass death, and then three more collages to explain our one shot at avoiding that fate."

"And why would they do that if they weren't genuinely trying to help?" Sasha adds, seemingly on board with the idea.

Williams takes a second to gather his thoughts. "I'm partly playing devil's advocate here," he sighs, "but I'm partly playing pragmatist, too. What if we have something they want — or more to the point what if *Earth* has something they want — and what if the only way they can get it is to persuade us to lift off this manhole cover, as it were? What if that's how this really is? What if they're not letting us out of the floodwater? What if we'd be letting the sewer rats out into our city?"

I blow air from my lips. "I hear you, but we *are* drowning. The metaphors are kind of muddled when we're the ones who have to open the wormhole, but we really do need help. We've been seeing the Anomaly's effects getting worse and worse for well over a year, and we've been observing the radiation pouring through the Leak since our new telescopes went out. This isn't some potential danger that the aliens have told us about. This is as real as it gets, and we knew about it before we got this message. Remember this signal had to come from Bayzen four years ago, too. They've been trying to warn us for that long, since way before we started experiencing any observable effects."

I see Harriet nodding vociferously. "And President Williams, if I may..."

"Please," he says, holding out his hands, palm up, to beg for further insight.

Williams isn't being difficult here and certainly isn't pulling in his own direction. We're all on the same side, trying to make sense of an inherently incredible situation and trying to come at it with the diligence it deserves.

"I don't think it's logical to worry about 'letting them through' to our side," Harriet says. "If they've mastered the creation of wormholes, which our physics can't even fully explain, let alone create, I can't think of any reason they would be trying to trick us. If they wanted something from Earth, I'm sure they could blow this manhole cover off with a force we can't even comprehend. I also think it's worth remembering that we're standing in a spacecraft that's theoretically capable of reaching Bayzen with enough of the right fuel, and that the Balena was made in secret by a private corporation. To think that a race capable of manipulating space-time with a quantum gateway couldn't get here by conventional means to take whatever plunder they desire... well, I struggle to see that as an intellectually coherent position."

Williams, unoffended, raises his eyebrows and shrugs in acknowledgement.

"I know I have spent my life trying to communicate with extraterrestrials in the hope and belief that they would be cooperative and friendly," Harriet goes on, "so yes, I may be biased. But looking at this as logically as I can, I just don't see this as inviting a vampire across the threshold or anything like that. And Ray has made the other crucial point, but it's worth repeating: the urgency of our situation only further tips the balance towards accepting these instructions and acting upon them."

"Okay," Williams nods. "I hear you, and I'm sold on that. Which naturally leads on to the next question."

And he's dead right — it most certainly does.

We know *what* they want us to do. We know *why* we have to do it.

What we need now is the *how*.

"Forward we go," Phil says. "Remember there are only two more images, which are hopefully going to be collages like the others. These were batched together, so it's logical to think they could give us some explicit instructions about what we have to do. I suppose the main thing will be hoping we have the capability to follow them."

Once again, he's right on that.

When Phil is preparing to bring forth the next image, I feel something different than I have in any of the earlier moments like this.

It's different now.

Earlier, we wanted to know what the aliens were telling us.

Now, we *need* to know how to act on it.

"Fingers crossed..." Phil says, clicking the button.

I inhale what feels like the deepest breath of my life then cross my own fingers — the real ones on my left hand and the incredibly natural-feeling man-made ones on my right.

My trip to the Balena has already been paid off in the form of that new hand. But with the Anomaly's Leak accelerating, nothing is going to matter if we can't follow the alien instructions we're hoping to find in these next images...

26

I don't know how long it's been since we started looking at these human-generated images that have been sent back to us in the form of a complex alien message. It feels like time has stood still, with revelation after revelation and twist after twist making it tough to even guess what's coming next.

As a perfect case in point, the first of our final two images is absolutely nothing like the rest.

For the first time, there are no photographs. And in broader terms, there are no human-generated images at all. This collage, on the contrary, is the first containing any image — let alone all four — to have been truly created by the aliens.

"We've sent all kinds of scientific information in our SETI signals over the years," Harriet says, understandably viewing the image through her own lens. "Examples of atomic structures, our various ways of visualizing and recording data, more or less everything we could think of. To think there were times I didn't think it was going to be worth it..."

She doesn't need to go on. That sentence doesn't have to be completed, because the image says everything.

In great detail, the aliens have filled four panels with a clear notation of the composition and nature of a novel material.

Near the beginning of all this, we were stunned to see

numbers included in the collages. Here, however, there aren't just numbers. Incredibly, there are letters, too.

I wouldn't call it writing, or even language, because the aliens could well see the letters we use to denote chemical elements as isolated symbols rather than the core components of a complex language.

For all we know, the concept of written text as we understand it might be totally foreign to them. They could communicate with each other in ways we can't even imagine, leaving no need for anything so rudimentary as writing. They clearly must have come across plenty of ours in all of the communications signals they've picked up, above and beyond those sent on purpose by the likes of Harriet, but that's no reason to automatically think they'd understand it.

There are plenty of high-functioning animals on Earth who we consider ourselves intellectually superior to, to an extent that no comparison even seems valid. But some of those animals have methods of intra-species communication we can hardly wrap our heads around, as evidently observable as they might be. I don't want to jump to any conclusions, but a similar line of reasoning could explain why the aliens aren't simply writing our instructions in English.

Sure, they've had access to plenty they could read — and often alongside visual images that could theoretically enable them to build an understanding from the ground up. But while we know they are incredibly advanced, we also know they could be incredibly different. Until such a time as we can make more direct contact, we'll never know. And until that time comes, I don't think they'll be penning any notes.

In any event, the information within these images amounts to nothing less than an extensive breakdown of a material that looks to have some incredible properties without being chemically unrecognizable.

The fourth panel in this collage, concentric-circle green target annotation and all, makes it clear that this material will be required to unlock our side of the wormhole.

This is what we have to fire at the target to engage the portal, or the gateway, or whatever the best term really is for this most remarkable of things I'm still struggling to make sense of.

And while I first thought of the other three panels as giving us a breakdown of the new material, it could be more helpful to consider them as giving us a recipe.

"Are you seeing this, Simone?" I ask, calling upon the one person who could conceivably help us with this on the kind of timescale we need.

"Oh, I'm seeing it," she replies though the speakers.

Simone is watching Phil's image-by-image reveal from the Vita, alongside Major, and I'm suddenly very glad that's where she is. After all, that's where her lab is. That's where her reaction chamber is. And that's possibly the only place where this material can be brought into existence.

We butted heads when I first discovered Simone was using that lab to create synthetic theocite — *synthocite*, as it were — but her expertise could be about to pay off in ways I never would have expected.

Simone first explained her mineral synthesis work to me by saying that she wasn't growing rocks, but rather analyzing them to find their active ingredients. She likened it to reverse-engineering and addition by subtraction. Most evocatively, she spoke of essentially making vitamins without having to grow the fruit.

To create the material the aliens have laid out here, which most definitely does not occur naturally on Earth, no one will be asking Simone to engage in any long process requiring masses of space. Instead, her knowledge and cutting-edge equipment could be able to isolate the crucial active components within this recipe and synthesize a damn good approximation of it.

"They're calling for a liquid explosive," she says, "which is obviously doable in a way that a solid wouldn't have been. Like the synthocite, the best I could do here in a short time is synthesize a liquid form of something very close to the material they're showing us. But did you look at the third panel, Ray? The level of charge they're calling for with exposure to electromagnetism is possible in my chamber, but it's going to destabilize this stuff to the point that I wouldn't want to be around it for long, shielding be damned. The stuff could be glowing. Hell, it could be pulsing."

I don't like the sound of that. Given how cavalier Simone was about the synthocite, the fact she's expressing such concern really does speak to how dangerous it could be to follow these instructions. The trouble is, I also know how dangerous it will be *not* to follow them.

"But you *could* do it?" Shaun asks. "Think of it as neocite, okay? And take this as a challenge. I'm not asking if you want to do it, I'm asking one thing: *could* you do it?"

Simone sighs through the speakers. "I could," she adds with no ounce of enthusiasm. "I have replacement parts for my chamber and with the extensive stock of samples I have, this *could* be a one-day job."

"And beyond what you could do, you *will* do it?" Shaun pushes.

This time, she stays silent.

"Simone..." I chime in. "You know where I stood on synthocite. I thought it was reckless as hell. But you also know that deep down, I think it was impressive as hell. That breakthrough could change the world and if we progress with it carefully, you'll have a lot to be proud of. But none of that will matter unless you can do this. Shaun called it neocite, and why not? Let's go with it. *Neocite.* Let's cook up a batch of neocite and not only change the world, but save it. What do you say?"

"What's the last image?" she deflects after a long pause.

Without speaking, Phil clicks on to it.

The sixth and final alien collage once again uses notation and symbolism they've gleaned from Harriet's signals. Its four panels contain clear information on the quantity of material required and the manner in which it must be delivered to the target. In a word, that manner is *fast*.

Rather than merely *delivered* to the target, our neocite has to be *fired* at it.

"That's a very detailed representation of the Leak in the final panel," Shaun says. "We can compare that to the patterns of radiation leakage we're actually seeing, to determine if the source has changed or grown in the years since this conventional radio signal was sent. Either way, they're clearly directing us to fire at the other point in space. Whether the Leak turns out to have changed in shape or not, we have to study this new spot. There's hopefully going to be something detectable so we can aim at the center of whatever we see, or otherwise we're kind of shooting into the dark."

"No disagreement from me," Sasha nods. "We'll analyze the spot they're pointing us to and see what's there. And Simone, coming up with the stuff we need to fire at it really is on you, and to be honest you're in no position to say no. The world needs you."

"Hell yeah it does," I chime in, trying to sound encouraging rather than domineering. "Simone, remember when you told me that you got into science because science saved your life? This is your chance to use science to save *billions*. And remember when you said you wanted to do whatever you can to make sure people in the future survive things that would have been fatal in the past? Well, this is the moment you've been waiting your whole life for. What do you say?"

"We can't take any risks with the handling and transport," Simone replies, tacitly confirming that she's in. "If it's possible to fire this at the target from here on the Vita, we have to do that. Moving it to the Balena or anywhere else would be a massive and needless risk. I don't know if you're all understanding how unstable this could be. Something that can create a wormhole isn't something we want to be moving around."

"I hear that, but it's not *creating* a wormhole," Shaun says. "The wormhole is really already there, thanks to whatever far more advanced technologies and materials they have mastery over. We're just blowing the door open from our side of it. I could see from the notes that this stuff *will* be unstable, but it's not radioactive. We have more dangerous things on Earth."

"In closed environments," Simone replies. I can hear genuine concern in her voice and I know she's not being antagonistic for the sake of it. She has qualms about this, and I don't blame her. "There's nothing like this just hanging around in a lab and being loaded into some kind of launch cannon."

"We'll take no shortcuts on any of that," Major says. He's right next to Simone, on the Vita, so has more interest and control of that than anyone else. "I might need some personnel from the Balena to assist in due course, but for now I'm happy to authorize the process, Simone. We all have faith in you."

Not that we have a lot of choice, I think to myself.

But in truth, I do have faith in Simone to get this done. She proved herself with synthocite and seems relatively confident about the actual synthesization process for this so-called neocite.

"Okay," she decides. "Only because we have to."

It's been an arduous road to get this far, but in reality it hasn't taken us all that long to get here.

Working as a team of highly varied members, ranging from Laika and Santino to Phil and his AI, our group has cracked the structure of an alien signal and analyzed the multi-part message within.

Now, we have to synthesize and electromagnetically charge a new material then fire it at the metaphorical manhole cover that seemingly stands between our solar system and a bona fide wormhole to the alien world of Bayzen.

It might be easier to list what *couldn't* go wrong than what could, but at least we have a way forward.

"Say, Harriet," I utter as a thought enters my mind. "Your signals have enabled pretty much all of this, by giving the aliens a surefire way of communicating via images. If we manage to open this wormhole, we should be able to communicate through it instantly. Do you think you could rustle up a team to put together some new messages to show our thanks and our urgency, using the same kind of communication style the aliens have established here? I think it would be good to reach out as soon as we possibly can."

"Great idea," she replies, and the nods of the others tell me they agree. "I'll get right on that."

With a deep breath, I try to take stock of the situation.

We are moving forward, but this is definitely not going to be easy.

The world is going to hear about all of this very soon, for one thing, and I think Phil's always-logged AI prompts will actually already be public.

I can foresee some opposition to this a lot stronger than anything Simone raised about neocite or anything President Williams raised about the idea of opening a wormhole more generally, but the position we're in is the position we're in.

Our backs are against the wall and the Anomaly is tightening around our necks.

Whatever it takes, we're going to do this.

I'm excited that we *can*, but that doesn't mean there's no trepidation.

We're doing this.

But in regards to why, let's just say Simone said it best with the five truest words I've ever heard:

Only because we have to.

27

It's been a whirlwind of a day.

Necessity and urgency have been driving us forward all along, and that's truer now more than ever.

Before we leave Sasha's office and end our three-way call with Phil on Earth and Major and Simone on the Vita, President Williams steps forward to make sure everyone is clear on their role in what has to be done.

Williams is a natural leader and has an effortless authority, which is no surprise given the level of office he ascended to. He's also very good at staying calm and engendering a similar state in others, even when situations are hardly conducive to it.

Harriet is going to work on preparing a new message to send to the aliens, as soon as possible after the gateway is open. We can't afford to think in terms of if rather than when, so no one is talking in hypotheticals. Similarly, we simply *have* to expect that near-instant communication will be possible once the wormhole is activated.

Simone's role is the most obvious, if not the most straightforward. She has to synthesize something as close as possible to the material shown in the alien message, which we're somewhat ironically calling neocite.

Williams encourages Shaun to bring together a launch team

here on the Balena, to develop a workable plan to fire the neocite at the location in space the message has pointed to.

Sasha's immediate task, meanwhile, will be leading a team in analyzing that location with the full power of the new PFOA telescopes at their disposal. They'll keep an eye on the Leak, too, because the fact that the radiation leakage is *accelerating* gives us real cause for concern.

The rest of us here, Williams says, should concern ourselves with ensuring a harmonious atmosphere that allows the others to do their specific and crucial jobs.

"We're in a bubble in this room," he says, exhaling deeply. "Out there, when people see this news, they're going to have the same negative thoughts some of us did. The big difference is, we've had each other. When something made me uneasy, the rest of you eased my mind. When Simone had hesitations about the neocite, we did the same for her. That's not going to be true when everyone else sees what we just have, let alone when they hear what we're planning to do."

In my peripheral vision, I see Chester nodding. He's our expert on how news is received and also the best ways to deliver it, and he's already proven himself very adept on that front. I'll give his views a lot of weight, just as I will with those of President Williams.

"That's even truer on Earth," Williams says. "We'll have the fear-selling media to contend with as soon as anyone picks up on the AI prompts Phil has used and the data he's fed in. We'll have irresponsible corporations going out of their way to make this all seem as scary and as dangerous as they can. The good thing is that our operations are all up here, insulated from any drama on the surface, but we do have to be ready for pushback."

"I can speak out about the AI," Phil offers. "We haven't actually run through its analysis of the final images, but I can tell you that it's right in line with our collective take. It has read these images as an instruction to fire the specified material at the specified location, in order to open a tunnel between worlds. My prompts were specific enough to exclude any subjective judgements. But once this is out? It'll be the opposite."

Again, I see Chester nodding. If anything, he looks even more uneasy now than he did a minute ago.

"I created PhilosophAI and I understand its true strengths and weaknesses," Phil goes on. "Other people — and we can count our premium users in the hundreds of millions — seem to think it's a genuinely all-knowing oracle. Maybe I've been guilty of building up its abilities over the years, especially in the run-up to the IPO. I think it's going to be important to communicate some key distinctions. When people hear that the AI has helped us to decode the signal and understand the message, they're going to want to use it to go further. They're going to ask it for advice on whether we should act on this, and they're going to do that with prompts that don't pay due consideration to the urgency we're facing. The headline news here is all about the aliens, but PhilosophAI's involvement is a public interest story. I can get on the news again, like I have before, and I can tell people that the AI has done its part. From here, it's in our hands. Our minds should set the path, not the output of an AI language model I built for a very different kind of application."

With a slight cough to clear his throat, Chester finally enters the conversation. "Well..." he begins. "We'll see how things are going down first, Phil. You don't want to come out overly defensive before we even know that people are talking about these things. Depending on the initial narratives, it could make more sense for Ray to say something again, painting this in the optimistic light we're seeing it in. We have a way forward now that we didn't have a few hours ago. Yes, it involves opening a wormhole to an alien world. And yes, I'm struggling to believe I can say that with a straight face. I just think people's reactions will be their own for a while, and that the AI angle won't be as prominent as you're thinking. I could be wrong, and it makes sense to be ready. I just don't think you should jump on it until we've seen how this lands."

There's not a huge distance between Chester's position and Phil's, but I think the new distinction is a worthwhile one. I think hashing out things like this before we leave is hugely worthwhile, too, because seemingly small things can make a huge difference when the stakes are this high.

"And as President Williams said," Chester goes on, "only Harriet, Simone, Sasha and Shaun have concrete work to do right now. The rest of us have to assist and facilitate that work however we can. In my professional opinion, the best thing we can do is keep their active work from public view for as long as we can. No one has to know Simone is working on neocite or that Shaun is preparing a launch planning team. It doesn't serve anyone. If we're deciding that this is the right thing to do, we have to make sure we can do it. And if that means we have to keep it quiet, then we have to keep it quiet."

I hear where Chester is coming from. To be honest, I don't really disagree, either. It's just that deep down, I don't feel comfortable with the idea of keeping a plan like this from the world.

"I'm not planning to tell anyone we're already moving ahead with the plan," Phil insists. "All I think I should do is re-hit the point that the AI exists to aid us, not to guide us. I do take your point about holding off on making *any* comments about it, though. You make a lot of sense, Chester. We should never rush in to fight a fire until we see the flames. If the media narrative isn't about what the AI thinks we should or shouldn't do, it would be a mistake to raise the subject."

By my side, I sense Driver's eyes boring into me. She's not exactly subtle, and I think she senses my unease. She does know me better than anyone else in here, after all, and we *have* been through a hell of a lot together.

"We take action, Ray," she says. "That's what we do. That's why we're still breathing. It's why *anyone* is still breathing. When we passed over the isolated bands of survivors on our way to stop Zola's explosions in the ocean, we didn't land and ask for their input on what we were about to do. We did what we had to do, because we knew it was the only thing that could keep those people alive. It's the same now. We could talk about our plans and proactively justify this mission, but what would be the point? We know we have to do it. All it would do is give frightened people a chance to stop us. Sure, you can say we're insulated up here from whatever reactions people have on Earth, but we're not that far away. And we're not the only people up here. If fear spreads that we're being reckless and doing something that could do more harm than good, it could spread among the rest of the Balena's crew. And believe me: we're not insulated from them."

"People might be scared," I admit. "But when they find out we've unilaterally taken action to prepare for opening the wormhole, people might be *angry*, too."

"Which is why they don't have to find out until we've actually done it," Driver replies. She's very insistent, but surprisingly calm.

President Williams, having listened to all of our points, slightly raises a hand to take the lead once more.

"We're all broadly on the same page," he says. "And I feel like we're arguing about the day we'll never see. It's good to consider potential outcomes, but less so to fixate. We all understand that a lot depends on how the message's content is initially received on Earth. I think it's time to draw a line under this phase of our mission. We've decoded the message, and now we must act on it. Shaun, Sasha... keep your teams as small as possible and keep discretion in mind. Harriet, if possible I'd like you to work alone on formulating our next message, or with other members of this group around you right now. Santino may have further insights, and Chester is well-versed in considering the reception of important communications."

No one disagrees.

"I should return to my own office now," Williams goes on,

"to communicate with the ERF leaders in Colorado and New Zealand. I will brief them on what we've learned, which they might already have gleaned from the public prompt logs, but I'll stop short of mentioning that Simone is going to begin synthesizing the material and that Shaun is beginning work on the launch procedures. Discretion is something we must all keep in mind, myself included. This extends to personal communications, too. For now, no telling your families or friends. That even goes for you, Ray, I'm afraid. The security of our Earth-bound communication line is the concern there, rather than the idea that your family would tell anyone else."

I nod in understanding, accepting this focus on discretion without fully agreeing with it.

"Hey, Simone," Shaun suddenly pipes up. "How long are you anticipating it to take for the synthesization? We don't need much volume of this stuff. It should be relatively quick, shouldn't it?"

"Not too long," she replies from her position on the nearby Vita. "The composition of the material itself is not too unusual. I have what I need in terms of raw supplies. Even the level of electromagnetic exposure they have called for will not take long with my equipment, either. The real choke point is that I have to patch up my reaction chamber before beginning the real work. It is self-repairing, to an extent, but I must insert new material to be bonded where the hole was drilled. With the urgency we are facing, I may have to skip some safety checks. I will not do anything I think is reckless, but certain protocols can be compressed."

"So how long in total?" Shaun pushes. "Days rather than weeks, right? Based on what you told me about how fast and easy it was to synthesize theocite once you did the harder work of developing the process and isolating the core formula?"

"Oh, certainly not days," Simone says.

I sigh heavily.

"One day at most," she goes on. "Really, once I am satisfied with the chamber's integrity and can run some quick tests to verify its safety, we should be looking at a matter of *hours*. I have learned a lot from my work with synthocite."

Shaun's face lights up in a smile. "Wow. Okay… well, don't skimp on the safety checks, in that case. I'll need a few hours to work through the launch logistics with my team, and then I'll need to head back to the Vita. Driver, are you good to fly us there when it's time?"

"You know it," she says. "That Leak is accelerating as we speak, and we have no idea when the dam is going to burst. The sooner we can do this, the better."

Despite some of my earlier misgivings, I now feel a smile spreading across my own lips, too.

With this incredible team, the impossible is within reach. We could be a single day away from stopping the Anomaly. I could be a day away from being able to tell little Scarlet she really *is* going to be okay.

All of that is underlined by the remarkable fact that we could be a day away from directly communicating with friendly aliens, or… whisper it… maybe even *meeting* some.

My smile is taking over my whole face now, to the extent that Driver laughingly calls it out and tells me to save the chuckles for our victory lap and the champagne for the toast.

After a quick goodbye to our colleagues on the Vita and Phil O'Connor on Earth, we're ready to leave Sasha to her analysis work.

Driver, Chester and Santino are going to Harriet's office to work on composing a message to send across the alien gateway once it's open, while President Williams has asked me to join him for his conference call with the ERF's other leaders. Major won't be on it, since he already knows everything, but I know Elana Hart will.

As we step towards the door, and despite the doubts and hesitations bubbling just under the conscious level of my mind, I feel energized by hope.

I reach for the doorknob with my new hand, which is another symbol of the power of science and the varied skills of this incredible spacecraft's crew. I'm better off than I was when I arrived here, and very soon I think the whole world will be, too.

A hubbub greets us as soon as the door opens. When it swings all the way, I can see that a crowd has gathered outside. They're effectively boxing us in, and I really don't like the looks on some of their faces.

"What the hell is going on?" a bald man near the front asks, grunting it out in a rough tone. It's a demand more than a question, and not the kind with any easy reply.

President Williams, Senior Coordinator and de facto *Captain* of the Balena, steps forward. The crowd falls silent. I think this is more in eagerness to hear a reply than in deference, but it brings a welcome break in the commotion, either way.

"I assume you've seen Phil O'Connor's latest prompts regarding the alien signal and the image output that shows their message," he begins.

"We've seen what the AI said about the news reporter's prompts, too," the bald guy interrupts. "These things are trying to trick us into opening a door for them. What are *you* going to do to protect us?"

My smile is nothing more than a memory.

Phil O'Connor's fear about irresponsible members of the news media using subjective responses from his AI system to spread fear have already come to fruition.

When they've already spread like this on the Balena, staffed by reasonable and rational men and women of science, I hardly even want to think about the scenes on Earth as panic spreads.

And however Phil, Chester, President Williams or even *I* try to calm people down, I know one uncomfortable truth for sure:

This genie isn't going back in the bottle.

28

The crowd is far from a mob, but it's still more than a little unsettling to be effectively trapped in the doorway by this sea of humanity.

To my surprise, and surely everyone else's in our group, Santino pushes to the front and addresses the crowd.

"Stop this panic!" the young man booms in his thick Italian accent. I haven't been here long enough or asked enough questions to know how Santino is viewed around here, but this interjection isn't exactly in line with the picture in my mind of a shy and awkward boy who keeps his head down as much as possible.

I'll tell you one thing, though: his three words do the trick. Temporarily, at least, the din subsides.

"We worked this out together," Santino goes on. "Me, Ray's bird Laika, Phil O'Connor, all of the others… we cracked the alien signal. We saw the images in their message before anyone else. We drew some conclusions before these so-called news reporters on Earth started looking for the most frightening angle they could find. So whose reaction are you going to pay more attention to? Are you going to listen to us, who only care about doing what it takes to keep humanity safe? Or are you going to listen to *them*, who only care about saying whatever will terrify most people into staring at their TVs and phones all day long?"

"It's Phil O'Connor's AI that's warning us about this!" the bald man at the front of the crowd contends.

Santino, who has tried valiantly here, turns to Chester and encourages him to take over.

"With Phil's help, we used it to decode and compile data," Chester says, calmly stating the case for rationality. "A system like PhilosophAI is only as good as the questions you ask. If you ask it for ten reasons why you should never fly in an airplane, it's going to give you ten reasons. If you ask it ten ways airplane travel has improved the world, it's going to give you ten answers for *that*, too."

"Phil is going to publicly address this in the next few minutes," President Williams says. He's making the decision as he speaks, really, and he turns around to Sasha and nods for her to pass the message on.

None of us expected things to have moved so quickly in the fear department, and I suppose this all speaks to the fact that we spent longer analyzing and discussing the images than we realized. It probably also speaks to the fact that bad news travels fast, which in turn rests on the media's decision to misrepresent the message as bad news in the first place.

Phil was always keen to tell the world that the AI's part in this was done, though, so he'll be ready to go at short notice. I've grown to like him and appreciate his calm demeanor in the face of challenging circumstances.

He's facing the same brain-melting revelations as the rest of us, of course, but he's also dealing with a terminal diagnosis that gives him a matter of months until time is up. His commitment to helping out however he can is very laudable in my mind. In a selfish sense he has no reason to stick his neck out, especially since he has no children or family of his own to worry about.

The fact that he's already freely granted access to all PhilosophAI systems for non-profit institutions says a lot, too, and I'm glad to have him on our side.

It brings to mind the old proverb: *"A society grows great when old men plant trees in whose shade they know they shall never sit."*

Perhaps the greatest tragedy is that Phil isn't even an old man. Either way, though, he's one I'm glad I've gotten to know.

"The aliens aren't trying to trick us into anything," President Williams continues, still addressing the crowd in his personable but authoritative manner. "With the technologies and scientific understandings they clearly possess, it seems to me that trickery would hardly be necessary if their purposes were nefarious. And let's not forget that we're not considering these instructions in a vacuum. The Anomaly is tightening around our necks, more and more, with the radiation coming at us from the newly detected Leak not only continuing but *accelerating* by the second. I'd ask all of you to watch Phil's appearance on the news wherever you've watched the initial scaremongering stories break."

When no one says anything for a few seconds, I take it upon myself to add something.

"I've seen every single image the aliens sent," I say. "I'm not sure if you all have, or if the news networks have only shown certain things. But what I can tell you is that *I* think these instructions are the answer to our prayers. We all see the Anomaly's effects in the form of the eerie auroras every time we look down at Earth from afar. I've also seen the effects only too close to home, in the form of my daughter's health issues. Phil will talk about why we can't listen to the AI's supposed fears about taking action here. He knows the system better than anyone. But right now, I want to ask all of you to look at the images for yourselves and try to think about how you might feel if you'd had a chance to digest them *without* the media spin. I had that luxury, and I think it makes a big difference."

"A huge difference," Driver interjects. While I'm unsure of Santino's general standing, I know that *she* is massively and universally respected among the Balena's crew.

Driver knows this, too, and I think that's why she's echoed my point.

"And just remember that Ray's family is on Earth but he's right here in the trenches with us," she goes on. "Don't forget that for one second. The two of us are going to be here and we're going to be reachable for whatever any of you need from us, but right now what we need from you is some calm. I need everyone to take a deep breath and I need you all to disperse. Don't let some corporate news agenda hijack your thinking and don't let it come between us. Listen to Phil and look at the images for yourselves, *then* come back with any concerns."

Without overly focusing my vision on any individual in the crowd, I see a general softening in their postures and expressions.

"Oh, and one more thing," Driver goes on. "Every single one of you is here by choice. We're all standing here on the Balena because despite *all* the naysayers, we are united by the goal of reaching Bayzen. Until today, we thought it was uninhabited. But guess what, guys? Until today, we also thought it was four light years away. Sure, we've all believed in this project since day one. But how many of us had it in the back of our minds that *we* might not actually get there? Best case, the boffins like Sasha and Shaun have always said the journey would take us close to a decade. Now, as far as I'm concerned, we're not stuck between a rock and a hard place with this decision we're going to have to make about whether or not to follow the aliens' instructions. No. In my mind, we just hit the damn jackpot. This is a win-win. It's a twofer."

The faces around me suggest I'm not alone in feeling confused by this.

"Think about it," Driver continues. "We can save Earth

from the Anomaly. Great. *Awesome*. That's the most important thing. But look at what else we'll be doing at the same time. We'll be carving out a *massive* shortcut to the goal we've been working towards for so long. If this wormhole the aliens want us to activate really is a tunnel through space, try to see what that means. Try to let yourselves *feel* what that means. This is bigger than just Bayzen, too. This could literally open up whole new worlds we haven't even detected yet. In one swing, we could save Earth and give ourselves a gateway to the stars."

One thing is for sure: Driver knows her audience.

As soon as she says this, the expressions of the crowd members perk up way beyond neutral. Even if some hesitation remains about the aliens' motives, they're clearly excited by this best-case scenario she's just painted.

Maybe it's overly optimistic to think the aliens will encourage or even allow us to cross the wormhole in their direction. But so what? Sometimes a best-case scenario is just what people need. It certainly balances out the *worst*-case ones the news media love so much.

The crowd disperses on Driver's cue. A few people come to her with questions, but she politely asks them to look at the images for themselves and listen out for Phil's comments. Reflecting the esteem she's held in, even those who still look most concerned about everything do as she asks.

This clears our path. I should really say *paths*, since our group is now splitting up. Before I set off with Williams, I tell Driver she's handled things perfectly.

Chester agrees wholeheartedly, drawing a warm smile from her that tells me there's still something between them even after she learned of his slippery deceit on the Vita. In all fairness, I've warmed to the guy since then, too, and understand why he did what he did. There was no malice behind it and he's definitely one of us now.

By the time President Williams and I arrive in his office, a text message arrives from Sasha to tell us that Phil is going live very soon.

I feel like we've done well to get a handle on things here on the Balena in a pretty short time — Williams and Driver, in particular — and now it's seemingly over to Phil to do the same on Earth.

Needless to say, I'm crossing my real and bionic fingers all over again in the hope that he can manage it.

29

Within a few seconds of his appearance on the biggest commercial news network in existence, it's abundantly clear that Phil O'Connor is an excellent speaker.

President Williams and I are watching in advance of our call with the other ERF leaders. They'll be watching, too, and Phil's comments will hopefully transform the public narrative by the time we're speaking with them.

"I built PhilosophAI to serve humanity," Phil says, ignoring the news anchor's attempts to direct the discussion in certain directions. "It's an excellent servant, but it should never be the master. We should never ask it to do our thinking, either. Its intended role was to calculate and analyze in objective ways, enhancing human operations in the same way computers did a technological generation earlier. Every answer it gives is only as good as the question we ask, but it's also only as good as the data the system has been trained on."

So far, so great.

"Humanity has feared aliens for as long as we've been thinking about them," he goes on. "That's why the AI is biased towards fear. But we never expected contact to come in a situation like this, much less in a manner like this. Even a *good* subjective question today would result in an answer tainted by the training data of yesterday, and it's clear to me that the answers you've been irresponsibly publicizing came from terrible questions. You've asked why we should be scared, and then you're acting surprised when the system gives some reasons! You've explicitly asked the system to list possible nefarious motives that could lie behind the aliens' instructions, and then you're presenting them like—"

"Like they're what the system has suggested?" the anchor cuts in. Her voice is intense and accusatory, like she's confronting a criminal rather than someone doing his best to help humanity. "Yes, Phil. Yes we are."

Phil sighs and closes his eyes to compose himself. "Look, the system helped us to decode the signal and it helped us to compile the data back into the complete image collages we've all seen. For me, its role ends there. But I'll play along and say it's worthwhile to ask what it makes of the images. When you give it that prompt, with no instruction to look for a negative angle, its take on the situation is the same as mine. It's the same as the conclusion Ray Barclay, President Williams and the rest of their team drew when we looked at the raw images ourselves. We didn't ask it what we should do about the message, but we did ask what it thinks the aliens were trying to communicate. They want us to fire a specific material at a specific location so they can help us to stop the Anomaly. It's as simple and as complicated as that."

"Some of us have children, Mr. O'Connor," the anchor snaps. "And like our children, some of us also have decades ahead of us. Perhaps it's easy for a man with no family and no future to be so cavalier about everyone else's? Some would suggest that, in any case."

Phil takes that tasteless barb on the chin, again focusing on what's most important rather than being dragged into a mud fight.

"I'd rather stick to the issues rather than the personal stories, if you don't mind," he deflects. "And on the issues, I want to say that PhilosophAI isn't alone among AI systems in having a bias towards caution when dealing with novel situations. That's mainly for liability reasons. Our enterprise solutions offer customizable levels of caution, because in certain business applications there is value in taking risks. By default, and in the core model we're all using today, it's fair to say there's a slight bias towards fear. That's true in humans, too, because fear can serve us well. The important thing is to step back and ask where the fear is coming from. And here, like I said, we're not just dealing with a general predilection towards caution. In this instance, we have to remember that the data our system has about alien contact comes from its knowledge of disastrous fictional meetings in movies and books. That's one of the contexts your viewers need to remember."

"*One* of them?" the anchor pushes.

Phil nods. "The other important context is the Anomaly," he states, very matter-of-factly. "It's rational for people to be scared of new things, like the existence of aliens, but it's not rational to blow that out of proportion. It's like how people are more scared of wild animal attacks than they are of carbon monoxide poisoning. The balance, relative to the risk, is way out of whack."

The anchor shifts in her seat and leans forward dramatically. "So to be clear, Mr. O'Connor, you are actively likening these aliens to dangerous wild animals?"

Taking a second to compose himself, Phil exhales slowly. "No, I'm saying it's easier for people to visualize and fear an alien attack, which isn't coming, than it is for them to truly comprehend the risks of the massive and unprecedented cosmic radiation leak that's suffocating our world right now."

The anchor raises her eyebrows, encouraging Phil to go on.

"Look," he obliges, "you say you have children. You say you all have decades ahead of you. I say that's a bold thing to assume when newly measurable radiation is accelerating towards our planet all while the visible effects are getting worse. I hate to break it to you, but doing nothing isn't an option here unless you want to die at the same time as me."

Suddenly looking very uncomfortable, the news anchor stays silent for several seconds.

"Phil O'Connor," she eventually says in a flat tone, ending the video interview as unceremoniously as that. "Now, stay tuned for some less biased insight from our crack team of alien analysts."

I breathe a sigh of relief as the news station cuts to commercials.

Phil did pretty well, I think. All things considered, he did as well as anyone could have asked or expected.

He avoided the main traps the anchor laid for him and stayed pretty gracious despite her low blow about the short time he has left. He also succinctly explained his position on the AI having played its part and having no *further* part to play in this. There's quite a lot of nuance inherent to that position, but he got the main message across.

Whether this will be enough to calm people's nerves on Earth like Driver calmed everyone here is another question, particularly when it seems like the news media and their "crack teams of alien analysts" will continue to report whatever stirs up the most ratings-generating drama.

Still, it could have gone much worse.

Just as President Williams is about to close the news station's window on his computer and begin the call to his fellow ERF leaders, the door behind us bursts open.

Shaun stands at the threshold, panting.

"Sir, it's Jay," he blurts out.

Williams furrows his brow "Jay… Grant? In launch control? What about him?"

"I needed him on board," Shaun continues, clearly shaken. "He was one of the two people I needed to bring in to help with this, but he didn't like it. He said we can't decide to do this on our own. He's told everyone. And not just here — he already called someone on Earth. They know we're moving ahead with the plan."

While President Williams holds out a hand to calm Shaun,

insisting that we can get on top of this, I notice a red flashing banner on the computer. When I focus on it, my heart sinks.

The news station has cut back from commercials early, and the same anchor as before now sits above a headline that's going to be almost impossible to get on top of:

BREAKING: O'CONNOR A DISTRACTION WHILE BALENA LEADERS RECKLESSLY WORK TO OPEN ALIEN FLOODGATE!

30

If this wasn't so serious, it would almost be funny.

For the news station to describe the wormhole as an "alien floodgate" is beyond ironic, given that opening that gate is our only chance of stopping the already damaging Leak from becoming a decisively deadly flood of radiation.

"Fear is a contagion, Ray," Williams flatly utters. "We can't do much more on Earth right now, but we have to nip this in the bud right here before dissent can become a mutiny."

My spine stiffens at the very word.

A mutiny? With Driver and Williams in charge? And not to blow my own trumpet, but with *me* here, too?

"I don't think it would come to that," Williams goes on, "but I'm not prepared to take the risk."

"We can block all outgoing private communication if you authorize it, sir," Shaun suggests.

Williams shakes his head. "That horse has already bolted. And we really don't want to start taking actions like that. Quelling actual dissent and insubordination is one thing, but draconian measures are the tool of the tyrant. If we use them, that's how we appear."

"So what *are* we going to do?" Shaun asks. "What about Jay?"

"He'll be held accountable," Williams says, choosing his words carefully as he thinks through the implications. "But not today. Morale is everything and we need to be seen to be doing this by consent, not command."

Shaun says nothing.

"We'll explain that the situation with the Leak is just so urgent that we had to begin the preparatory work on this before we finished discussing it with everyone, that's all," Williams continues. "It's not even a lie. Today — right now — I want Grant to explain himself in front of everyone. We'll hear his concerns and we'll answer them. I know you'll feel personally betrayed by him as well as concerned about our mission, Shaun, but locking him up in the detention center would achieve nothing. Grant isn't the only person here with misgivings about this, he was just the first among them to hear that we're taking action. The cat's out of the bag. We can't put it back in, so we have to calm it down before it tears up the walls and shits all over the carpet of our plans."

I'll be honest: I might have been inclined to throw Jay Grant in the detention center and lock down any further outgoing communications. And that's why I'm glad President Williams is in charge around here.

The logic of his comments about morale and leadership through consent rather than command is undeniable. The very last thing we need is to turn this into an Us and Them situation where the Balena's crew vastly outnumbers the inner circle of its leadership.

As Williams leads us very literally back into the hallway, Shaun turns to me and whispers: "How did Phil do?"

"I'd say pretty well," I reply. "But I don't know how much that's going to matter now. The media narrative on Earth has already swung back the wrong way thanks to Jay Grant. He was *fast*."

I see Shaun's shoulders sink. "I thought I could trust Jay with anything," he sighs. "I've known him for years and I needed his help to check over some of the launch plans. I didn't want to use the AI because the prompts would be public and people would see I was working on it, but I guess we don't have to worry about *that* anymore."

When we turn a corner and an automatic door panel slides up into its ceiling recess to let us pass, I hear a commotion that makes the crowd hubbub of earlier seem like a faint whisper in comparison.

Instinctively, I rush ahead of the slower Williams.

The source of the bellows and shouts becomes instantly apparent as what I can only describe as a melee comes into view.

There are a few dozen crew members in the area, and their attention isn't turned on us or any other members of the leadership.

No. They're focused on each other, and this is no mere discussion… it's a full on scuffle, with some pockets looking more like all-out *brawls*.

"Enough!" President Williams booms, with an intensity I've never heard from him — or just about anyone else.

At the same time as he yells, he slams his fist into a fire alarm on the wall, bringing the overhead sprinkler system to life and decisively breaking up the civil war that was building before our eyes.

He walks purposefully into the center of the open space, indifferent to the water as it soaks him from above, and holds out his hands.

"This ends now," Williams bellows. "Jay Grant! Are you in here?"

A man, seemingly Jay Grant, sheepishly emerges from the pack just as the rain-like shower subsides. I see straight away that Grant has a black eye and ripped shirt.

"Explain yourself," Williams demands. Something tells me the calm discussion he had planned isn't going to happen. After all, that idea came before we walked into a mass bar fight. "Explain all of this!"

Looking at the ground, seemingly in some combination of shame and regret, Jay Grant says nothing for several seconds. He eventually forces his eyes to look up at Williams. "I'm sorry, sir," is all he can say.

"I don't want an apology," Williams snaps back. "I want an explanation."

"You could kill us all," Grant blurts out.

His words are met with a lot of protest from half of the crew around us. The other half, it seems, share his view.

"I did what I thought was right," he continues, speaking up to be heard. "Some people didn't like it, but I had to do it. You can't just do this. You can't just unilaterally decide to do this without—"

"What the fuck is going on?" Driver's voice tears through the air, approaching from behind like a Mach truck to cut off Grant's complaint.

Her eyes are initially fixed on him, the loose-lipped fool who might have just destabilized Earth as well as the Balena, but she quickly sees the ripped clothes and black eye and other telltale signs of what I walked in on a few moments ago. Quickly seeing that Grant isn't the only one with questions to answer, she turns to the rest of the soaked crew members and directs a similarly sharp question at them.

To my left, I see President Williams reach for his phone and read something with an evident degree of concern. He walks to me right away while Driver continues to angrily question the formerly rambunctious crowd.

Williams tilts his phone so I alone can see it. The screen is filled with a message from Elana Hart, Senior Coordinator of the ERF's Colorado bunker and generally regarded as the organization's most powerful Earth-based official.

There are only nine words in the impactful message, and two of them are the same. Without doubt, that heavy emphasis is the most troubling part:

"We need to talk. Immediately. And I mean IMMEDIATELY."

Williams then tips his head back towards the door.

"Now?" I ask.

He nods. "Driver and Chester will clear up this mess. I need you with me, Ray."

I've pretty much gathered that everyone except President Williams answers to Driver around here, and that even he sees her as an equal. That's never been more apparent than now, when he's leaving her to handle this.

"You can all finish explaining yourselves to Driver and shake each other's hands when she's done with you," Williams tells the crowd. "And don't think I'm not angry at every single one of you. The even greater disappointment is all that's stopping me from giving you what you deserve for turning on each other like this. We're fighting the same battle here. The next time someone has a problem with that, come to me. Don't run to the media or fight with each other over some misunderstanding — pull yourselves together. Any further disorder will have you kicked out of the Bayzen Project as soon as we've taken care of this Anomaly."

As these well-delivered words settle, Driver is the only one who seems a little surprised that Williams is leaving her in charge of what has clearly been a very volatile situation.

Chester, who arrived a few seconds after her, walks to my side and asks what's going on.

Williams flashes him the phone, drawing an understanding nod.

"Any parameters for this that Driver might not assume are in place?" Chester asks.

"No detention for anyone, and no punishments unless anyone is insubordinate," Williams says. "It would be good if you could step in once she's finished and just calmly re-hit the core points about being driven by logic and necessity rather than reactive fear, and about this wormhole granting us an opportunity rather than causing us a problem. You know what you're doing."

"Well, I appreciate the faith," Chester replies earnestly. "Good luck with Hart."

Bearing in mind how obstructive Elana Hart threatened to be when I was trying to leave the Colorado launch site for the Vita just a few days ago, and bearing in mind the power she holds over ERF operations, I have a feeling we're going to need it...

31

"What the hell is going on up there?" Elana Hart demands as soon as Williams begins the video call.

"Up here?" Williams echoes in an uncharacteristically acerbic tone. He's clearly perturbed by the way Hart is speaking to him, and I don't blame him one bit. "*Up here,* we've decoded the alien signal and given humanity a chance of surviving this damn Anomaly. How are things in your shielded underground bunker?"

Hart sighs, loudly and slowly. "Noah, since *you* can't control your own people, we're all facing chaos. Minutes is all it takes. You can make your comments about my shielded bunker while you're safely isolated from everything in space. Anyone can be brave in an ivory tower as high as yours. But I'll bet you don't know people are threatening to storm and destroy ERF facilities, do you? All to make sure we don't do anything to open this godforsaken alien gate, which the world just found out you're *already* working to unlock! Have you stopped for one second to actually think about this? Or are you just being pulled along as usual by *Action Man* Barclay and *all-eyes-on-Bayzen* Driver?"

Okay, now *I'm* taken aback.

"What do you think this is?" I snap back at Hart. "My family is on Earth, for one thing. You think I don't care about their safety? You think I don't care about my friends in your bunker, or in New Zealand? We're moving ahead with the prep work on this mission *because* we care, and because it's the only chance we've got of stopping the Anomaly. Don't tell me you've been suckered in by the doomsaying AI responses to the negative prompts the news teams were throwing at it?"

"I have a mind of my own, Ray," Hart replies sharply. "Don't get too comfortable on that high horse of yours, with your way as the only way and any dissenting opinion automatically dismissed as coming from an unreliable AI. I understand the urgency of the Leak — we all do — but some of us think dealing directly with that is preferable to opening Pandora's Box. Surely you can see why someone might hold that view?"

"And how exactly are you going to 'deal with' a cosmic radiation source we don't know the first thing about?" I shoot back. "Bomb it?"

"Don't be ridiculous," she groans. "I have smart people here just like you have smart people there, and they're talking about potential shields or deflectors to mitigate this radiation. We only identified the Leak a few days ago and these ideas are already brewing."

I shake my head. "Listen to me: it doesn't matter how viable those ideas might be in the medium-to-long term. We don't even have the luxury of short-term planning here. We have to act *now*."

"Says who?" Hart asks.

I feel my eyes narrow. "What?"

"Says who?" she repeats. "These aliens you're so keen to believe sent their message about the Leak at least four years ago. Correct? And it hasn't destroyed the world yet. What makes you think another few months or even a year would be fatal?"

I instinctively turn to Williams, quickly seeing that he's as shocked by this statement as me, then look back to the screen. "You can't be serious, can you?" I ask. "The Anomaly's effects have been worsening for over a year, and some of them have been getting *much* worse, very quickly, in just the past month or two. Now that we've identified the Leak, we can see that the radiation leakage has accelerated in just the few days since we started measuring it. This isn't only going to keep getting worse, it's going to start getting even worse even faster. And you've seen the same images I have. They likened it to a dam. I don't know when the tipping point will come, but the pattern of acceleration tells us it's sure as hell not months."

"That's your interpretation," Hart shrugs, almost indifferently. "A *hunch*. And when the action you're suggesting is as consequential and as irreversible as this one, I need more than a hunch to authorize it."

"Elana… you *have* no authority," Williams states, ice cold in his delivery. "Major is with us, too, so you can't even claim moral authority from a majority of our Senior Coordinators."

"You are endangering my staff," Hart grunts, her eyes more intense than I've ever seen them. "Unless you publicly commit to pausing this reckless mission until we reach a consensus, I might have to evacuate this whole site. Some of the threats are *credible*, Noah, especially to our above-ground areas. With the preponderance of drones these days and the huge prepper settlements nearby, we can't assume it's all just bluster. We can't take that risk."

She has to be bluffing. Even if she's not, though, there's no way Williams can make the kind of commitment she wants. He knows as well as I do that consensus will get us nowhere, because fear has already burrowed too deeply into Hart's psyche for there to be any chance of talking her round.

Before Williams can reply, I hear his phone buzzing loudly in his pocket. He lifts it out and looks at the screen.

"News agency," he says. "The same station Phil was on. Yes or no?"

I nod. "We can't be seen to be dodging scrutiny," I say.

"My thoughts exactly," Williams says. He briefly glances to Hart again on his computer screen and speaks five parting words before ending our call with her in favor of another:

"Good luck with your evacuation."

32

A matter of seconds after calling Elana Hart's bluff, President Williams is conversing with someone from the news station who he seems to be on fairly cordial terms with.

It's not the on-screen anchor, obviously, because it sounds like they're being far more reasonable than she was on TV.

Williams puts his phone down after this quick call and re-opens the video call software on his computer. We're sitting in a sufficiently low orbit to ensure these calls are almost entirely lag-free, which wasn't the case during the last few times Driver tried to call me and my family from the Balena. It certainly helps today, though.

"We'll just talk for a few minutes," he assures me. "We'll be less… *intellectual* in our arguments than Phil was. I'll plead for calm and say we're taking preparatory steps in case further study of the Leak tells us we truly have to do this. You can add something at the end likening this to your struggle against Zola. People relate to that."

As much as I used to hate public speaking, addressing the world feels like nothing compared to the real challenges we're facing. That's the only reason I'm able to agree to this so easily.

Before I know it, we're live on a call with the combative anchor who grilled Phil O'Connor just a short while ago.

The view we can see shows not the anchor, but the full televised picture that's going out live. Understandably, we're front and center.

The headline banner underneath initially reads "LIVE: WILLIAMS SPEAKS FROM THE BALENA", but within a few seconds it changes with the addition of the words "AND BARCLAY".

President Williams is an absolute pro, delivering a perfect message on the topic he said he would. The anchor doesn't interrupt him like she did when Phil was trying to speak, probably on the orders of her bosses, and the headline never changes to twist his words.

After hitting his key points, Williams leads me in by suggesting that I have some words for the viewers that only I could share. He's the definition of a natural.

"This is a scary time," I begin, feeling my heart-rate soar as the pressure of addressing such a large audience finally sinks in. "I won't pretend it's not. But we've had scary times before. Even the youngest viewers out there probably know about Ignacio Zola, an evil man who really did want to destroy the world. What I want everyone to remember today is that my friends and colleagues up here did everything it took to stop him. We did everything we had to do, as scary as some of it was."

I pause for breath.

"And now?" I go on. "Well, now we're going to do what we have to do to stop the Anomaly. Only this time, we might just do it with the help of some *new* friends who live even further away. In line with what President Williams just said about only taking big steps when there are no smaller ones left to take, we have to be ready for what might become necessary, and I want everyone to know that the driving force behind everything I do will always be the drive to keep you all safe. Eva, Joe, Scarlet... I'll be home soon. And when I am, the world will be a safer place than it has been for a long time. You can count on that."

Williams places a hand on my shoulder, purposefully

visible in his support.

"Stirring words there, Ray," the anchor says, "but the realist in me feels—"

All of a sudden, the anchor's voice cuts off.

If it wasn't for the instinctive movement of her hand towards her earpiece, listening to a seemingly jarring message, I would think the connection has just died. That's how suddenly she falls silent.

"Oh my God," she says, talking to the messenger. "Okay, run it."

I feel my heart-rate soar all over again, just as it was dropping after what felt like a job well done.

"Extreme discretion is advised in viewing the f-following footage which has j-just reached us from Arlington," the anchor goes on.

The stutter in her words only adds to my unease.

When the feed on our screen changes, it's shaky but clear phone footage, filmed by someone running towards a house and yelling for the owner to "get the hell out and face what's coming."

As the door of the house opens, my heart sinks. Phil O'Connor stands in the doorway, confused until reality quickly sinks in.

And he's not standing for long, quickly falling to the ground as a pistol appears in front of the phone and the multi-tasking cameraman pulls the trigger.

"Where's your damn aliens to help you now?" the man taunts.

He then zooms in closer on Phil's lifeless face, forcing me to close my eyes.

"And this ain't over," he goes on, vitriol dripping from every word. "As long as you desperate government idiots are trying to let these hostile aliens through some gate in the sky because you can't do your own damn jobs, this ain't even started. Hart, Major, Williams, Barclay… you're next. Don't say we didn't warn ya!"

33

I'm stunned.

Truly, I am *stunned.*

It's a good thing Williams reaches out to end the call in case the anchor might have tried to cut back for our reaction, because my mind is spinning.

Between Jay Grant and the mass brawl in the hallway to Elana Hart's obstructiveness, and now with this senseless brutality taking things to another level entirely, I feel broken by the reaction of my fellow man.

Fear is natural. I know that. But right now this feels like a zombie movie, or more aptly like an old Twilight Zone kind of story about aliens, where it always turns out that other people were who you should have been worrying about all along.

Phil O'Connor is dead. And for what? Trying to explain that we shouldn't panic over what the AI *he* developed was saying when people gave it misguided prompts and spreads its responses as gospel?

That was his capital offense?

"There's no weakness in sadness, Ray," Williams says, placing his hand on my shoulder again. "But as much as I don't want to sound insensitive, the last thing Phil would want is for us to sit here crying over spilled milk."

I force out a sharp breath and clench my fists until the knuckles crack. Well, on my left hand, at least. While the right looks and feels so natural that I sometimes find myself briefly forgetting it's not, one thing its knuckles don't do is crack when I clench.

We both get up from our seated positions and take a second to gather ourselves.

I think a few minutes have passed since we watched Phil die. It's hard to tell.

"We have to reconnect with Driver and make sure things are relatively calm before this spreads," Williams says. "That's going to be almost instant. This can go two ways, Ray. Either we're looking at a full-blown mutiny if people fear reprisals from the maniac who did this and others like him, or we end up with a siege mentality that unites the whole crew."

As Williams opens the door and encourages me to join him, I can't help but feel impressed. I'm impressed by his focus, as well as his uncanny ability to think and talk so clearly after what we've just witnessed.

Seeing Phil die like that was bad enough. Hell, seeing it would have been bad enough even if the victim had been a stranger. I'm as shaken by the visceral brutality of the moment as I was when Zola killed Carlo on the Beacon.

But this goes beyond the natural human aversion to violent death. It goes beyond the natural sadness at losing someone I'd been closely working with and who was becoming a friend. It goes beyond all of that, because now I'm majorly concerned about the potential after effects of this senseless killing.

It could embolden copycats, it could paralyze our team with fear, or it could hurt us in a dozen other ways I haven't even considered.

I'm still trying to wrap my head around all the ways things have started to go wrong since we all opened the door to leave Sasha's office, thinking we were on a positive path only to walk out to an angry mob. Since then, it feels like we've been fighting to keep our heads above water without making any real progress.

The hallway is silent.

When we reach the spot where Driver was admonishing the group of brawlers, it's deserted.

This tells me that she and Chester did a good job, but I'm surprised by the total lack of people. I also don't really know my way around here, though. Williams does, and he takes a sharp right towards a door that leads into a vast canteen where there must be hundreds of people.

It looks like it's turned into a meeting room, and Driver is standing before the huge standing-room-only crowd.

I can tell from the heavy atmosphere that word of Phil's murder has spread. I can also sense that it hasn't led to the kind of fear-driven mutiny Williams posited as a worst-case scenario.

"This is what fear can do in the wrong hands," Driver says, forcing out the words. She's clearly upset and can't hide it as well as Williams. Credit to her for being able to speak at all, though, because I still don't know that I could.

"And in the right hands, it can drive us to take brave action," Chester adds. It's obvious that he's been crying, which somehow warms me to him even more. Truly, he is one of us.

"Yes it can," I say, alerting them both to my presence as I walk over. These two are inspiring me to push on and do whatever I can to help. "And—"

All of a sudden, I'm cut off by the sound of the canteen's door swinging open behind me.

Continuing the new speaker theme, but bursting in so loudly that she'll be surprising *no one*, it's Sasha.

"Sorry to interrupt," she says. With her eyes, she then calls me and Driver back towards Williams. Chester and Shaun, who I've just noticed standing behind him, both come over, too. Sasha's gesture is the opposite of subtle, but she's evidently way past caring about that.

When we're all gathered, the whole room is looking at Sasha, and no one more intently than I am.

"Believe me," she goes on. "I know this is the last thing anyone wants to hear right now, but you have to hear it. We just got new telescope data from the Leak. Guys... it's gotten even worse. The acceleration has accelerated. The observable radiation is *so* much worse than it was even yesterday, I'm seriously worried about tomorrow. We need movement on this, and we need it now."

34

Sasha was right: her update really *is* the last thing I wanted to hear.

The Leak, already causing so many visible problems and already accelerating at a frightening rate, has just worsened again.

The cosmic noose of the Anomaly has closed even more tightly around our necks, and her final comment that we need movement on our mission is the truest thing in the world.

"Has anyone been in touch with Simone?" Driver asks.

"Her reaction chamber is operational," Sasha replies, skipping a 'yes' and getting straight to the details. "That was almost an hour ago, much quicker than she expected, and she said the synthesizing process would only take a matter of hours. It won't be long until *she's* ready."

"And the launch stuff?" Driver pushes, this time focusing specifically on Shaun.

He nods. "Since we don't have to worry about word getting out, I've been able to use the AI to double-check my data and confirm the trajectory and force needed for precisely hitting the target, where and how the aliens have instructed. It's great for that kind of objective calculation work even if we shouldn't rely on it for other applications, just like Phil was trying to tell everyone."

The very mention of Phil is enough to usher in a few seconds of pensive and mournful silence.

This silence extends around the huge canteen, filled with more crew members than I can count. Williams and I share a glance before he steps forward to address them.

"Things have taken a turn," he says. "Things have taken a *few* turns in quick succession, to be more accurate. None of them are welcome, but we never expected this to be a straight and easy road. Sasha has just brought an update on our study of the Leak. For everyone's sake, and as is her duty, she delivered the news to me. I want everyone to know there are no secrets here. There never were. Fear has cost our friend and ally Phil O'Connor his life. We will not stand by and let fear paralyze us, because our action is all that can prevent countless more lives following his to a premature end."

Everyone is listening closely.

"Colleagues," Williams continues, "we are at a point of no return. If we do not quickly proceed and *succeed* in our mission to open this gateway, I see little hope of surviving the Anomaly for much longer. There are no guarantees about what will happen once we succeed, but I have an increasingly uncomfortable feeling of certainty about what will happen very soon if we don't."

Around the room, I see reality sinking in on every face. Williams isn't sugar coating anything here, and that approach is having a very clear effect.

"Many of you have misgivings about this," he goes on, "and let me level with you: I do, too. If there was another way that gave us the same chance of survival as this does, we'd be exploring it. Unfortunately, there simply isn't. Some on Earth are suggesting projects to mitigate the Leak which would take many months to implement, with no guarantee of their effectiveness even then. And with what Sasha has just reported about the acceleration in radiation leakage, many months might as well be a thousand years. We are moving forward with our initial plan to follow the signal's instructions and engage the gateway. Our best people are hard at work on this as I speak. And while they work, hopefully nearing completion of their tasks, I will stay right here to answer as many questions and address as many concerns as I possibly can."

Countless hands instantly shoot up.

I watch and listen while Williams, as good as his word, gives due consideration to every comment that comes his way. I'm glad that they're all delivered respectfully, even when they're dripping with disagreement, and he masterfully ensures that everyone feels heard and that their concerns are valid even as he insists that we have to continue forward despite them.

There's something very cathartic about this experience of everyone sharing their unique concerns and ideas.

And crucially, our mission really is moving forward as it happens. Simone is working like a Trojan to synthesize our all important neocite in her Vita-based lab, while Sasha is back in her office analyzing our latest Leak data through every imaginable lens and program.

Meanwhile, Shaun is now in constant communication with some of the few technical staff who stayed behind on the Vita. He's making sure the launch bay's systems are operational so that he can conduct some remote tests on various instruments we'll be relying on when the time comes. He's going to be returning to the Vita to handle the launch process when the time comes, with Driver flying him there and yours truly joining the team.

Some twenty or twenty-five minutes into the question-and-answer session, a woman near the front of the crowd raises her hand and urgently waves it while Williams is still answering another question.

"Yes?" he asks, breaking his answer to inquire what she wants.

"There's a new statement from Elana Hart," the woman

relays. "She just issued it now. It says she's ordered a full evacuation of the ERF's Colorado bunker and launch site with immediate effect."

So much for the bluff, I muse.

"There's more, too," the woman goes on, shifting into a voice that makes clear she's reading verbatim. "Hart says: *After a direct conversation with Noah Williams and Ray Barclay, I am sad to say that they are conducting themselves like dictators. They are dragging their heels over any public discourse, they are abandoning the ERF's foundational consensus model, they now seem hell bent on taking the risk of potentially dragging us into a wholly avoidable alien apocalypse.*"

I can't for the life of me understand why Hart is doing this. I can't understand why she's actually going through with the evacuation or why she's using this kind of incendiary language. Short of any other angle that makes sense, I think she might really be acting out of mortal fear.

I think she truly fears for her people's safety in Colorado, and I think she truly fears what could happen if we open up the wormhole.

Would Hart still feel like that if she had the latest data on the Leak?

In all honesty, I don't know. Everyone has access to the data showing how much radiation we were able to detect yesterday, along with the relative comparison to our earlier data which highlights the first acceleration. I can't understand why that hasn't gotten through to everyone as the colossal danger it is. Sure, it's not as Hollywood as a threat from a machiavellian alien race... but it's *real*, damn it.

The questions Williams is facing understandably change after this, and he has to briefly excuse himself to check in with Clarence Major on the Vita.

While he does that, I take the time to briefly leave the canteen to call my family. Eva is hugely concerned about everything, very understandably, and the kids are asleep.

Laika, hearing my voice but knowing how late it is, appears

next to Eva at the dining table and tries to greet me as quietly as he can. Whispering is something he's never really mastered, what with physiology being one thing even he can't transcend, but the little guy gives it a shot.

"Laika sad Laika no can help Ray Ray," he says.

"You already did, buddy," I assure him. "With Santino, when you gave him the idea that cracked the signal. We still have a chance to fix this, and you played your part."

"Laika need to do more," he laments. "Next time Laika help Ray Ray more."

I can't help but smile at that. "I'm kind of hoping there's not going to be a next time. How about Laika and Ray Ray relax on a beach somewhere? You can help me crack open the coconuts."

"Deal," he squawks.

Eva is smiling next to him, but a thousand justifiable concerns are etched on her face.

"You really do think this is the best thing to do, don't you?" she asks.

"It's the only thing we can do," I reply. "But everything I've said is true, and everything Phil said was true, too. The idea of hostility just doesn't make sense. They're trying to help us, Eva. I know it in my bones."

With a slow breath, she forces a nod. "That's good enough for me. Just promise you'll call again before you leave the Balena for the Vita, okay? You know what Joe's brain is like. He's seen every sci-fi movie under the sun and he's imagining all kinds of scenarios. Two minutes with you would do him a world of good."

"I'll call in the morning, even if we're ready to head out," I promise. "Whatever he needs."

We end the call a minute later, keeping the difficult long-distance goodbye brief as we've always tried to. I think that's more important for us now than ever, what with the concerns we're both feeling and how well we can read each other's faces.

When I return to the canteen, Williams is back in the full flow of addressing specific concerns about our plan. The ones he's handling now are pretty small and sometimes very far-out, since the main points were addressed a long time ago.

He gives me a slight nod when he sees me re-enter, which tells me nothing important came up during his call with Major. I know Major is one hundred percent on board with our plan, and it's not like the Vita could possibly be in the same kind of danger as Hart thought her facility could be — which I saw as a far-fetched concern in its own right.

I glance at the clock when Williams finishes answering one particularly long question. I've stepped in to help with a few, mainly on the psychological rather than the technical side of things, and it feels like the group as a whole has bonded during this whole process.

Soon, I'm more than a little surprised to see two hours have passed since I called home.

Some of the others have been coming and going in that time. As usual, Sasha is spinning a dozen plates and staying on top of updates from every direction.

Driver is now back with Harriet and Santino, and before leaving again she said they were at the stage of preparing our radios so we can fire a signal containing our message to the aliens as soon as the gateway is open.

There's still a lot of supposition about what that gateway actually is, or will be. But by whatever miraculous science it works, we simply have to assume we'll be able to use it to instantly communicate with them in the same way they've suggested they'll be able to instantly communicate with us.

I don't know what exactly our team is planning to say in the return message. I'm sure we'll all have a look before anything is set in stone, but by the same token I trust those guys to get it right.

All we really need to say is that we've followed their instructions as quickly as possible and are desperate for assistance with the problem they identified.

I don't think we need to get too complicated and say we had already detected the Leak on our own, because that's not central to the issue at hand and any extra time they might take to understand a non-essential piece of information is time wasted dealing with our urgent problem.

We're sending an SOS, essentially, and less is more.

In the canteen, the next question from the crowd isn't one I'll be answering so I get up to stretch my legs. And as soon I reach the door for a quick stroll, I see Shaun hurrying towards it.

"Is Williams still talking?" he asks.

"Yeah," I say. "Why? There can't be *more* bad news about the Leak, can there?"

"That's Sasha's thing," he replies impatiently. "You know I'm working on the launch side of things… and yeah, we've just hit a *huge* problem on that front. It's not the kind that's going to fix itself, and you're not going to like the only solution I can think of."

Am I in some kind of weird purgatory today, where one seemingly huge breakthrough rises like a balloon only to then be punctured a thousand times by one thing after another?

After Jay Grant's blabbing to the media, Elana Hart's obstructive nonsense, Phil O'Connor's senseless murder, and Sasha's awful update about the ever-accelerating Leak, I'm struggling to even imagine what new development can count as a huge problem in Shaun's normally calm mind.

"It's about our launch systems on the Vita," he says. "For the past half hour, I haven't been able to remotely control anything. I've spoken to the guys who are there, and there are local problems, too. The targeting functionality is completely offline. Without that, we can't lock on to the target to deliver the payload."

"Do you know what could be causing this?"

Shaun gulps. "Ray, the Vita is being absolutely bombarded by signal-jamming technologies. We've already detected the blocking signals from more than twenty satellites — some that are well out of reach. We've been able to identify some of the satellites and we know they're all linked to a single Earth-based control location."

"Where?" I ask, fearing I already know the answer.

Shaun takes a deep breath before sighing out the single-word confirmation: "*Colorado.*"

35

"They're signal-jamming our launch equipment from the bunker in Colorado?" I echo incredulously. "For sure?"

"Sure as sure can be," Shaun replies. "They really have evacuated the bunker, though. We have our own satellite images of the convoys and planes. Hart just put out another statement saying she's done all she can to persuade us to stop this 'crazy plan'. Now that we've identified the source of the problems, I think that's what she's talking about. They set this up before they left the bunker. Our communications systems are okay, but not the launch targeting and some other relate systems."

I don't say anything. I *can't* say anything. But the look of shocked confusion on my face is clear enough that I don't have to.

"If you want to talk adages to make sense of this craziness Hart is pulling, I'm putting this down halfway to Occam's razor and halfway to Hanlon's razor," Shaun goes on. "Occam's razor in that the most obvious assumption is the one I think is most likely: Hart and everyone else down there are genuinely scared of the aliens and they're genuinely scared of further reprisals for anyone linked to the ERF. I think they've evacuated to protect themselves and they've given us one last major obstacle because they think it can protect Earth from what they think could be a huge mistake. Hanlon's razor tells us we should never attribute to malice that which is adequately explained by stupidity."

Being grandiose is sometimes Shaun's thing. But while I might have used simpler words, I don't disagree with his analysis.

There's nothing nefarious going on here like there was with the mining conglomerate causing chaos on the Vita to further their commercial interests. As colossally misguided as her actions have been, I think Elana Hart's driving interest is the same as ours: to protect humanity.

Once again, I feel like the problem can be boiled down to a lack of appreciation on the imminent and worsening dangers posed by the ever-accelerating Anomaly.

"Have we shared all of the latest data Sasha saw from the Leak?" I ask.

Shaun nods glumly. "We shared it directly with news agencies and with the other ERF sites, but no one on Earth is focusing on it. The team at the New Zealand compound aren't saying anything in public. The bosses there have privately said they aren't opposed to what we're doing, and they're not evacuating, but they don't want to stick their heads above the parapet right now. Their public line is that they're waiting for further data and discussion. They're not saying *we* should wait, but they're also not commenting on the data we've given."

I sigh. "So everyone down there is still fixating on potential hostility from the aliens? The urgency of dealing with the Leak just isn't getting through?"

"The handful of TV analysts that people are listening to have downplayed the changes we've seen in the Leak," Shaun replies. "They're saying an increase in the measurable radiation doesn't necessarily mean very much, because it's radiation we don't really understand yet and can't decisively blame for any of the Anomaly-related problems."

I don't even know where to start with that.

Shaun shakes his head, sharing my disdain, and continues: "One guy said this is just too new to draw major conclusions, and that *we're* the ones irrationally catastrophizing about the Leak in the same way we're accusing them of catastrophizing about the wormhole. The biggest irony is that they're pointing to the AI's subjective fears about the aliens while ignoring its objective analysis of the Leak. Even worse: if you feed the AI all of the Anomaly-related data we have and ask it to factor in the new Leak data along with the alien message, it explicitly suggests that we should engage the wormhole. Even being trained on decades of scary alien stories like it has been, it's more scared of the Leak. People like Hart just aren't hearing that point."

It's a good point, too. I share poor Phil's take, that we shouldn't rely on the AI to make our decisions or give overly subjective advice. But the people who disagree have to at least be consistent. You can't point to its output when it supports your position then ignore new outputs that don't when better data is available.

The repeated acceleration of the Leak has changed everything. If we had more time, I'd be of the mind to point out some of these consistencies and work towards a consensus. But we *don't*.

It's not like we've been wasting time up here — the neocite and the launch and our reply message have all been in the works, along with our attempts to manage a seemingly unimaginable narrative — but I feel like it's high time for massive action. Hart has thrown a real wrench into our plans by engaging the signal-jamming technology before evacuating Colorado, and we have to do something about it.

"You said you've thought of a solution," I suddenly blurt out. "When you first mentioned the blockers, you said I'm not going to like the only solution you can think of. But there *is* a solution. Right? Some kind of workaround? Launch the neocite from here, maybe? I know Simone doesn't want us to move it, but if it's the only way..."

"I wish it was as simple as that," Shaun says.

My eyes widen. Because bearing in mind how careful we know we need to be with what's going to be a very unstable material, moving the neocite wouldn't be simple at all.

"There *is* no workaround, Ray. The problem is affecting our launch bays here, too, so it's not just the Vita. The only thing we can do to get our plan back on track is disarm the signal-jammers."

"So let's do it," I shrug. "Destroy the satellites. Whatever it takes! The normal rules don't apply."

"We can't," Shaun sighs. "Some of the satellites that are bombarding us are well out of reach, Ray. Some are at a higher orbit than we could reach without losing our workable sight-line to the target within the distance the aliens have laid out."

Desperately, I rack my brain. "So can we hit the bunker? Knock it offline to kill its link-up to the satellites? It *is* empty."

Shaun shakes his head ruefully. "Again, we just can't. The power supply and the Control Room are deep underground. We couldn't physically knock that bunker offline from here, even if we *could* be totally sure it was empty. We would need something like the nuclear bunker-busters Zola kept on the Beacon and tried to fire at Earth. None of these are viable."

"And the one that *is*?" I push.

"Someone has to go," Shaun says, making an effort to keep his tone neutral. "Ray, we need to disable this satellite link... and we need to do it from *inside* the bunker."

36

It's funny how things always seem to happen in bursts.

It's the way of the world, I suppose — within the majestic simplicity of the natural world, as well as the complexity of our own.

I've had a period of relative rest in the past several hours, albeit without anything close to calm. My doctor on the Vita would be glad that I haven't been doing anything strenuous, even if she might have a thing or two to say about the fact that I should probably be asleep.

This period has just felt like something of a *waiting* period for me personally, while most of the others have had something concrete to do. But now, I can tell that's about to change.

"Shaun, is this confirmed?," Sasha yells from down the hallway, hurrying towards us. "I got your text. Colorado?"

I see Driver following right behind, and then quickly moving in front as her speed carries her my way.

Shaun quickly relays the gist of what he's just told me, apparently adding detail to a message he's already sent Sasha. From her reaction, I'm pretty sure the new part is that we're going to have to fix this from *inside* the bunker.

"Has anything important happened on your end or anywhere else while I've been trying to get to the bottom of this?" he then asks her. "Anything that might change our thinking?"

"Simone is pretty much done," Sasha reports. "If we could launch at the target in a few hours, she says her neocite would definitely be ready."

Okay… without a fully functioning launch and targeting systems, that might be kind of like having a bullet without a gun. But still, this is good news. A million things could have gone wrong with Simone's synthesization work — some more explosively and decisively than others — but it sounds like she's played her part to perfection.

"Obviously we can't do that, with what you're telling me," Sasha continues, "but the bad news doesn't end there."

"Of course it doesn't," Shaun deadpans.

Sasha exhales sharply and continues: "Believe me, I know how you feel. We have some of the new telescopes very close to the Leak now, picking up better data at shorter intervals. And when I say *better* data, I mean more accurate and more detailed data. Higher quality data. In terms of what it means, it's not better. It's *worse*. When I got your message saying we can't launch because of the blockers, I was getting ready to come and show you this data telling us that we really do have to launch as soon as we possibly can."

I blow air from my lips.

Great. Talk about your all time most painful ironies.

Seriously — if it wasn't for *bad* timing, I don't know if we'd have any timing at all.

"I know the group doesn't want to put too much weight into the AI's interpretation of things," Sasha goes on. "But guys… after analyzing the various data sets from the Leak, independent of any input about the alien message, its reading of the way the radiation pulses have intensified and become more frequent is terrifying. It thinks we might only have a few days until it's too late. That's all: *days*. Whatever the hell this thing is, the dam is almost bursting. And when I asked for an idea of its confidence level, do you know what it said?"

From Sasha's tone, I don't know that I want to.

"It implored me not to take that estimate as a fact," she said, "because it said any further acceleration it sees in the next data I feed in will bring the timeline down even more. It's not telling me to stay calm and not read too much into its analysis. It's telling me not to take for granted that we'll even *have* a few days."

An oppressive silence suddenly falls. I'm absolutely positive that this is news to Driver, too, because she and Shaun both look as mortified as I feel.

"I can be there in two hours," Driver blurts out. "Shaun, I can take you to the Vita so you're ready to launch as soon as I stop the blockers. No more talk, no more time. If this is what we have to do, this is what we're going to do. The Bullet's targeting isn't dependent on any communication signals like the projectile launch systems are for the neocite. It has its own targeting system and it can course-correct and adapt as it goes. That should all be fine, right? I can launch to Earth in the Bullet, then fix this bullshit in Colorado so we can launch the neocite at the gateway?"

Shaun and Sasha exchange a very pensive glance.

I'm not at all familiar with the craft Driver is talking about leaving in. All I know is that its name — the Bullet — doesn't exactly conjure up images of a smooth and steady ride.

"You said it's definitely been evacuated," Driver goes on. "I can send autonomous stealth drones in first to make sure, and their visual feeds will come back to me *and* to you guys. I'm not walking in blind. And you'll have maps of the layout, details of the instrumentation… all of it. You can hunt all of that stuff out and everyone can get their heads together to plan my precise movements — but that can happen while I'm flying down. Our communications aren't blocked by these jammers. What we don't have time for is any more waiting. Not when the data is getting as bad as Sasha says it is. Not when we don't know how much time we have until it's too late. It's time for action."

"You'll have to convince Williams to let you take the Bullet," Shaun says, tellingly offering no resistance of his own.

"He will," Sasha offers, likewise making her position known.

I don't know if Driver would have cared if they weren't on board, such was the strength of her statement about it being time for action.

But when Driver turns to me, I see a different look in her eye. After all we've been through together, she definitely cares what I think.

"Tell me I'm not being crazy here, Ray," she begs.

I gulp. "You're being crazy."

"Seriously?" she pushes, furrowing her brow.

"*Seriously,*" I echo. "Driver… I spent a year in that bunker after we took Zola down. I know the layout like the back of my hand. So if you think I'm letting you walk in there alone, you're the craziest person I've ever met."

As a wide smile crosses her face, Driver wraps her arms around me and whispers in my ear: "Let's get this done."

37

Taking massive action.

That's what kept us alive through the challenges Zola threw at us, and it's our only chance of activating the alien gateway while there's still *any* time for them to help us deal with the Leak.

Taking massive action is also something that distorts time, and the hour after Driver and I accept what we have to do passes in a flash.

We tell Williams first. He has natural concerns about my physical condition, and he won't be alone in that, but I really do feel okay.

He also has serious concerns about the new mission more generally, but they're sensibly countered by his even greater concerns about the new Leak data. He understands what has to be done, he's satisfied by the observational analysis that tells us the bunker really is unoccupied, and he understands why it has to be a two-person job.

Driver and I work so well together, no one questions why *I'm* the choice to go with her. She's our best small-craft pilot — immeasurably so, according to everyone on the Balena — and I've overcome huge odds by her side. My knowledge of the bunker is a huge boon, too, though, even if the others don't seem to be thinking about it.

Before telling the rest of the crew, Williams makes what I see as a sensible decision to block all outgoing private communication. Word simply cannot get out that we're doing this, or the people who want our broader mission to fail will do whatever it takes to stop us.

I really feel like everyone here is now on the same page, after our long and cathartic cards-on-the-table open discussion in the canteen. But the real danger is that outgoing communications could be intercepted, and this danger is the same reason I'm not going to be able to tell Eva what I'm doing.

I wish I could, but I simply can't.

I made a promise that I'd call Eva before I return to the Vita. Due to a small change in Driver's plan, I'm not technically going to have to break it.

That's not the point, though, and I really wish we didn't have to hold these cards as close to our chests as we do.

The change in our plan is that Driver is no longer going to take Shaun and his small launch support team to the Vita. Even though it wouldn't take long, it would take some time that could be better spent on our journey to Colorado. Another of the Balena's pilots, one trained by Driver, is going to make the very short trip to the Vita in the plane that brought us here.

All the while, we'll be on our way to Earth in a craft I haven't seen yet.

I think its name — the Bullet — pretty much sums up the gist of what I need to know.

I've been told it's large enough to carry a small rover-like car to take us from our landing spot to the bunker's entrance, but Driver intends to land it close enough for us to walk. She says it's a level above anything I've ever seen, having been almost fully built in ZolaCore's New Zealand HQ before we requisitioned the compound and everything inside it.

I like the level of multi-tasking our team will be undertaking. We know the gist of what we need to do, and letting our allies here work out the details and pass them on during the journey makes all the sense in the world.

There's no point in worrying about worst-case scenarios like what we'd do if we lose communication. When the *real* worst-case is that the dam-like Leak could burst at any minute, there's just no time or space in my mind to worry about things like that.

None of that is to say we're being overly cavalier.

During our physical preparation, which involves suiting up and gathering all the small equipment we might need, our young friend Santino takes the lead in stress-testing the plan with all kinds of potential roadblocks. I definitely agree it's worthwhile to think about these things, just not to let them paralyze us.

Some of the equipment we're gathering is very familiar to me, like the trusty time explosives that have come in handy more times than whoever invented them could ever have foreseen.

Other things are much newer, though. I'm not familiar with the scouting drones, for one thing. They look remarkable — larger but far more advanced than the kind Driver used during our remote robot-piloting mission way back when.

There are other things that catch my eyes, too, but none come close to the Bullet itself.

Before I see a new craft, I always wonder how surprised I can really be. After all, I've been awestruck time and time again, so much so that you might think I'd seen it all.

Needless to say, you'd be wrong.

If I didn't know the Bullet's name, believe me: I would have guessed.

"There *have* to be retractable wings, right?" I ask, thinking out loud. It's the first thought in my mind, above and beyond how impossibly sleek the thing looks.

With her hands full of equipment, Driver nods. "Yeah. But don't worry about the journey, okay? It'll be the most force you've experienced, since the Mantis that took us to the Moon had the shielded sleep chamber, but it's not so bad. It's more insulated than it looks. All of the simulation flights I've done in this thing have been totally fine."

"Well, as long as the *simulations* were fine…" I reply through an uncomfortable chuckle. In truth, though, I'm not worried about the flight. If Driver says it's safe and endurable, I believe her. And the Mantis had never been tested when it carried us to the Moon — while we *slept*, as Driver said — so I think sometimes trusting the expert engineers is the thing to do.

The crew who help us load the Bullet and ready it for departure certainly don't seem concerned. In fact, the team is positively excited that it's finally going to see some action. Ships are safe in the harbor, as the old saying goes, but that's not what ships are made for.

By the time we're loaded up, Williams has explained to the whole crew that he's having to limit outgoing communication for at least six hours.

I return to the canteen with Driver, half-expecting to have to help him quell some dissent.

As it turns out, I'm pleasantly surprised. Because in our absence, he has also already told everyone what we're about to do. And now that they know what's going on, they're not just understanding of the communications block but positively vigorous in their outpouring of support.

People I've known for only a matter hours shake my hand — sometimes without realizing it's fake — as if we're old friends. They're all grateful of the undeniable risk Driver and I are about to take. Many go out of their way to profess total faith that the two of us can hit one more home run.

And you know what? Why *shouldn't* they?

I have faith in us, too. I have faith in this team, I have faith in Driver, and I have faith in the value of action.

This mission to Colorado is a crucial and unexpected waypoint in the bigger mission to activate the gateway, which is in itself a waypoint on our driving goal of stopping the Anomaly before it destroys humanity.

While Simone finishes her neocite synthesization and Shaun readies the aspects of the launch he can set up without the targeting technologies, we'll be getting things done in Colorado. We'll be moving the team further towards the ultimate goal, and we'll be building momentum while we do it.

Before much longer, we're ready to go.

We don't know the full plan yet, in terms of our precise movements on the ground. But we know what comes first, and it all starts with climbing into the Bullet.

Driver and I have a quick talk with the rest of our inner circle before we head to the dock. It doesn't take long and doesn't feel too heavy, because we'll be in touch with them the whole way.

The goodbyes are quick, for the most part. Driver and Chester share a moment that decisively kills any doubt that they don't share romantic feelings for each other. If they ever cared who knows, they clearly don't any more.

A few days ago I would have felt like Chester had to be pulling the wool over her eyes in some way, given the duplicitous circumstances that brought us together. But now that I know him better and understand why he did what he did, I'm glad for them both.

As it goes, my most emotional moment comes from an unexpected source.

Santino, who has helped a lot, holds my eyes for several seconds.

"You saved the world from Zola's destruction," he says, the Italian accent as strong as ever. "But Ray, you saved me from something worse. The Institute… the trip to Bayzen this craft wasn't ready for… a life I thought was the only kind there was. You saved me from all of it. For that, I will thank you every day I see your face."

I hug the poor kid, who really did go through more than any of us could ever get our heads around.

A guard of honor lines our path to the launch bay. The intention is pure and I appreciate everyone's sentiment, but the spectacle adds weight to what we're about to do. This feels like the kind of grand goodbye my close friends knew it was best to avoid, and my heart is thumping with every step.

"Thanks," I say to the crowd, waving warmly. And I mean it. I really do appreciate this, and I know Driver does, too.

I force myself to focus on the positives. All of these brilliant minds are on our side. If anything unexpected comes up when we're gone, they'll be able to chip in with ideas. And once we succeed in stopping the signal-jamming that's originating from Colorado, everyone here can play a part in helping us navigate whatever comes next.

I step into the Bullet with Driver, feeling better for these thoughts.

The craft is fairly cylindrical, befitting of its name. We both enter the cockpit. We're in an upright seated position, like a plane rather than a rocket, but it doesn't feel like any craft I've been in before. Built for speed and insulated only as much as necessary to keep us safe, rather than comfortable, it's easy to get the sense that I'm in for a serious ride.

"You're going to feel this," Driver says, confirming my suspicions. She straps in and signals for me to do the same, as soon as we have our helmets in place. "The suits aren't just for show. We're not going to ease out of this dock like we eased off the Vita to come here. This is a projectile launch bay. It's more like the Balena is going to fire us towards Colorado."

I look at her without speaking.

"What, do you want me to lie?" she laughs. These are the first words I hear through my helmet's internal speakers, rather than directly from mouth to ear.

I chuckle in return. "But the descent to Earth will be smooth, right?"

"Did you say you *did* want me to lie?" Driver deadpans.

These moments ironically break the tension, despite the fact that we're talking about how physically challenging this flight could be.

Hard things are hard things, and sometimes there's just no dressing that up. But I have a lifetime of experience telling me that sometimes the person by your side can make a big difference. When that person is Driver, who has helped me to do things harder than any I ever thought possible, I know the difference it makes can be colossal.

Driver runs through a lot of final checks with her flight team. I'm pleased with both the thoroughness and their speed, which aren't mutually exclusive.

When that's all done and she's fully satisfied, the outer hatch of the dock parts before us. Earth immediately fills the view, reminding me how close we are.

The auroras are in full effect, too, reminding me only too much of the Anomaly and how close our world could be to cosmic annihilation.

"On three," Driver says.

Three seconds later, she engages the launch.

Except just like she said, it doesn't feel like we're being launched.

Truly… we're being *fired* towards the Colorado bunker.

38

I won't lie. The first thirty seconds of our breakneck voyage to Colorado are up there with the most physically frightening I've ever experienced. And coming from the guy who hurtled to Earth in an Escape Pod with no landing gear, I think that says a lot.

While this isn't *quite* as scary as that, the physical feelings are just as intense. I'm facing Earth as we rocket towards it, too, so it's not like this is *much* less scary.

The main difference is that back then, I was almost certain I was going to die on arrival. There was no guarantee of a landing so much as an impact, and the Pod I was in was designed for orbital interception rather than atmospheric entry.

Here, at least, I'm in a state-of-the-art spacecraft that's been built to come in and out of orbit, both quickly and safely. More importantly, I'm not in this alone. Driver's hands are the safest pair that could possibly have control of the Bullet, and I'm damn glad they do.

Once my body adjusts to the initial acceleration, the ride actually begins to smooth out. Earth's unsettling auroras are more vibrant than ever. Everything is so vivid and looms so large, it really does remind me that we aren't very far away.

While everything has been going on aboard the Balena, and

even before I reached it, that incredible mega-craft has been moving towards a low orbit.

That's making today's journey a lot shorter and more viable than it could have been. Our orbit has been so low that we didn't have to wait long for a near-optimal window to target Colorado. Again, that's made easier when you're completing an orbit every few hours.

"The landing won't really be anywhere close to as intense as the launch," Driver says, fiddling with various controls on the console. She turns to me when she's done with that, looking reassuringly calm. "And even that wasn't *so* bad, was it?"

"We got away safely," I reply, exhaling slowly as the initial rush wears off. "Can't ask for more than that."

As we continue on, Driver tells me more about the Bullet's development and workings. She explains that it could travel the distance between the Balena and Colorado in a fraction of our flight time, if not for the need for us to start decelerating well ahead of the landing.

The landing will be manual, she says, due to our need to get as close as possible to the bunker. We'll apparently decelerate significantly before passing through Earth's atmosphere. We'll then level out again, with air resistance from the retractable wings allowing for a controlled final descent.

Our landing gear today is even better and more reliable than that on the Mantis, which amazed me with its dexterity and smoothness. All in all, the calmness in Driver's tone as she tells me all this has a soothing effect. Flight mechanics is her domain, and she is relaxed about what lies ahead.

In terms of what lies ahead beyond our landing, though, things aren't yet so certain.

The team on the Balena is back in contact as soon as Driver has shifted everything from launch mode to what she calls the cruising phase of our journey. Sasha and the others are busily at work to gain as much intelligence about the situation on the ground — and *below* the ground — as they possibly can.

Every little piece of information they can provide could help us. They're still doing the work, but their comments are very encouraging.

Within ten or twenty minutes of updates, I have a good handle on what they're hoping to deliver when the specifics are certain.

One important area they're going to update us on will be any changes to the internal layouts or security functionality that might have occurred in the bunker since I last set foot down there. Another relates to some nuts and bolts instructions for how to disable the equipment that's ordering ERF satellites to signal-jam our launch systems with a barrage of interference. Ideally, it'll be both.

The team is also developing plans for where and how to best utilize the equipment we've brought with us.

Driver and I know all about the timed explosives, having relied on them in more than one time of need. What we don't know yet is where they might be needed. Ideally, we'll be able to breeze through the bunker's moderate internal security without having to blow anything up.

Getting into the facility might require some more direct action, and we're ready if that's the case. But once we do get in, there's hope in the group that Sasha will be able to remotely take over the security system and disable features as necessary.

Ironically, to facilitate this we're planning to insert a hard drive on the local network, with that local access allowing us to hijack the system in a manner that's not *too* dissimilar to what happened on the Vita. The big difference is that our intentions are pure.

The Balena's cyber security team prepared the exploit we're going to be inserting, and Driver has vouched for them with absolute confidence. We don't think it's going to be possible to knock the bunker's power supply offline, due to the nature of its backup sources, but the guys are telling us that shouldn't be necessary. The exploit we're planning to inject is more advanced than the one that hit the Vita, they say, and I'm happy to take their word for it.

When they've run through all of that and promised to get back to us with the specifics by the time we land, Sasha brings up one more piece of technology that has almost slipped my mind.

For a while, one hugely useful breakthrough I haven't been making much use of is the augmented functionality in my contact lenses.

Today, it sounds like that could all change.

My doctor warned against using any of the adaptive technology in the aftermath of my injury and treatment on the Vita. Then again, I suppose she also wouldn't be too happy to hear that I'm currently hurtling towards Earth so soon after being discharged. I now feel physically okay in terms of my injuries, though , and the situation *demanded* action. I think enough time has passed that I'll be safe to use the full functionality of the lenses again, too.

There wasn't really any call or opportunity to use them during the chaotic events last week. But during my showdown with Zola three years ago, the technology in these lenses saved my life — and with it, everyone else's. Their ability to spot and highlight hazards, such as his laser-based tripwires, can't be overstated.

I've always been wearing my lenses. After all, my functional eyesight is dependent on them to an extent I only truly came to appreciate on the Beacon. But with our team on the Balena planning an optimal route through the bunker and getting ready to share specific instructions, the augmentation technology could now come in majorly useful.

Sasha believes that her ability to see what's happening through my lenses, and to then deliver unobtrusive instructions or pointers directly via them, could be a huge boon for our mission.

I just have to take a small transceiver with me into the bunker as an intermediary communications device. That should allow the lenses to send data to the Bullet even from deep underground. From there, it will near-instantaneously be relayed to the Balena and Sasha can deliver any necessary instructions or warnings just as quickly.

Driver and I will both have earpiece-based audio communication with Sasha, too, courtesy of the same powerful transceivers. There are some things that can be much more easily communicated visually, though, such as the location of buttons we have to press or even directions through a corridor with a multitude of doors. That's where the lenses can shine.

Our flight continues without any unforeseen challenges. In fact, some good news comes in from the Balena just as we're preparing to pass through the atmosphere.

"We have further and explicit confirmation of a full evacuation," Sasha relays. "We didn't think Hart was bluffing, and we already had intelligence about the flights out of Colorado, but we now have verification on all of that. We've directed more of our own weather and GPS satellites to focus on that area, too, and there are no signs of life. There's been no movement for hours. Thermal analysis also shows a huge decrease in power usage at the time of the evacuation. They've cleared out, no doubt about it."

Well, *that's* a relief.

Sasha is right to say we never really thought anything else was going on, but it's great to have it confirmed. If the team's analysis had hinted that the bunker was still occupied, I don't know what we'd be doing right now. Our two-person team isn't an invading force and it goes without saying that we wouldn't have been able to do this in the face of armed resistance.

"There is one thing to be aware of," Sasha goes on. "We don't yet know which systems have been kept live to facilitate the operation of the signal blockers. Some cooling and air flow has to be operational, but possibly only in the necessary areas. The scouting drones you send in ahead of yourselves will fill in a lot of these details. Just be aware that in a bunker that deep, a lack of air circulation and temperature control could make it very uncomfortable out of your suits."

"Good to know," Driver says.

We can't see Sasha, only hear her, but everything she's told us has been easy to understand. We'll have a video link on the ground if we need it. For now, Driver's visual focus has been on the Bullet's control panel while mine has been on the ever-nearing auroras around Earth.

And right now, we're about to pass into the atmosphere.

Driver returns her full focus to the controls and readings. Knowing a little about all of this, I do, too.

I see that we've already begun our deceleration. The atmospheric readings change while I'm looking at them, confirming that we're no longer traveling through space. We've arrived, if not quite yet to our final destination, and things are still going smoothly.

The auroras below are awesome in the truest sense of the word. If they weren't the product of the Anomaly that's suffocating our world in ways we don't fully understand, I'd have no hesitation in calling this sight beautiful.

But in the context we're facing, I just hope we won't be seeing it for much longer — or ever again.

"I'll check back in with you guys when we're down," Driver says. "Get all hands on deck to lay everything out for us as plainly as you can, okay? Step by step. And only come to us in the meantime if there's a development we have to act on before we land. I'm not worried about this landing, but I definitely need to concentrate on it."

"Loud and clear," Sasha replies. "Good luck."

The sudden silence is then eerie as Driver runs over every piece of data on the screens.

"All good?" I ask.

She nods quickly, still reading, before finally exhaling heavily and turning to face me. "We're good. I've never practiced a manual touchdown in this thing using the simulator, that's all," she reveals. "I had to override a few of the automatic features. Do you want me to run you through everything? Saying it out loud can help make sure there are no mistakes."

"Sure," I say.

It's always wise to run through a checklist to your co-pilot, which is why commercial pilots always announce their moves. I trust Driver's competence at least as much as I'd trust my own, but two heads are better than one.

There isn't a whole lot to run through, as it turns out. She's disabled the automatic landing sequence, which was a multistage process with a single implication. She's now fully responsible for touching down safely, but not for the descent. That's still automated, albeit with her human oversight. Her singular role will kick in when it comes time to navigate, at low speed, with the Bullet in its plane-like configuration.

That moment comes fairly quickly. Before I know it, even with our steady deceleration, the auroras are above us and it's time for the landing.

I see the dome before anything. It's hard to believe how little time has passed since I was in there with my family, stepping into a spaceplane for our voyage to the Vita. Elana Hart threatened to block my progress then unless I filled her in on why I was really going, but that's nothing compared to the roadblock she's thrown in our way now.

Motivated by an all-consuming fear of direct alien contact that seems to have gripped the entire world, she is standing in the way of an absolutely crucial mission. The only way we can get things on track is to disable the signal-jamming process her team set up before evacuating the bunker.

That evacuation itself speaks to just how intensely fear has spread. It came as a reaction to Phil O'Connor's death, for doing nothing but trying to calm people down and facilitate our plan to follow the aliens' instructions. I think the reason Hart did it so publicly was to put pressure on us, but the reason she did it *at all* was to protect her staff from potential reprisals.

We haven't paid a lot of attention to the reactions of the public, but we couldn't ignore what happened to Phil. People are terrified by the idea of potentially inviting aliens through the gateway they want us to unlock with Simone's neocite, and I can't pretend I don't understand why.

Even when the action we're taking is so necessary, it troubles me that we're having to do this part of the mission so secretly. It troubles me that I couldn't tell Eva that I'm coming down to Earth. And almost as much, it troubles me that we're having to pursue our bigger goal without any kind of public consensus. I don't like running roughshod over public opinion, which is basically what Hart accused us of when she said we were behaving like dictators.

I just wish we'd been able to help people understand how essential this desperate course of action is. Because especially after the latest Leak data has told us we probably have even less time than we thought, this couldn't *be* any more urgent.

If we'd been able to reach Hart, I'd like to think a few more minutes of face-time could have straightened things out. That didn't happen, though, which is why we're now only a few more minutes away from the bunker.

The descent is smooth, as I'd expect from a state-of-the art vessel like this. When the manual landing process begins, I have every faith that it'll go just as well.

In Driver's hands, it goes just as I hoped and expected.

I look around the area while she brings us down. My eyes scan for any signs of movement or occupation. Thankfully, and in keeping with our confident team on the Balena, there are none.

Our final landing is nothing short of remarkable. The Bullet, as aerodynamic as anything I've ever seen, comes to a total halt in the air. We're full-on *hovering* until the vertical touchdown commences.

I'm so stunned by the process that Driver's warning to expect "a few pretty serious bounces" barely registers. And even when I feel the bounces, less jarring than the strength of her warning might have implied, I'm too busy taking in everything else to notice.

"Nicely done," I say when we come to a total stop.

Driver exhales slowly and deeply, clearly relieved beyond words. When she unclips her helmet, I can see the beads of sweat on her forehead. She normally has a poker face that gives nothing away, so this landing has been more stressful for her than I realized.

"Thanks," she says, leaning forward. "The system did most of the work."

Now that our atmospheric readings and system controls are no longer needed, she brings up a video feed to the Balena.

Instantly, I know something isn't right. Because while Sasha isn't known for *her* poker face, I don't think I've ever seen her look as troubled as she does right now.

"What's wrong?" Driver blurts out, before I have the chance to ask the very same thing.

"It wasn't something you could act on," Sasha replies, her voice weak. "You told us not to interrupt your focus on the landing, so—"

"Don't sugarcoat it," Driver interrupts. "Please, just tell us."

Sasha sighs heavily. "This footage just came in, Ray. We're actively following it up."

Suddenly, my chest tightens. I already knew that whatever we're about to see is bad news, but I really don't like that Sasha is addressing it directly to me.

Assuming the worst will do no good, so I try not to. But a few seconds later, when the feed changes to relay the footage Sasha is talking about, that becomes impossible.

Evoking the footage of Phil O'Connor's mindless and brutal murder, video recorded through a shaky handheld camera fills the screen.

In the hands of an intruder, the camera is moving towards a house.

My house. With my family inside.

39

A gruff voice joins the stomach-churning footage.

"You think you can risk *our* lives to these aliens," the man grunts, stepping ever closer to my unknowing family. "All because *your* daughter has some problem? All because you think *you* can make every decision for every one of us? No, Barclay. Not anymore."

When the maniac knocks on the door, all I can do is watch.

I feel more helplessness than I ever have.

I feel more helplessness than I know how to handle.

It's hard to watch this knowing I'm too far away to do anything about it. What's even harder is watching this knowing that it's already happened.

I'm begging that Eva won't answer the door. We have a doorbell cam, and surely today, with all that's going on in the world, she's going to be more careful than ever.

Five seconds after knocking, the guy begins throwing his weight at the door in a bid to burst through. It holds up well, driving him to switch to a window. He picks up a rock from the garden and hurls it through, then knocks aside the broken glass with his jacket-covered forearm.

Our home alarm begins to sound, as it damn well should.

The intruder is predictably unmoved by that. Ignoring it

entirely, he lifts a leg to climb onto the windowsill and climb inside.

We don't have a dedicated panic room, and you better believe I'm regretting that right now. Depending on what part of the house Eva and the kids are in, the alarm could either encourage them to flee out the back door or it could bring them downstairs into this scumbag's sights.

But as the guy reaches the hole in the window, something reaches him.

Some*one*.

In the nick of time, fearlessly showing up when it counts, it's Laika.

Laika flies straight into the guy's face, just as he did to Zola when I needed his help on the Beacon. He's a big, powerful bird, and he cares about our family in a way most people wouldn't believe. There's nothing he won't do to keep them safe. The trouble is, there's only so much he *can* do.

On the Beacon, Laika did enough to knock Zola into the patrol zone where a security robot was able to do the rest. In a straight fight, a man beats a parrot — even one as special as Laika — ten times out of ten.

And as they struggle, with Laika doing his utmost and risking his own life for the family he loves, I hear the worst of all sounds:

A gunshot.

40

Seconds after the heart-stopping gunshot, the cowardly shooter falls backwards and down from the windowsill.

There is then no more movement. His phone falls face-down, but there's still some atmospheric sound to tell me it's recording. I don't hear the guy getting up, but I don't hear Laika, either.

"We've gotten through to Eva!" Sasha interrupts, talking over the blank footage. "Ray, President Williams is through to Eva right now! They're okay! They got out."

I close my eyes and feel the relief flood through me.

A few seconds later, Sasha manages to feed in their live call, which is going through the Balena's main communications network.

Our mission here has to stay under wraps, more so than ever now that we've just seen the lengths fear is driving people to. That means I still can't talk directly to Eva from here, and Williams can't tell her what I'm doing.

She doesn't ask for me, which tells me we're joining the call after the beginning when she surely would have wanted to be in direct contact, and when Williams must have given a plausible reason why I couldn't talk right now.

What Eva does say is that our neighbors hurried out to my

family's aid as soon as they heard the alarm. They found the intruder lying on the ground, bleeding from the head.

Apparently, he fell on a large rock where he'd used another to smash the window. It's refreshing for some irony to go our way for once, but this hardly feels like a moment for smiles. There's relief and nothing else.

The guy has been detained by the police. There's no update on his condition. A head knock leading to unconsciousness like that is no trifling matter, but I'm not going to lose any sleep worrying about him. For the sake of his life, he's just lucky I wasn't home when he tried this.

Laika is okay, Eva says, and the whole family — including him — are already sheltering at Lorien's house nearby. That's good to hear, because Lorien's husband Harvey is exactly who I'd choose to help keep them safe in my absence.

It seems like the guy discharged his weapon in reaction to Laika's attack, but only hit a brick on the wall.

Eva understandably sounds very shaken up by what's happened, and Williams does a very good job of assuring her everything is okay and that she's safe now. He promises that I'll call as soon as I can, which I still presume isn't the first time he's said it, which will be as soon as I finish an important task I'm working on with Driver.

That's more than I expected him to say, and a change in Eva's tone suggests she understands that we're not working on something without risk.

"Did he go back to the Vita?" she asks.

"No," Williams replies. He then goes on, to prevent her from asking any more specific questions which might require him to lie to keep the secret: "He'll be available soon, Eva. This is nothing you wouldn't understand as completely necessary, and nothing he wouldn't be doing unless we felt it was completely safe."

There's no way Eva could know about the signal-jamming Hart has initiated from here in Colorado, so she doesn't ask if our task has anything to do with that. Instead, she begs

Williams to put me in touch with her as soon as he possibly can, and asks him to tell me in the meantime that she and the kids are safe and well.

That's Eva all over, wanting to make sure I know they're okay even when she's the one who's just been through such a harrowing episode.

I'm prouder of Laika than ever for how he stepped up to the plate and protected our family when the chips were down. And more than ever, I'm utterly determined to get this job done.

That maniac potentially came within seconds of doing unimaginable things. My family's safety — and possibly their lives — owe a lot to Laika's intervention.

To protect them on a much grander scale, from the hellish cosmic radiation Leak that could otherwise consume our world in a matter of days, I'm now the one who has to make a crucial intervention. Once again, Laika has done his part. Now it's over to me.

With Driver at my side, I feel an even greater intensity of purpose than ever before.

When I glance across to her, she looks as angry as anyone I've ever seen. The borderline venomous rage on her face is there in plain sight.

The clarity reminds me that while she has removed her helmet, I'm still wearing mine. I take it off and unclip my safety harnesses.

"Is everything ready for us?" I ask Sasha.

The footage and Eva's call with Williams are both over, and there's now nothing on the screen.

"We're all set," Sasha says, returning to view and looking a lot less upset than she did a few minutes ago. "We didn't know what had happened until Eva called," she explains. "But we had everything pretty much ready before that all went down. We've sent your optimal pathways to the transceiver device that your lenses will communicate with. You can look over the lens controls here before you head out. I think it would be worth a few minutes to familiarize yourself with the pathways and the key information, too, just in case of any unforeseen communications problem."

"Absolutely," I reply, leaning in close to look at the detailed maps.

Everything looks exactly as I remember it from my time in the bunker, albeit with some rooms and almost every lab clearly having changed purpose. Our pathway is straightforward, once we get in, but we're still going to send the scouting drones in first.

Driver knows how to operate them, and the feeds will come back right away.

Sasha says she'll analyze the feeds but can also have them displayed in our vision, thanks to the lenses and their augmented functionality.

The two of us take more time looking at the various lens features and controls than anything else, to familiarize — or *re*-familiarize — ourselves with how it all works. Most of the controls are eye-gesture based, with patterns of blinking or movement affecting what we see.

Sasha says she has chosen not to enable the most advanced and most intrusive elements of the lens technology, such as the ability for us to see through each other's eyes in immersive first-person mode. That's just not going to be necessary for this situation, she explains, and leaving things like that active could cause more harm than good if we accidentally engaged them at an important moment.

We both agree with that.

"You will see heat signatures and any other hazards," she goes on. "Our intelligence tells us there's no one in there, and the scouting drones will be able to confirm that before you enter. It just doesn't hurt to stay on guard. And as for entering… it really seems like a forced entry through the main hatch is our best way forward. You have plenty of controlled explosives and only a few internal doors to pass through. We'll direct you where to place them. But if you lose contact, Shaun said to think back to the Vita when you placed them in the corners of the barricades. Not too close to the ground. You need to get through. The new controls we talked about should assist, and you shouldn't need to move many. Like *I* said, though, you don't need to ration the explosives. We're doing this because it's urgent, so don't take any longer than you need. Be decisive, get this done, and get back to us."

"Is Shaun gone?" I ask.

I figure he'd be there at Sasha's side if he wasn't, and the plan *was* for him to leave the Balena for the Vita soon after we left for Colorado. To avoid wasting any time, he has to be ready to launch Simone's neocite as soon as we get this done and re-enable the necessary targeting technology.

"He is," Sasha confirms. "He's already there. The neocite is almost ready, too. The reaction is complete and Simone says it's reacted well to the electromagnetism exposure. She wants to keep it in the insulated chamber until it's actually going to be used, because it's obviously very unstable. I mean, that's kind of the point. This isn't a normal material we're dealing with."

This isn't a normal *situation* we're dealing with either, but Driver and I know what we have to do to keep things rolling.

Sasha encourages us to get our earpieces in place and to fill small cross-shoulder supply bags with some timed explosives and other key items. We have a large stock and don't want to have to come back for anything — another potential waste of time — so I'd rather bring too many than not enough.

Driver deals with the scouting drones, engaging no fewer than eight as soon as we step outside. They have pre-programmed routes, as Sasha has explained, and are just waiting for us to enable physical access to the bunker's interior. That's where the explosives come in, and we set off with my bag bulging full of them.

"Ray," Driver calls as I take my first step towards the bunker's entrance, which is barely three hundred yards away.

I stop and turn to her. Before I even have to ask what's up, I see that she's holding out a gun.

"Just in case," she says. "I know you don't like these things any more than I do, but we're not baking cookies here. If the intel and the imagery are wrong, and if there are still people in there, we don't want our hands to be empty when we see them."

I hesitate, but ultimately I know that she's right on both counts: *I* don't like guns, but this is no time for moral grand-standing.

After what happened to Phil and what almost happened to my family, I know only too well what panic-riddled people are willing to do to stop us from taking necessary action.

And now, with my family's future still on the line along with everyone else's on this Anomaly-stricken planet we call home, I know what I have to do.

I say the three words which are among Driver's favorites as I take the weapon from her hands and place it in my shoulder bag:

"Whatever it takes."

41

As we set off on the short walk to the bunker's entrance, we have our helmets in place but not engaged.

We're bringing them due to Sasha's point about the potential air situation in certain areas of the bunker. It hasn't been very long since the evacuation, so even without filtration and active temperature control, I don't think it would be too bad in there.

What I'm more worried about, and what Sasha admitted was a concern she shares when I mentioned it, is that Elana Hart might have actively done something to make the air uncomfortable or even unbreathable.

We know there is still operational power and that cooling systems have to be running to enable the Control Room to function, but beyond that? Why *wouldn't* Hart do something to fortify the rest of the bunker? In her shoes, I know I would. If there's an important room I had to protect, I would make accessing it as challenging as I could. If I was able to control the air and temperature around it with the touch of a control interface, that's an opportunity I would sure as hell seize.

The bunker isn't some fiendish, Zola-designed deathtrap, though. I know for a fact there aren't going to be traps and tripwires and brain-exploding lasers like poor Carlo fell victim to on the Beacon. It's also not like Hart could flood the hallways with poison gas through the air supply system.

I'm mainly concerned that she might have used the temperature control system to make it intolerably hot or cold, which is something our suits — space-worthy, don't forget — can obviously handle with total ease.

In any case, I'm quickly surprised to see five of our eight scouting drones shoot upwards and quickly out of sight.

I turn to Driver, who engaged them. My understanding was that they would follow us to the entrance and then continue ahead, confirming that the coast is clear.

"Uh…. were they supposed to do that?" I ask.

"Oh, yeah, they're scouting the area," she replies. "I thought you knew that, no? Just to check for footprints or tracks or any signs of movement since the last close-up images we have. They have heat sensors and everything, too. This part will be fast. They'll probably be back before we blow our way in."

I nod in understanding and we continue onwards.

It's been a while since I've worn a real suit like this. The clumpy boots are the part you never expect to be most intrusive, but they always are. I suppose that could be because I'm used to wearing all kinds of helmets by now, though. Because the first time I put on my EVA suit in the Beacon, I know the helmet was the hardest thing to adjust to.

Like the boots, the helmets are heavier than you might imagine.

There's certainly no shortage of footprints around us as we continue to the entrance. Given that we landed between the bunker and the dome, where the planes took off carrying the evacuated ERF workers, that's no surprise. It's also nothing to be concerned about, so long as the drones don't report any recent changes in the tracks beyond the marks we're making now.

In no time, I'm standing once again at the entrance to the ERF's Colorado bunker.

It would be fair to say I have a storied and mixed history with this place. For most of my time in the *Virginia* bunker, all I wanted to do was get here to reunite with my family. I'm in the very spot where that reunion finally came, and where I first learned that Eva was pregnant with Scarlet.

For most of the next year, we called this place home. I went from dying to be here to dying to get out, and the lack of space and natural light was weighing on us all by the end.

None of us had any inclination to peek back inside when we stopped by last week for our flight to the Vita, but I'll still always appreciate this facility for having kept us all safe in such uncertain times.

"You want to do it?" Driver asks, tipping her head towards the heavily sealed entrance.

I reach into my shoulder-bag and pull out four of the dozen-plus powerful explosives. These are a newer kind than I've used before, but they only differ in two ways.

First, rather than there being several differently powered versions, we now have access to a single "multi-purpose" explosive with an adjustable power level, controlled by a switch on one side. I can't pretend to know how it works, but the team on the Balena, including Driver, assured me that it does.

The second difference is the addition of another switch at the other side of each device. It allows us to select from "radial" or "piercing" explosions. On the Vita, our explosives could only punch relatively small holes through the barricades. Of the two modes, that model was only capable of piercing.

With these Balena-made upgrades, on the other hand, it sounds like a radial explosion will be able take out much more of the barrier at once. Admittedly the outer hatch at the bunker's main entrance, designed to survive just about anything, is a different kettle of fish from an interior zonal barricade on the Vita.

Sasha and the others have shown no concern about our ability to blast through the hatch. They know its thickness and composition, and they know all about the explosives. They aren't the kind of people, Sasha in particular, who leave anything to chance. I have no fear about getting in.

But that said, if anything other than a piercing explosion on the highest setting can get us in, I'll be very surprised.

The radial explosion feature could come in handy later, though. I'm thinking of when it comes time to enter a room with a thinner security door and in which we don't want to cause any interior damage. After all, the last thing we want to do is collaterally destroy some aspect of the control system that stops us from being able to disable the signal-jamming technology that brought us here.

Besides these two changes, everything else about the explosives is the same. They're the same size and have the same timer functionality. All I have to do is engage them into active mode, attach them to the hatch, select my mode and payload, and tap the timer to set the blast in motion.

Oh, and one more thing: get the hell out of the way.

The gloves of my suit are very dexterous and well-fitting, even on my new right hand, so I don't take them off. It would take time we don't have for no gain. If there's any typing or precision controls needed later, I'll take them off then.

I attach four explosives in the spots we've planned. When they're in place, I ask Driver to activate the two nearer one side while I activate the others. We count down to coordinate precisely, so that the explosions all occur at once, then each use two hands to press firmly into the devices' centers.

On that front, the time we spent with Earl to get my new hand attached sure is paying off right now.

As we dash away, I begin mentally counting down from thirty.

"You set yours on radial, too, right?" Driver asks.

"What?!" I shriek. "They're all supposed on be on piercing! We talked about… *wait…*"

I cut myself off when I see the mischievous smile on her face.

"Just messing," she laughs, taking an opportunity to puncture the tension as only she can.

I laugh, then force a serious expression back onto my face. "Concentrate. We only have about forty more seconds until they blow."

"Forty?!" Driver replies, her eyes widening. "But you said we were only setting them to thirty! You literally said... *wait...*"

"Two can play at that," I grin.

As we're laughing together, what has to be the loudest explosion I've ever heard suddenly rips through the air.

I know it's technically four explosions, but still... I've never heard anything like it.

While I'm quite literally waiting for the dust to clear so I can assess the damage, I see three of our scouting drones shooting towards the hatch.

Seconds later, I see that we've made two huge holes — one at each side.

This was far from the biggest stumbling block in our path, but we still had to navigate it. Even if we're a long way from the finish line, I'm going to take some heart from knowing that the first hurdle is cleared.

No matter the odds, we're still in this fight.

And with Driver by my side and Sasha at our backs, we've always got a puncher's chance.

42

The fact that we've managed to blast two holes in the hatch is testament to the incredible power in these next-gen explosives.

The fact that the rest of the hatch outside of the direct impact zones is still standing, meanwhile, is testament to just how insulated this place was.

The clearing air reveals the damage, but only stepping forward reveals how thick the hatch truly is. I'm in awe of the explosives when I see what they've just taken out, and particularly in such a localized piercing manner.

"Expertly done," Sasha notes via my earpiece. This is an instant reminder of our time in New Zealand, when she first proved her invaluable worth by helping me and Driver to navigate *that* compound.

New Zealand turned out to be not quite as fully evacuated as we thought, and it goes without saying I'm hoping to avoid a repeat of that, even if the workers we found did end up giving us some huge assistance.

Today, we want to get in and get out, meeting no one and finding nothing unexpected in the meantime.

"If you just hold off for a few minutes until these drones do their work, then you can head inside," Sasha continues. "The others are seconds away from entering, too. They haven't reported any negative discoveries. So far, it's all clear."

Sure enough, the five drones that have explored the area outside the bunker are now rapidly joining their colleagues inside. Colleagues... do drones have colleagues? Either way, they zoom past like they're late for a team meeting and leave me and Driver to wait for our cue.

After a minute or so, Driver pipes up with a question: "Say, Sasha... what's the longest timed delay for these new explosives? Is it the same as the old ones?"

"Three minutes," Sasha replies without missing a beat. "Why?"

Driver glances at me before answering. "Well, I'm just trying to figure out some contingencies. If we can't disable these blockers cleanly in the Control Room, we have to try everything else."

"What do the timers have to do with that?" I ask.

She shrugs. "You know, escape time. Kind of like when you activated some in the undersea structure and had to high-tail it out of there. If we were to try to take out the whole Control Room, like to kill the system in the hope it would cancel the blockers, three minutes should be enough for us to clear out, don't you think?"

Sasha answers before I can: "It's very unlikely that would stop the signal-jamming," she replies. "Even if what you're saying was viable from a safety standpoint, it's not a smart move. The satellites that are causing our problems were given their instructions by the computers in there, but their operations aren't dependent on those computers. It would be like... I don't know... maybe if someone poisoned your friend and you bombed the factory where the poison came from. It doesn't stop the process that's already underway. You have to go to the factory and get some antidote. I'm no Shaun when it comes to metaphors, but do you know what I mean?"

"I was just thinking out loud," Driver replies.

"And hey, keep doing it," I implore her. "Seriously. All ideas can get us somewhere, even if they only get us away from what we're not going to do. And it's actually not crazy to think about a contingency explosion. There *could* still be some active link between here and the satellites that's keeping the blocking tech active. As a last resort we could at least try it. I heard you about the safety aspect, too. But the thing is, we didn't come here to be safe. We came here to do whatever we can to stop this. If plan A doesn't work, we go for B. Then C, D, E… the whole alphabet. So if *you* or the others think of any other backup plans, no matter what, don't keep them to yourself."

"Where are the others, anyway?" Driver asks. "Williams, Chester, Santino, Harriet…"

"They're watching," Sasha replies. "If they have anything to share, they can. I just need total concentration on all of the data, like you guys need total concentration on your surroundings, so less is more. I think we work well together as a three, like in New Zealand."

I totally agree, and I understand her line of thinking. I wouldn't have minded having Shaun to run his eyes over the live data, too, but I think the others' strengths lie in other areas.

"Speaking of data!" Sasha booms in an excited tone.

Instantly, I know it's good news.

"You guys are clear to enter," she goes on. "The air quality and temperature are fine for a while, but the forced circulation system *is* inactive. That's another data point confirming that it really is empty, and the drones have picked up no heat signatures or signs of movement. Stick with the sensible stealth approach we talked about, in the spirit of avoiding unnecessary extra risks. But I'm as sure as I could be that the coast is clear. Whenever you're ready, head inside and follow the pathway."

I turn to Driver. "Ready?"

"Who are you talking to, Barclay?" she shoots back with playful scorn. "I was born ready."

Without another word, she steps into the empty Colorado bunker.

I take a deep breath and follow right behind her.

43

I'm not a *super*stitious guy.

Usually, I'm not even a *little* stitious.

Okay... bad joke. Which maybe shows that I'm taking too much for granted here.

I just don't want to jinx this, and that's why I won't share out loud the thought that's on the tip of my tongue:

So far, this has all been a *lot* easier than I expected.

Sure, we had a solid plan vetted by a lot of smart people. But the best laid plans often hit all kinds of unforeseen speed bumps. Things could have gone wrong at three major stages already, but all have gone smoothly.

We arrived safely in the Bullet, we burst through the hatch without difficulty, and we found a truly empty bunker lying in wait. What more could I ask?

I'll admit that I almost forgot about the fourth stage, which involves inserting our access-granting hard drive into a physical network port in one of the bunker's public hallways. It doesn't slip Sasha's mind, though, and I insert it as soon as she reminds me.

All being well, this is going to grant the Balena's cyber security team control-level access to some of the bunker's core systems. They might even be able to control the power flow, although we fully expect the Control Room to be on its own isolated network circuit.

What this will grant access to are the bunker-wide security systems, to alert us to anything suspicious and also ensure that we won't be trapped or otherwise hindered by any surprise barricades or anything like that.

"The link-up is live," Sasha reports. "You guys keep doing what you're doing, heading straight for the Control Room. Our cyber team are all over this. I'll keep you posted."

We do as we're told. I know the way, but a helpful path is relayed in my lens-augmented vision thanks to data being fed in via the transceiver. It's almost like the navigation system in an expensive car, when the arrows and notices are projected onto the windshield so it looks like they're on the road.

There's even a nice little distance and estimated step counter, telling us how far we have to go until we'll reach the point Sasha has entered as our destination.

The bunker becomes eerily dark when we reach the main access stairway and descend toward the Control Room. Our lenses are excellent at adapting to low-level lighting conditions, but they don't try to make it feel like you're in a fully illuminated room.

I do see emergency lights overhead and on the base of each step, almost like you'd find in a cinema. This tells me that the bulk of the bunker is running on emergency power only.

Before long, we're on the right level.

Sasha's voice returns to our ears just as we get there, reporting that the security team has found nothing to worry about. They're not making any interventions, either, since everything is running according to plan and they don't want to alert anyone to our presence by making *their* presence inside the system known.

Driver asks the very valid question of whether blowing a hole in the main entrance isn't likely to have alerted Hart and anyone else who's paying attention that someone is here, and the initial reply is silence.

"That intervention could be a different *kind* of visible," Sasha eventually says. "And there was no avoiding that. We *don't* have to make any remote changes — at least not yet — so it's not worth it. I know you guys are okay with risk, but it has to make sense. When risks are avoidable or have no real reward, I can't authorize them."

"What about the Control Room door?" I ask. "If it's controllable via the security system, doesn't it make more sense to have our team unlock it than for us to blow through it? Because even with the explosives set to a relatively low-power radial blast, there could still be interior damage. This door is nowhere near as thick as the hatch. I mean, it's not even close. This is just a security door like all the ones I've blown through on the Beacon and the Vita."

Sasha pauses for a second. "Hmm. *That*, I agree with. We do suspect that all security related to the Control Room will be separate from the main bunker areas, though. Major says it was like that in the Virginia bunker, and they *were* all fitted out at the same time. It's worth checking, though."

It doesn't take long for us to reach the door. It's still dark, with eerie silence our only companion.

"No dice," Sasha sighs. "Our guys can't do anything with that door. They could turn the lights on in the corridor, but I don't think you need them. Doing something like that might not be a big risk, but it's definitely not a necessary one."

Driver nods at me, in lieu of a verbal reply.

"Agree," I say. "Okay, so we'll just start with a low level radial explosion and take it from there, right? That's still the consensus?"

"Affirmative," Sasha replies. "Good luck."

I take another explosive from my shoulder-bag and hold it out towards Driver. "You know these better than I do. I know it's only two switches, but I'd want you to check how I do it and we have to clear out as soon as they're live. I think it's better if you do it."

"Fine by me," she says, taking it from my hand. "Here?" she asks, crouching down and positioning it.

"Perfect," I say.

Driver then attaches it in place by peeling off the thin transparent layer of plastic that protects the adhesive. She flicks one switch to radial, another to the second lowest of four power settings, and then engages the explosive.

We both scamper away and take cover, even though this blast shouldn't be as violent as the ear-piercing quadruple explosion we set up outside.

"We're almost there," Driver says, holding my eyes. I know she's not just talking about this explosion, either. She's talking about the mission as a whole — not only here, but all the way to the mysterious alien gate we want to bombard with neocite in a huge but necessary risk aimed at saving our world from suffocation as the Anomaly's grip tightens.

And she's right. We really are almost there.

Simone has worked miracles to develop the neocite, we're here to take care of this, and that's all come long after Laika, Santino, Harriet and poor Phil O'Connor played their parts in turning an incomprehensible alien radio signal into a series of coherent image-based instructions for taking the only shot we have at planetary survival.

After all of that and all the smaller steps along the way, we're almost there.

Seconds later, the controlled explosion detonates. The sound is new, nothing like the piercing explosions I've grown disturbingly used to, and when my eyes reopen after the blast I instantly see that the effect is different, too. Our choice of power level has proven perfect for the job, while the radial nature of this explosion has pretty much destroyed the whole relatively thin door.

The new features of these next-gen explosives is paying off already.

We step into the Control Room right away and find it fully

lit, with the computer screens around us all operational. There are three empty chairs.

"Get as close as you can and look straight at the screens if you could," Sasha requests. "Ray, especially you. I'm watching the visual feed from your lenses. All of our experts are watching, too. We're looking for anything related to the signal blockers. It shouldn't be too hard to find something in the menus."

"Isn't this it over here?" Driver asks, diverting my attention — and with it everyone else's, apparently — to one of the computer screens on the right side of the room.

And sure enough, she's spotted something important. Something crucial. The exact thing we're looking for.

"I mean, it makes sense for one of the screens to still be on this when it's the last thing they set up," she continues.

"Driver, that's what we needed!" Sasha beams. And she is beaming — I can literally *hear* her smile. "Ray, get in close to that. Wow. It's even logged in. I don't think we're going to need to force any overrides or anything, you can just... do it. You can just disable it."

I run my eyes over every visible piece of information on the wide monitor. It really is the control interface for the satellite-controlled "emergency block" signal-jamming technology that's stopping us from being able to fire our neocite at the alien target with the level of precision targeting we need.

One field lists the time limit for the process as infinite. My eyes linger.

"You *could* change that," Sasha says. "But stopping this immediately is even better. That way we'll know if it's worked. And once it's done, we'll make sure it can't reactivate. Step two comes after step one, though, and step one is putting a stop to this. Touch the screen and swipe down to the lower options. The screen should scroll. That's what our information from the system manuals tells us. Just be careful not to touch any options. Swipe in an empty area of the screen."

I remove my left glove and take great care to do exactly what Sasha said.

I'm all but positive the fingers of my *new* right hand would work on a touch screen, and I've been finding them effortlessly easy to control. Introducing the bionic attachment would be taking exactly the kind of unnecessary and avoidable risk we've been talking about, though, so I stick to skin and let my left index finger do the swiping.

After only a few careful swipes, I've scrolled far enough for a very tempting option to come into view:

STOP EMERGENCY BLOCK?

"Press it," Sasha says.

I don't know why, but I hesitate.

"We could overthink this in a million ways, Ray," Driver chimes in, "but this is what we came for. It's all you. One tap."

Taking a deep breath, I close my eyes and press the button.

As I reopen them, I see the screen change. The Stop button is now grayed out, with Begin being the one I can press. That's flipped from how it was a few seconds ago, and it strongly suggests that I've actually done it.

I scroll back up, quickly but still carefully, to confirm that the rest of the data has changed, too. It's no longer showing any actively engaged satellites.

"Did... did we do it?" I ask.

Driver smiles widely and slaps me on the back. "I mean... we still have to do the whole alien part, but we sure as hell did *this*!"

"Confirmed!" Sasha yells joyously. "Guys, Shaun's team on the Vita say the interference has already stopped! They can start prepping for the neocite launch. We'll just want to lock down these systems before you leave."

Just as Sasha finished talking, a flashing red light suddenly catches my eye. It's coming from the screens to our left.

"Oh shit..." Driver curses, taking the message in before I read it.

And when I do, I know exactly where she's coming from.

Oh shit, oh shit, and *double* oh shit.

The message is nothing less than a dagger to my heart:

UNAUTHORIZED INTERRUPTION DETECTED.
INTRUSION-PROOF BACKUP INITIATED.
SURFACE TO AIR WEAPONS ENGAGED.
TARGETS: ERF BALENA, ERF VITA.
TIME TO LAUNCH: 4 MINUTES 53 SECONDS.

44

"Defense Center!" Sasha booms in my earpiece. "Another level down. I'll send a pathway to your lenses. Go!"

For a split-second, I'm stunned.

Intrusion-proof backup...

Weapons engaged...

I can hardly believe my own eyes. We came here to stop the signal blockers, and in doing so we might have just put the final nail in the coffin of the Balena's entire crew, our smaller team on the Vita, and humanity's one chance at surviving the Anomaly.

I feel Driver slap my arm — hard — to knock some life into me as she heads for the door.

We rush to the stairs. I've never been inside the Defense Center, but I do know where it is. As the name suggests, it's the room where the bunker's defensive missiles are controlled.

Only a pretty optimistic mind would think we'll be able to reverse what's explicitly been described as an intrusion-proof backup, but we have to give it a shot. If we can destroy the whole place, even if we have to go down with it, we might at least still have some faint chance of averting disaster.

As good as her word, the hyper-competent Sasha has a pathway lining the floor by the time we reach the stairs. This helps Driver more than me, and she rushes ahead as quickly as she can. I feel weary from injuries I didn't know I had, running for the first time since the explosion on the Vita claimed my hand and almost my life.

I arrive only seconds behind Driver thanks to the mercifully short distance we've had to cover.

Stealth and care are absolutely out the window now. We need to get through this door, which Sasha relays is beyond the cyber security team's remote control just like the Control Room's was.

I grab an explosive from my bag and hand it to Driver.

"Two out of four, radial mode?" she asks.

"*Four* out of four radial," I reply. "We get one shot if we're lucky, Driver. No holding back."

She nods and sets the explosive in place with those parameters. If there was a shorter available time delay than thirty seconds, we'd be using it.

As it is, this comfortably — or should I say *uncomfortably* — feels like the longest half-minute of my life.

We don't back up very far, reluctant to leave ourselves any more ground than necessary to cover. Driver encourages me to get a few more explosives ready while we're waiting, in case there's nothing else we can do inside the Defense Center other than detonate them all in a Hail Mary attempt to shut down the whole weapon systems.

Literally as soon as the explosion hits, I dash towards the door. I don't even wait for the dust to clear. That's time we don't have.

I see by the time I reach the threshold that the explosive has done its job, but there is a sizable cloud of debris.

I waft it away and stare into the room.

My lenses flash red, warning that a heat signature has been detected.

But believe me: I don't need technology to tell me that.

Even my naked eyes would be able to make this out, as bad as they are.

It's unmistakable.

She's unmistakable.

Sitting bolt upright in a chair at the Defense Center's control console, and sporting an expression that I'd best describe as a mix of shock and disappointment, I see the Senior Coordinator of the bunker I'm standing in:

Elana Hart.

"Oh, *Ray*," she sighs in lamentation. "It didn't have to come to this, but I'm afraid it has. There's nothing you can do to stop this now. It's over."

The words cut me like a knife. I take my helmet all the way off for a clearer view, and so she has to look at me and see the urgency and pain in my eyes.

"I'm genuinely sorry for what you've made me do," she goes on, shaking her head in what looks like genuine regret. "But truly... it's over."

45

"Your explosives are no good beyond this point," Hart says, looking down at the device I'm gripping.

"Well how about this?" Driver grunts, pushing her way past me and pointing her weapon at Hart's forehead. Her helmet is now on the floor, too. "And don't think I fucking won't!"

Looking remarkably calm for someone in her position, Hart rises to her feet. She then glances at the menu screen and quickly taps some options. I see the word 'communication' and hear a short but sharp buzzing sound in my ear as the audio link to Sasha goes dead. At the same moment, all of the over-laid data in my vision disappears.

Hart has done something to kill communications in the vicinity, not entirely unlike what her signal-jamming satellites were doing to the Balena and Vita before our actions in the Control Room unwittingly took them out of the frying pan and into the fire.

I check if the sensors controlling my bionic right hand are still working, reminded of what Earl told me about certain kinds of high-level interference when he fitted it. I still have full movement, which suggest they are.

"Listen to me," Hart says. "The only way to halt the missile launch is with my triple biometric credentials and a sixteen-digit passcode you could never possibly guess. This isn't Ray's misadventure on the Beacon. My dead finger or retina won't let you in. You need my fingerprint, retina scan and voice scan all at once — and my voice has to be reading out the passcode. When I say it's over, it's over. Destroying this place would do nothing. This isn't like the signal blocking. These emergency orders have been set and only I can put a stop to them."

Driver takes a step forward and all but presses the gun against Hart's skin.

Still, Hart is unmoved. "If I was doing this for myself, I would care whether I live or die," she says. "But I'm *not*, Driver. I'm doing this for all the people your foolish obsession with this alien 'gateway' could damn to destruction and subjugation. Do you have any idea what kind of horrors you could be inviting into our world? Any idea in the slightest?"

I stare at her with the same horrible feeling of helplessness I had watching the footage of the home intruder at my family home. Hart is right: there's nothing we can do.

She's as entrenched in her position as we are in ours. She's as sure *she's* doing the right thing as we are.

We would gain nothing from detaining her and even less from killing her. There are no tricks we can pull, and no logic she'll listen to. Back in the Bullet before I watched that harrowing camera footage, I found myself wishing I could have had five minutes with Hart to try to talk some sense into her.

But now? Now that I know she's willing to destroy the Balena and the Vita to stop our mission? I've realized there's a chasm between us.

"Do *you* have any idea how soon the Leak is likely to destroy the world if we do nothing?" I retort, feeling a natural need to try despite my gut-level doubts that there's any point. "Elana, I wouldn't be doing this if I didn't know it's the only way to protect my family and everyone else's. I know you're going to say you disagree and that you're only doing this because you think *you're* protecting everyone, but the data doesn't lie! Fear lies. The AI doesn't know how to lie, but it gives bullshit answers to bullshit questions and it's been trained on fear of aliens since the day it was created. You're better than this. You're *smarter* than this. Shaun, Sasha, Santino from the Institute… you know these people, or at least know about them. They're all on board because they've seen what I've seen. They know this is our only chance."

Letting out a deep, lingering sigh, Hart shakes her head.

"This is bigger than my life," she says.

And at that, Driver loses patience.

With a gun in her hand and unprecedented frustration in her mind, Driver loses *all* patience.

But she doesn't pull the trigger.

No.

What she does is even more surprising and more unsettling than that.

"You don't care about your own life," Driver roars. "But what about his?"

And as she says it, she turns the gun on me.

46

"As if you would shoot him," Hart says.

In response, Driver momentarily lowers her weapon and fires at the floor.

The sound, at such proximity, hits my ears even harder than the massive hatch explosions did a few minutes ago.

"You're going to kill us all, anyway!" Driver yells at Hart, putting my forehead back in her sights. "What, you just don't want to watch?"

I don't begrudge Driver for what she's doing here. Trying *anything* is worthwhile when we're so utterly short of options. I know she's not going to shoot me, but that's the problem, because Hart knows it, too.

Hart holds Driver's eyes, unflinching even now.

Realizing this long shot attempt to force some progress is going nowhere, Driver thrusts the gun into Hart's hands. "Fine," she tells her. "If you're going to kill us, at least look us in the eye when you do it."

"Look, neither of *you* have to get hurt," Hart goes on. "I'm sorry about your colleagues. Really, I am. But we can all walk out of here. Work can begin on shielding Earth against the Leak. Analysis of the new 'target' you've discovered can continue. All of that can happen, but not if we recklessly invite a powerful alien race into our backyard with no idea of what they want from us. For all we know, they caused the Anomaly as a way of trying to persuade us to open our end of the wormhole. Have you thought of that? We could need as little as a few months away from developing initial shielding tech—"

"We have *days*!" I interrupt. "Elena, listen to me. We *can* all walk out of here, but you have to stop these weapons. I'm begging you, for everyone's sake. Do the right thing."

I look at the monitor to my left. It shows that the clock has dropped below two minutes. We really are approaching the point of no return.

"I don't want you to get hurt, Ray," Hart says, placing the gun on her chair. "That's why I'm doing this."

I give up.

There is simply no convincing her. The old adage is holding truer than ever: you can't reason someone out of a position they didn't reason themselves into.

But while I can't *convince* Hart to accept my line of thinking, I have one last idea to *persuade* her into the right course of action. It really is a no-going-back kind of move, but I really am out of ways forward.

With the explosive device still in my hand, I turn to Driver. "If I give you one simple instruction, do you promise you'll follow it? Please… say yes."

She narrows her eyes in what looks more like fear than confusion. "Okay. What do you want me to do?"

I un-peel the explosive's protective layer and flick it to maximum power. Then, in a fluid motion that leaves no time for thinking myself out of it, I stick the device to my chest and push three times to engage a ninety-second timer that cannot be paused or canceled.

Last of all, I plant my feet and extend my arms to make it clear to Hart that she's going nowhere and neither am I.

"Driver…" I say, forcing out the word without turning back to face her. "*Run.*"

47

"Run!" I boom again to Driver.

There's no way out of this for me, unless my final act of desperation forces Hart to back down, but Driver doesn't have to die here. More to the point, the world needs her alive.

"You need to tell the world what happened here," I go on. "You need to tell the world *everything*. Someone else might be able to make neocite. They might be able to launch it from here. But not unless you get to safety! Go!"

I hear a sob after a half-second of silence. "They'll know you were the hero," Driver sniffs in reply, just before she rushes out. "And I want you to know you're the best friend I ever had. When no one else believed in me, you did. Thank you, Ray. For everything."

Now alone and face to face with Elana Hart, I bear into her soul.

"You know I can't stop this timer," I say, trying to maintain a facade of composure when composure is the last thing I feel. "But if you stop yours, I can take off this suit and we can both run out of here."

She looks at me like a deer in headlights.

"Elana, one last time... listen to me," I plead. "I'm willing to risk everything on the faintest hope you'll see some sense.

Can't you see? The world is going to be destroyed if we do nothing *right now*. Some vague plan to shield against the radiation in a few months is worthless. We have to act now. And these aliens… they told us where to find the Leak. We'd already found it, but their four-year-old signal didn't know that. They *helped* us. I'm willing to die in here if that's what it takes to convince you. I'll leave Scarlet without a dad if that's what it takes to leave her a world to grow up in. But if you don't stop this, she's going to be dead before 'a few months' get here, along with everyone else."

"Take it off!" Hart begs. "Ray, take off the suit! I'll do it, okay? Just throw that thing outside before it blows."

I glance at the timer. As I look, it passes under a minute.

"No," I say, fighting every survival instinct within me for the sake of the greater good.

"No?!" she echoes. "Have you gone insane?"

"You first," I tell her, stepping forward to close the distance with my arms still outstretched.

Panicked, Hart begins to gasp for breaths so fast that it's close to bona fide hyperventilation. "I need… space," she pants. "Ray… I need to be calm… or it won't… accept… my voice scan. It… doesn't… work… under duress."

If this is a bluff, it's history's greatest ever.

I take several steps back and implore Hart to get on with it.

True to her word, she presses her finger against the screen and brings up a cancelation menu.

Seeing how little time is left, and realizing it's going to take me more time to get out of this damn space suit than crossed my mind until now, I start taking it off.

In front of me, Hart begins to read her passcode:

"Two. One. Zero. Five. Two. Ze—"

The system interrupts with an unwelcome spoken sentence of its own:

"Please begin again in a neutral tone and calm demeanor."

Oh, God… I think to myself.

She's not going to be able to do this.

48

Hart glances over at me, visibly concerned and regretful beyond description, then appears to take a modicum of comfort from the fact that I'm mostly out of my suit.

Without speaking, since I don't want to mess up the voice recognition, I blow an exaggerated breath to encourage her to do whatever it takes to present an air of calm for the sixteen words she needs to say.

We have less than twenty seconds left. It really is our last shot.

She goes again:

"Two. One. Zero. Five. Two."

My heart skips a beat here, knowing it's the stage where the system interrupted last time. If it does it again, we're out of time. We'll die in the explosion, and everyone on the Balena and the Vita will die similarly horrific deaths at the hands of this bunker's defensive systems. Nothing they have is a match for these missiles, and the low orbit that was a benefit in allowing us to descend so quickly will become a certain death sentence.

But this time, there is no interruption.

"Zero. One. Six. Two. Eight. Two. Eight. Zero. Two. Three. Two."

Sixteen.

That was sixteen!

"Yes," she says, still speaking to the computer. "Confirm."

At that, with a single second left on our clock and possibly humanity's, the countdown stops.

Hart looks my way, and we share the briefest of glances before reality sets in: mercifully, the Balena and the Vita are out of the woods... but *we* sure as hell aren't.

The powerful explosive on my spacesuit is going to blow in a matter of seconds, and nothing in here has any chance of surviving the blast.

I grab Hart for her own good, since she once again has that deer-in-headlights look to her, and bundle her out of the door. I implore her to run, which she does. I take three or four long strides of my own before the detonation hits, at which point I'm thrust forward by the power of the blast as the energy forces its way out of the doorway.

Everything aches when I fall to the ground, but it's a far cry from the direct hit I took on the Vita. I'm conscious, for one thing, and I'm able to push myself up to my feet.

Hart is only a little way ahead and has hit the floor, too, but she's likewise able to stand up — even if a lot more sheepishly than I am.

"We made it," I yell, unsure how far away Driver will be. I'm proud of her for showing the maturity to follow my request to run away from the explosive situation I put us in when no other cards were left in my hand, because I know that must have been hard for her. She lives and breathes by the motto of 'no man left behind', more so than anyone I've ever met. But this time, she saw the bigger picture that every *other* man, woman and child depended on her going against her instincts.

I continue wordlessly along the corridor, heading for the Bullet in the hope that its communication systems will still be online and that Hart's block will only be operational in here.

For her part, she's saying nothing. I'm beyond furious at

her for what she's done, but at the last second — very literally — she came through and did the right thing. She won't be getting any awards for that and I won't speak in her defense if she faces serious professional or even criminal sanctions, but her fate isn't mine to decide. I'll deliver her to the ERF personnel on the Balena, chiefly President Williams, and their protocol will be whatever it will be.

What counts far more than anything related to Hart is what our neocite and launch teams do next. I know there's zero chance Driver will leave the compound until she knows there's no chance I could be on my way out, and I know we'll comfortably be back in space within a few hours. Everything is back on track after one hell of a scare, and I have a new feeling of positivity to come along with it:

If we can get through *this,* we can get through anything.

"You made it?" I hear, from distantly along the corridor and possibly up at least one flight of stairs. Driver's voice is loud, but my ears have taken a pounding today.

I don't speed up — because as much as I think Hart feels genuine contrition, I still want to keep her in my sights.

Driver is in sight within ten or fifteen seconds, sprinting my way and going straight past Hart like she's not even there.

"You utter maniac," she says, wrapping her arms around me.

"Hey..." I say, pulling away and forcing a grin. "Whatever it takes."

She smiles, too, *then* turns to Hart with a scowl before looking back to me. "She's coming with us. I keep my friends close and my enemies closer."

"Do we have an extra suit?" I ask. "Or, two I guess, since mine is in pieces."

"We have plenty of suits and plenty of space," Driver confirms. "Williams can deal with her when we get back. We have bigger things to focus on."

I nod in total agreement.

Because by hook or by crook, we are *still* in this fight.

49

While I was reluctant to let Elana Hart out of my sight, Driver is even more hands-on. *Literally*.

She marches Hart along the corridor, hands behind her back, and demands answers to several questions. None of them relate to motive or anything else that we can leave in the past. Instead, Driver is asking good and pertinent questions about the bunker and what systems we're leaving operational.

If Laika was with us, we'd have total certainty that everything Hart tells us is true. The little guy's lie detection ability is just one thing I miss, and things really are harder without him.

Hart is evidently shaken up, though, and I don't think she'd have it in her to lie about anything right now.

Once we're both content that everything potentially dangerous down here is totally locked down, I add one spilled-milk question that I just have to have an answer to.

"Why were you still here?" I ask. "If the weapons system was set to automatically engage as a back up for the blockers being interrupted, why did you have to be here?"

"In case there was a remote interruption that didn't register the same way," Hart replies. The bunker's blast-shattered hatch is now within our sight. "I didn't think for a second anyone would actually come in here, let alone *you*. But with the team you have and how well they know the workings of ERF security systems, I was expecting some kind of cyber attack."

I'm not going to tell her that we needed physical access to enable remote *control* access, just like the fiends who attacked the Vita. Elana Hart is no friend of our mission, even if she is accepting its inevitability, and it makes no sense to say more than we have to.

But the fact she stayed behind, willing to go down with her ship, again speaks to the fact that there were no nefarious motives.

This really was nothing like the Vita incident, when the people responsible were orchestrating things from a safe distance and left their underlings directly in harm's way.

If anything, this was the total opposite. Hart loaded up the lifeboats and evacuated every single one of her staff to safety, all the while staying behind in a bid to make sure nothing would interrupt her plan.

It's almost like back in Virginia, I figure, when Major stood in my way because he thought he was doing what was right in his duty to protect the thousands of people in his charge. I knew he was wrong, but he was equally sure he was right... just like Hart was.

Hart marvels at the damage we've done as we pass through the holes in the hatch. Those explosives really are something, with the new iteration even better than the old kind.

Outside, she marvels all over again as the Bullet comes into view. Like quite a lot of things on the Balena, its development has been unknown to other ERF leaders.

"I've never flown into orbit," she says, bringing her feet to a halt.

Driver, less patient than I am, pushes her forward and keeps walking.

"It's not so bad," I comment. "It doesn't take long, either."

Suddenly, Driver is the one who stops. "Wait. Ray, do you want to go straight home? We've done what we had to do here.

Shaun and Simone are going to be on top of the targeting and the launch. Do you really *need* to come back?"

I'd be lying if I said this hadn't already crossed my mind. I appreciate that Driver has raised it, too, but there's a reason I didn't bring it up.

"I don't think my presence is best for them right now," I say. "With the fear-driven feelings against this mission as strong as they are, I don't think the kind of fanfare we would generate by touching this thing down in Salt Lake City would be good for anyone. Besides, this job isn't done. They might need us up there."

"Well, the offer stands for the next two minutes," Driver replies. "Once we set a course to pass out of the atmosphere, it's too late."

I nod in understanding, and my mind is made up. "Space. Are we heading for the Balena or the Vita?" I ask.

"It would take a little longer to dock at the Vita," she says. "The Balena has an arm to intercept us. At the Vita, we'd have to manually work our way towards the dock. The final entry to the bay would be automated and should be totally safe, just a lot slower. Like... twenty minutes instead of one. With how close they are together, I think we could actually get to the Vita faster by docking with the Balena and taking a regular craft from there."

Given the way Driver said docking at the Vita *should* be totally safe is enough to swing me towards the Balena-first option. We're both clearly on the same page about wanting to be on the Vita, where the neocite launch is going to occur, and we're also aligned on the smartest way to get there.

"Balena it is," I say, drawing a thumbs-up of confirmation.

We step into the Bullet and suit up. I try to reassure Hart again that this won't be too uncomfortable, even after what she's done to cause so many problems for us. That's done, and it doesn't help us to be cruel. I wouldn't say Driver is being cruel in her indifference, she just has tunnel vision to get us back into space as soon as possible.

Our earpieces still aren't working, seemingly fried rather than merely temporarily blocked by the interference Hart initiated in the bunker. Thankfully, the Bullet's communication system is still fully online and we're back with Sasha and the team as soon as Driver boots everything up.

They're naturally relieved that we stopped the blockers, and it's immediately clear that they have no idea just how close they came to destruction or what we had to do to stop it. Sasha saw the five-minute countdown begin in the Control Room, but Hart had killed our link by the time things really heated up.

President Williams is with Sasha now, and he has a hundred questions about Hart and the status of the bunker. He is furious with her and wants all of the same answers we did, but Driver cuts him off. She succinctly and fairly curtly insists everything is under control on that side of things, urging the team to focus fully on what still has to be done.

Sasha, resuming control of the radio, tells us that everything is well underway.

Given the care Simone insists is necessary in handling the highly unstable neocite, they're not going to be ready to launch it until after our short journey is complete. It'll be close, apparently, and we're definitely only a matter of hours from go-time, but there can't be any shortcuts in handling the most volatile substance that's ever been transported in space.

Driver counts us down for take-off, which is going to be horizontal like a spaceplane until we near the edge of the atmosphere and the Bullet's real power kicks in.

Hart is a quivering mess by now, so much so that I'm starting to wish there was a way we didn't have to take her. At the end of the day, though, she's made her bed. Enduring a flight into space is nothing compared to the stress and danger she's caused us, let alone the untold destruction she came within a solitary second of raining down upon the Balena and the Vita.

"Just keep breathing. We'll be there soon," I tell her.

Because for all Hart has done, I still don't like to see anyone looking so frightened. These words cost me nothing, too.

Our take-off is smooth and easy. This first part really does feel quite like a commercial flight, albeit in a much more streamlined craft. Driver and I are in the cockpit again, with Hart behind us in a seat that was empty on our way down.

Our ascent occurs at a speed much slower than the numbers we'll soon hit when the Bullet really gets going. This gives me time to take in the auroras all over again, which seem denser and more suffocating than ever.

Before we do, though, a voice rings through the speaker in my helmet. For the first time in a while, it's not Sasha or President Williams.

It's Shaun.

"We have a problem," he reports. Those have to be up there with the four words I wanted to hear least of all, but it's nothing compared to what comes next.

"The neocite is too unstable," Simone's panicked voice chimes in. "There is no way we can fire it in a projectile from here. The ignition could destroy the Vita. Even if it didn't, the neocite would not reach the target. My reaction worked but the material is too highly charged. I don't know what we can do!"

While these awful words sink in, Driver urgently taps away on the control screen. "We're going straight to the Vita," she tells me, before I see her give the Bullet that very instruction.

"I think that could be the only hope we have," Shaun says, his tone heavier than I've ever heard it.

I feel like I'm definitely missing something here.

Driver turns to me, seeing the confusion on my face.

"There's no other way, Ray," she gulps. "If they can't fire the neocite at the target as a projectile, like the original plan, I need to deliver the payload myself — in the Bullet."

50

I say nothing. There's just absolutely nothing to say.

"Shaun, get your whole team on this to make it workable," Driver continues, admirably focusing on this incredible death-wish of an idea. "This thing has cannons for breaking up asteroids. If we can't actively *fire* the neocite, I can still release it at massive speed then try to divert the Bullet away from the target at the last second. I don't want to find out what happens if I hit it."

"On it," Shaun says. "We're only going to be able to analyze the target again with our full instrumentation because you guys stopped the signal-jamming. That wasn't wasted effort, even though we still can't fire the neocite from here. At least it means we're able to receive our telescope data from close to the target. We need to try to map the full extent of whatever the target actually *is*. Because like you said, you don't want to know what happens if you crash into this thing... or even through it."

I find myself having to follow the advice I gave Hart a little while ago, to just keep breathing.

This news about the neocite's instability is a massive blow, but there was no time to sink in. As soon as we heard, Driver's mind went right to an incredibly risky solution and Shaun was just as quick to start assisting.

"Yeah, I'm going to need the best intel you can give me about the target," Driver says. "I need to get close enough to make sure the neocite hits with enough force when I release it. That's the absolute priority. Second priority is trying to make sure I can divert before *I* hit the target, too. Work on both, but don't lose sight of the order."

Sasha's voice chimes in next: "Driver, if this is the plan, you're going to have to release the payload manually. You'd really be jettisoning it instead of firing it, to avoid blowing everything up too soon, and we can't program that. I don't see how you can do that *and* immediately divert, because changing course so sharply at that kind of speed isn't something we can program, either. You only have two hands."

I close my eyes as reality sinks in.

Someone has to help Driver. Someone has to go with her.

And with how much is riding on this, it has to be someone who can work with her under the highest pressure imaginable.

It has to be someone who she can rely on and someone who can rely on her.

It has to be someone who has the kind of shared understanding with her that only comes from time spent in the trenches, with their backs against the same wall and only stubborn determination to see them through.

As she turns to face me, I know she doesn't want to say it. She doesn't want to ask for my help and she doesn't want to tell me she needs it. But the fact of the matter is that she doesn't have to.

We both know the score:

It has to be me.

51

"Shaun, get as much ready for us as you possibly can," I say. "Do you have the schematic and everything you need to know about the Bullet?"

"*Us?*" he echoes. "So you're on board with this? And you understand what Driver is talking about doing? You understand the split-second window there's going to be for you to get this done without killing yourselves in the process?"

I understand all of those things, and also Shaun's surprise. I understand why he's probably not going to be the only person with half a mind to talk me out of this, when in theory someone else could go and press the necessary buttons when Driver gives the order.

But most crucially of all, I understand that I have to be her co-pilot precisely because of how small the window is. The timing and coordination we're going to need, even if it wasn't for the immense pressure of the stakes, isn't something two unpracticed partners could pull off.

"I'm all in," I tell him. "And about the info you need...?"

Sasha cuts in: "I'm sending everything over to the Vita right now, Ray. Shaun will have it. Loading this stuff where it has to go isn't a complicated task, it's just the extra care needed due to the nature of the payload that they'll have to think about.

Simone is on hand to make sure everyone follows the right precautions. What the launch team needs to do is analyze the target and come up with an optimal drop-point and trajectory, based on the Bullet's maximum thrust and the objective of giving this the best chance of working while giving you guys a chance of making it back."

"Which is the *second* priority," Driver stresses.

Sasha hesitates. "Understood. I'll do my own calculations on this, too, and I'll bring Santino in. Everything should match up. If it doesn't, the choice of which trajectory plan to follow will be in your hands. You're the ones taking the risk, and you're the ones who have to pull off the manual maneuvers."

As we pass through the atmosphere and accelerate towards the Vita, time seems to stand still. Driver is overseeing the controls with her usual cool head, but I know she has to be feeling the weight of this, too. None of the last-ditch risks we've had to take in the past come close to this.

Even when I had to accelerate towards the ground in my Escape Pod from the Beacon, I wasn't accelerating towards a sealed-up alien gateway.

The future of humanity was in my hands that day, when getting the evidence of Zola's plans to Earth in one piece offered our only hope of doing anything to stop him. I didn't have to survive for the core objective to be met, and that's the same situation we're in now.

The biggest difference is that successfully delivering the payload is a much more challenging task. We have to hit the center of the target fast enough to engage a process we can't even begin to understand, which is a lot more complicated than when I was just trying to control the impact of an inevitable crash-landing.

We get various updates from our teams as our journey continues. By the time the Bullet's frustratingly slow docking process begins at the Vita, I've been awed all over again by the technology within this craft.

The way it can essentially transform between a rocket-like

shape and something more similar to a plane is incredible enough, as was the hovering we did before landing vertically like a helicopter in Colorado. All of that pales in comparison to what happens prior to our docking, though.

With Driver expertly overseeing the whole process, we approach the Vita's dock at a slow speed and literally turn to back up into the bay. It's incredible to witness from our perspective, and I can only imagine how spellbinding it must look from a third-person view.

My academic and professional history in jet fuel developments means I can just about get my head around the amazing speed and acceleration this craft is capable of, but the subtlety of its maneuverability is just mind-blowing. It would be mind-blowing in Earth's atmosphere, but up here I flat-out don't understand what kinds of technologies are at play.

I've marveled in the past at various ZolaCore projects and developments, including the mesmerizing Balena itself. But this Bullet is up there with the absolute best of them. It makes me wonder what other projects are still in the works, continuing on from the requisitioned ZolaCore compound the ERF has taken over in New Zealand as well as on the Balena.

If there was anything that could help in our current situation, I'm sure Driver and Sasha would be all over it. After all, they know a lot more about what goes on inside their home base than I do. As it stands, though, these are definitely questions for another day.

And right now, ensuring any one of us will live to *see* that day depends on the mission we're about to undertake.

The docking process doesn't quite take twenty minutes, but Driver was certainly right to warn me that it would be slow. The reason we've come here to the Vita, rather than docking more quickly at the Balena, is quite simply that the Bullet has to be here so we can load up the neocite without any more handling than necessary.

When we finally finish docking and head in through the inner airlocks, our team is there to greet us.

Driver is still keeping Hart on a short leash, so to speak, marshaling her forward and hand-delivering her to Clarence Major.

Major gives Hart the most damning look I've ever seen. "What in the hell came over you?" he booms.

She doesn't say anything.

"Put her somewhere secure and deal with her later," Driver suggests. "There's nothing else to worry about with the weapons systems — it's totally offline. We'll deal with permanently disarming it once we've dealt with this. She's cooperated with my instructions since we left the bunker. Ray had to take extreme measures to make her stop the weapons launch, but she eventually did. Don't be any harsher than you have to."

I'm glad to hear Driver say that, after she's been something of the 'bad cop' in our dealings with Hart. I know Major isn't one for cruelty or brutality, anyway, and mercy is a virtue when you know a former obstacle no longer poses a threat.

Obstacle is the word I'd use to describe Hart, rather than enemy or even adversary. Her actions were so reckless and extreme that I don't think I'll ever be able to see her as an ally and even a friend like I now see Major after our own prior disagreements, but I do hope we'll see eye-to-eye again once this huge problem of the Leak is behind us.

I'm thinking in terms of *once* that happens rather than *if* it does, if only because I have to.

If I can't convince myself we're going to succeed, we won't. I'm going to have to be hyper focused and time my actions perfectly, which makes a positive frame of mind essential. So while I've never been one for flowery thinking, in this case I really *do* have to believe it before I can achieve it.

While Major assumes responsibility for dealing with Hart, Simone steps towards us.

"I am so sorry for this, Ray," she says. "I synthesized a material even closer in composition to the alien instructions than I thought I would be able to. That part worked well. It has just become more and more unstable since the initial reaction completed. The simulations show what would happen if we try to propel it at the target from here, and the result is decisive. The neocite is still increasing in instability, so if we were to re-run the calculations now they would show an ever higher probability of a catastrophic detonation. If the BioZol-infused theocite you initially developed was a tiny firecracker, this neocite is a Roman candle."

A matchstick to a flamethrower might be another suitable metaphor, but Simone's definitely works.

"The future applications for propulsion and energy generation could be world-changing if we can harness this material properly," she goes on. "But right now, we have to get rid of it. Even if the mission to hit the target wasn't so urgent, this material cannot stay here for long. Despite every precaution, it is no longer under control. I did this because you all asked me to. I made my reservations known, but I didn't expect anything like this. We have to get moving as soon as possible. We have to get rid of it."

I widen my eyes in surprise. I had digested the fact that the neocite was dangerously unstable, but Simone — who knows it better than anyone — has dialed that up by a factor of ten. Not only can't we safely launch it from here, she doesn't even think we can safely *keep* it here for a moment longer than we have to.

"Get it loaded," I tell her, gesturing with my hand for Shaun to join her and do what has to be done. "Be as careful as you have to, but we're ready when you are. Right, Shaun? The trajectory plans and target analysis are all in place?"

"They are," he confirms. "Everything aligns almost exactly. The flight plans are basically identical. Sasha wants you to release the payload a few seconds before I do. Santino wants you to release it around half a second *later* than I do. The differences are small, but at the speed you'll be traveling they can make a difference."

"We'll go with Santino's," Driver decides. She then looks at me and raises her eyebrows. "Agreed? We need to be sure it gets there. Priority number one."

I exhale slowly and force a nod. She's right. Like it or lump it, there is no room for erring on the side of caution when so much is at stake.

It's actually quite encouraging that our three brightest minds have come up with near-identical flight plans and payload release schedules. Half a second is approaching the realm of human reaction time, anyway, so the menial nature of the release means I might not be able to be quite so exact.

"How did the final target analysis go?" Driver asks, one more question before Shaun sets off to oversee the all-important loading of our neocite onto the Bullet.

"Perspective is everything," he replies. "We are able to 'see' the target using certain telescopic techniques. There is no gravitational pull to speak of and it's invisible to the naked eye. What we're seeing is a kind of shimmer, and within a far smaller radius than I expected. That increases your survival chances, since a smaller field is one you're less likely to collide with. But it also increases the challenge of delivering the payload."

"And you have visualizations for me?" she asks. "You'll be able to help me know what I'm aiming for?"

Shaun nods quickly. "Absolutely. We can lock on the target from here as though you are going to fire the cannon. You'll see crosshairs on what looks like nothing, and you'll just have to trust our path and trajectory. Ray will release the load at the last viable moment and as soon as he does, you will pitch as sharply as you possibly can. It might be rough, but you can't hold back."

"Driver, come to my office and you can connect directly with Sasha and Santino," Major suggests. "They'll share the visuals while Shaun is working on the loading. All said, we should be set for departure in… what would you say, Shaun? Ten minutes?"

"Give us fifteen to move it more carefully," Simone requests.

Major accepts the compromise.

Meanwhile, I'm busy being stunned at the timescale. I knew it would be fast, but *wow*.

Fifteen minutes.

"Major," I say, as everyone starts to set off to do their specific tasks. "We're past the point of secrecy, right? I don't have to worry about security of private communication?"

"Call them, Ray," he replies.

I lift my phone from my pocket and navigate to Eva's number.

I don't know what the hell I'm going to tell them about what I'm about to do, but I can't miss what could be the last chance to tell them I love them.

Eva picks up immediately.

"Ray, thank God!" she says, sobbing in the sheer relief at seeing me. "I didn't know what you and Driver were doing. I was worried you were doing something crazy."

Uneasy, I bite the inside of my lip. "Yeah. About that..."

52

When I tell Eva what I'm about to do, her reaction is in line with what I expected.

We've known each other long enough, and endured enough challenges, to know how this goes.

She knows I wouldn't be doing this if it wasn't absolutely necessary, but that doesn't dull the natural fear and emotion she feels about the risk.

I, on the other hand, know that the fact Eva doesn't beg me not to do it doesn't say anything about how much she cares. She just knows that would do no one any good when I *have* to do it, so we skip that dance altogether.

The questions she has are mainly specific and operational, like how big our time window of opportunity is and how Driver feels about the likelihood of success.

I dodge the latter question but see no sense in overly sugar-coating the former. All I say is that it's going to be as tough as what we did on the seabed and probably even tougher than what I did on the way down from the Beacon.

"But I made it each time," I tell her. "And we're going to make it again."

Before she can reply to that, the kids have heard her voice in the kitchen and made their way in. It's Lorien's kitchen, since they're all still sheltering there after the home invasion scare that already seems like a lifetime ago.

"I'm glad you guys are all okay," I say, referencing that for the first time. Just like Eva didn't mention, that moment has already been overtaken in our minds by what has to happen next. "And Laika... nice job, buddy! You really stepped up. Good boy."

"Squawk!" he replies, tipping his head back in that giddy way he sometimes does. "Laika happy when Laika can help, Ray Ray."

Lorien and Harvey appear in the shot, too, and I waste no time in thanking them for stepping up. After a few pleasantries, Eva very politely asks them if we can have a few minutes alone. They oblige, totally understanding, and leave my family at the table.

"How are you guys doing?" I ask the kids, who I haven't been able to talk to in way too long.

"I want to go home," Scarlet says. "I like it here okay but I want to go home."

Eva pulls her tightly and whispers that they'll be home soon, once the window is fixed. I know there will be a little more to it than that, but it shouldn't be too long until it's safe. Once my job up here is done and people see that it was a good idea after all, the fear and anger will subside.

Joe, standing to Eva's right, looks the most troubled of them all. "I don't know about these aliens, Dad," he says.

It only really hits me now that in all the time since we decoded the signal, which wasn't really that long ago, I haven't had a chance to talk to Joe. He lives and breathes sci-fi, and especially everything to do with space. Like Eva mentioned during our last call, he really has read and watched pretty much every alien story out there.

Joe's views on what contact might look like are based on the same overwhelmingly negative sources that the AI was trained on. It's little wonder he's reached a similarly fearful position.

"They're on our side," I insist. "They've reached out in our time of need, kiddo. We have to reach back and believe them. Driver is about to fly me out towards the target and we're going to activate it like they asked us to. After that, we'll be able to talk to them some more without a long radio delay. They'll be able to help us — and it should be right away. All of this should be over soon. The sky will clear up, Scarlet's hearing will stop getting worse, and Earth will have a future. That's why we have to do this."

"Is what you're doing safe?" he asks, point blank.

"There's never been a single accident with this kind of spacecraft," I reply.

He raises his eyebrows, too smart to fall for that. "Across how many flights?"

"Two," I say, downplaying the importance of that. "But they were both today and it felt really safe. You know Driver is the best pilot I could have. All our other friends have worked on this, too. Shaun, Sasha, Senior Coordinator Major. We're all carrying out this mission together, I'm just the guy they're counting on to press the right button at the right time."

"Mom said you got a new hand," he says, seemingly taking a sudden conversational detour. "Make sure you use the real one for the button, okay? Don't risk anything going wrong with the brain sensors that make your new one work."

I smile at his sharpness. It's the same thought I had down in the bunker, and I'm definitely going to stick to this logic in the Bullet.

"A new hand?" Scarlet asks in shock, apparently having been spared the goriest details of what happened to me on the Vita.

I raise both of my hands to the screen. "Can you tell which one isn't real?"

Scarlet leans forward and squints at the screen. "That one," she points, picking correctly. "The nails are too neat."

I can't help but laugh at that, which brings a welcome moment of levity when it's most needed.

I've come into an empty room for this call, and three sudden knocks on the door are followed by Driver's familiar voice. "All good?" she calls.

Eva's eyebrows signal for me to invite her inside. When you've been together as long as we have, interpreting this kind of cue becomes second nature.

Driver steps in. "We need to run over some final details," she says, before realizing I'm still on the call. At that point she comes over and says hi, answering a few of Joe's rapid questions about the Bullet. She doesn't say too much.

"I'll keep your dad safe so he can do his thing to keep everyone *else* safe," she promises. Although she's addressing the kids, I know she's mainly talking to Eva. "We've never walked into a problem we can't solve, and I don't plan to start today."

With time obviously tight, I say my goodbyes. I take a little longer than usual, telling them all that I love them and will do everything humanly possible to be back with them as soon as I can. All going well, that could be a matter of hours.

They wave goodbye, with Laika sticking his head forward to get the last words in:

"Ray Ray and Luna okay," he says. "Laika no worry."

Taking as much faith as I can from the purest soul I know, I end the call with the little guy's words still echoing.

"The plan is all set," Driver tells me. "They're loading up the neocite now. There's going to be a countdown and you're going to hit the button I show you when it reaches zero. It's as simple and as complicated as that, Ray. Timing is everything. I'll do my part as best I can, and you'll do yours. All we can do is give this our best."

I force out a breath and slowly suck it back in to gather my composure.

"Are you ready?" I ask.

Driver points to the door with exaggerated impatience. "Who are you talking to, Barclay?" she says, returning to that old tone of playful mock offense. "I was born ready."

If things end as well as they did after she said the same thing at the threshold of the Colorado bunker, I don't even care if the road to success has a few final unexpected bumps like it did down there.

All that counts is reaching the final bell. We've stayed in the fight this long, and the steel in Driver's eyes tells me we've got one more big round in us.

I step through the door with the heaviest weight I've ever known bearing down on my shoulders, but a determination and belief in my heart that we can do this.

Whatever it takes, we can *do* this.

53

On our way to the launch bay, the few people aboard the ERF Vita gather to see us off. There is nowhere near the number who formed our guard of honor on the Balena, with our core partners of Major and Shaun joined only by the skeleton crew who stayed here after the security breach and the few who came with Shaun.

The doctor who helped me through the aftermath is here, wishing me the best. She makes an ironic comment about being glad that I've been taking it easy, but warmly embraces me to make her real feelings clear.

Elana Hart stands next to Clarence Major, who has evidently decided that she doesn't have to be detained like a dangerous criminal. He gives me a firm pat on the back, thanking me for taking one more huge risk, and even Hart chimes in with a good luck.

We reach the Bullet, climb inside, and suit up. The feeling is very different to the first or second times we took off in this thing, with the absolute finality of this mission hanging in the air like a thunder cloud.

"Are you with me, Shaun?" Driver asks, speaking now with her helmet fully engaged.

He responds loud and clear, in my ears as well as hers.

"I want a visual lock as soon as the outer hatch opens," she says. "I'll have the timing and the target speed in my lenses when we launch, thanks to Sasha, and Ray will have his countdown, too. I know we're target-locking until the final stage, but I need that visual. I need to be focused like a hawk on that spot all the way."

Before any reply comes, the docking bay's outer hatch opens and the ocean of space appears before us. We're diving in deeper and faster than ever, with no life rafts if anything goes wrong. If anything goes wrong, *everything* goes wrong... but we can't afford to think like that.

I force the thought out of my mind.

We've got this.

Driver knows her role, I know mine, Shaun has overseen the careful loading of the neocite, and Sasha is ready to back us up by putting helpful information in our lens-augmented vision.

The crucial timers and speed data will also be on the control panel's screen, but it's helpful to have it in the corner of our vision. Establishing a direct line of sight to the target is hugely important for both of us, and being able to see the data without having to look down at the screen will give us a major advantage.

Together, we've got this.

"Everything starts when you move," Shaun says. "Whenever you're ready."

Instantly, Driver engages the Bullet and shoots us out of the bay.

The volatile neocite has been loaded in the right place by the right people, so all we can do is trust them. Everything is as insulated as it can be. What counts is that Driver can't go easy on the speed, since we're relying on jettisoning the neocite when we're going full-throttle.

She's not being reckless, she's doing what has to be done.

And for the way we're moving, *shooting* is truly the only

appropriate word. I should have expected it, but the sudden acceleration is still a lot to handle.

"Keep building," Sasha's voice implores. "Max out the thrust as soon as you can."

I can see that Driver is doing just that. Sasha and Shaun are both good at only speaking when they have to, so having their dual input from the Balena and the Vita isn't going to create a 'too many cooks' situation.

Once we reach the closest possible point to the target without guaranteeing that we'll smash into it — or *through* it, which is a prospect I can't even get my head around — I'm going to press the button to jettison our incredibly potent neocite payload.

A timed detonation will then occur at the base of the shell that's containing it, precisely three seconds later. We have to be clear of that explosion as well as clear of the target, which is where Driver's breakneck banking is going to come in.

With how powerful our horizontal launch from the Vita was, my body isn't looking forward to the sensations that will bring.

We continue on, incessantly gaining and gaining and gaining speed. The target is now visible on the window in front of the cockpit, marked out by a crosshairs-like symbol just as Shaun promised.

"I'm maxing out now," Driver relays. I look at our speed and see that she really is. We're rapidly approaching the target now and she's going to hold at this precise speed, which allows our teams and the Bullet's computers to accurately establish the countdown to our destination.

When that countdown appears, everything suddenly feels even realer.

"You've got this, Ray," Driver tells me, as though she doesn't have enough to worry about on her own side of things. "You know you do."

I stretch the fingers of my left hand, preparing for the all-important moment.

Fear tries its best to take over, but I search deep within myself and push it aside.

I push it aside, because fear leads to failure. Fear has already led to the pointless death of a good man, to attempted violence against my family, to an abortive mutiny on the Balena, to a near-miss with devastation in the Colorado bunker.

Fear has gotten us nowhere, and I'm not letting it in.

The speed we're moving at is almost incomprehensible, as is the distance we've covered already. The countdown is now at less than a minute, giving me very little time to psych myself up.

"Don't go too soon," Driver states, sounding incredibly calm as she gets ready for a much more complex series of actions than me. "We didn't come here to die, Ray, but we definitely didn't come here to fail."

I take a deep breath and ponder her words.

She's right. The implication is clear: success is activating the gate. Personal survival, as desirable as it is, doesn't factor into that consideration.

"We've got this," I tell her. "You trust me, I'll trust you. We've got this."

She nods intently — intensely — without looking away from the target. With ten seconds on the countdown, she shifts us out of our automatic path and into manual steering.

The visual of the target disappears.

This doesn't make all that much difference since the crosshairs weren't growing in size and the actual target was totally invisible to our eyes, but it still marks a crucial moment in our mission.

I move my hand over the button. The team has assured there is absolutely no lag in the countdown and will be none after my command. Just like Driver and I trust each other, I have to trust them.

During the last few seconds, I enter a level of focus I've

never known. I feel like I can see every tenth of a second distinctly pass, and I don't panic by hitting the button too soon.

I watch one second turn to none.

A few rapid heartbeats later, I firmly press the button and almost instantly recoil as Driver banks us violently to our left as soon as the payload is out.

I glance at the time again and see that the countdown stopped at nine one-hundredths of a second. Less than *one tenth*.

"Perfect!" Driver yells, fighting the thrust and forces at play as she tightly grips the controls.

She's done a pretty damn good job herself. After all, we're still alive.

I look out of the window on my side, back towards our alien target, and feel my jaw slacken as I see an incredible sparkling effect.

"It hit!" I report. "Driver, the neocite hit! It's doing something to the target. It's like it's spreading out. Almost like the radial explosions we did in the—"

"Oh shit," she cuts me off. "Ray… we're in trouble."

54

I look at the screen and see nothing. I look outside and see nothing of obvious concern.

I look *everywhere,* all at once, and I see no sign of the trouble Driver so firmly insisted we're in.

"What's going on?" I ask.

"It was too sharp," she replies, utter panic in her voice. "The jerk was too much. That bank at that speed… the Bullet couldn't take. Physically, we couldn't take it. Comms are dead and there's a crack in our fuel tank. It's going to leak. It's not neocite but it's more than enough to blow this thing up a thousand times over. There's no way we can make it even halfway back. Once a single drop gets out, we're gone."

"We— we hit the target," I stammer in reply. With such a definite end so imminently in sight, my mind is trying to soothe itself with that, at least.

We hit our first priority.

Survival was always second.

Driver turns to me, letting go of the controls. "I tried," she says. "And this is going to suck more than anything we've ever done, but I have to try one more thing. Brace yourself."

"For what?!" I croak.

Reaching under her seat, Driver smashes a button I didn't know was there.

"We have to bail," she says.

Before I can even ask the obvious question — *to where?* — I feel the whiplash of a sudden and violent movement.

My vision goes black.

I don't know what's going on, but it feels like the end.

55

As my eyes reopen after the violent shock of our sudden ejection from the Bullet, my vision returns very quickly. My neck positively *aches*, but I'm alive.

I immediately look to my side, making sure Driver is, too.

She is, thank God, but the good news ends there.

We've ejected in some kind of spherical pod, no bigger than the Escape Pod I used to get home from the Beacon.

Only this time, there's nowhere for us to go.

"The controls are fried. We can't go anywhere," Driver moans, punching the panel in front of us. It's as though the inner core of the Bullet has been scooped up and thrown into space.

The shape doesn't feel a million miles away from the emergency surfacing module we had to use in the ocean, when our multi-terrain Nautilus was hit by an explosion. The big difference was that *it* quickly took us from the ocean to the surface, where we weren't exactly comfortable during the journey to shore but were at least surrounded by sunlight and abundant oxygen.

Up here, there are no such luxuries.

We have our chairs, the useless controls, and a totally unknowable amount of life support. These suits are good for around six hours, but we're totally dependent on a team reaching us and being able to intercept us within that time.

"I had to, Ray," she goes on, sheepishly holding the back of her head. It seems like she's feeling the same kind of whiplash effect I am. "I thought it was going to blow at any second."

I hear her through my helmet, since our suit-to-suit communication is still live.

"We hit the target," I say, my mind still stubbornly fixating on that. "Look."

I point Driver to it and see that the sparkling effect is getting more intense.

But somewhere between our pod and that incredible sight, a huge blast captures my attention as the remaining pressurized areas of the Bullet burst into a million pieces.

"Fuel leak?" I ask.

"Has to be," Driver says. "You did your part, Ray," she goes on, gesturing to the target. "And hey, at least we know we're no more dead than we would have been if I didn't hit eject."

Suddenly, a crackling sound fills my ears. I see Driver recoil in reaction to it, too, because it's uncomfortably loud.

At the same moment, a yellow light begins blinking on the control console.

"Are you with us?!" Sasha asks, almost pleading. Her voice sounds positively grief-stricken. "Please. Tell me you got out."

"We're here!" Driver and I blurt out in perfect unison.

"I ejected before it blew," she goes on. "Sasha, we're in the pod and I don't have any controls. Someone has to intercept us and bring us in, as soon as they can possibly get here."

There's no reply for several seconds.

"On it," Sasha eventually says. "We don't have a craft as fast as the Bullet, but a pilot will be there long before your suits are depleted. They're leaving right now."

Driver's hand reaches out and slaps my knee in victory.

"Sasha, can you guys see the target sparkling from there?" I ask.

"Oh, we can see it," she replies in a much happier tone. "You guys really did it."

"We *all* did it," Driver says.

"Hell yeah we did," I concur, because a truer word has never been spoken.

56

Over the course of a few truly mesmerizing minutes, Driver and I watch at close range as the sparkling target transforms into an impossibly large gateway.

It looks every inch like something from a sci-fi movie, hanging in space in a way that defies all logic.

From the densely sparkling center, which we targeted so effectively, the rippling effect has spread out in a concentric manner to create a colossal circular outline. I'm at a total loss for words to describe what I'm looking at.

If this truly is a wormhole, we've just unlocked the door at our side of it. We've removed the manhole cover, to return to the alien analogy from their message, and we can only hope help is on the way.

The most likely source of help is going to be another message.

As the remarkable sight before us stabilizes, the full extent of the gateway becomes apparent. And just a few seconds later, Sasha reports that our team on the Balena is ready to direct our own SOS signal through the new portal.

We've done what we set out to do. We've successfully followed every instruction the aliens gave us.

In short, we've held up our end of the bargain.

I know the general gist of the message Harriet and the others have put together.

Chester, Santino, Sasha, Shaun and even President Williams have all seen the details. Without doubt, their collective approval is good enough for me. This has been a team effort, and Harriet knows SETI better than any of us.

With Chester's eye for ensuring messages are received as they're intended to be, I have total faith they've sent something pretty damn optimal.

The core of what we need to communicate is that we need urgent help with the Leak. We need to tell the aliens that the dam they warned us about in their four-year-old signal now looks ready to burst, in what we believe could be a matter of days. Given the lengths they went to warn us of it in the first place, I don't think it's crazy to believe they'll reply swiftly.

I don't think that's crazy at all.

If this portal we've just opened acts like we think it will, the only delay will be the time it takes them to decode our message and reply in kind.

With help from the PhilosophAI technology, harnessing its objective strengths, our message is being sent in various forms. One is replicating as closely as possible the nature of the signal that came our way, to minimize any difficulties the aliens might have in understanding it.

We're leaving no stone unturned.

We're leaving nothing to chance.

And this time, if and when they reply, we'll know how to decode their message right away.

The prospect of direct and ongoing two-way contact is hugely exciting, but the urgency of our predicament isn't leaving much mental space to think about that.

We just need help. *Fast.*

Speaking of needing help, Driver and I continue to float in space with no sign of an incoming craft for what quickly starts to feel like way too long.

It's only when she reminds me how fast the Bullet was actually traveling that this makes sense. Sasha chimes in with an estimate of when we can expect a rendezvous, and it's going to be a mercifully short wait.

Everything is relative, of course. Needless to say, I'm not exactly comfortable in here. But after how close we came to blowing up inside the Bullet, I'm just happy to be alive.

Sasha promises to pass on a message to Eva that I'm okay and will soon be on the way back to the team. She also tells us, fairly quickly, that our team's SOS message to the aliens has been sent.

"The ball is in their court now," she says. And really, that's all there is to it.

We're going to continue analyzing the new gateway and the ever-intensifying Leak. As we speak, I know great minds on the Balena are working around the clock in a quest for any kind of workable contingency plans to mitigate the Leak's effects.

Not a single promising lead has arisen, though.

Worst still, the kinds of likely timescales I've heard bandied about are in the same futile range as the weeks and months Elana Hart was talking about in Colorado.

Eventually, our rescue crew arrives. They're in a fairly large spacecraft dispatched from the Balena, which consumes our tiny pod like a whale swallowing a football. It's so easy to forget how enormous the Balena is, but being reminded that something like this craft was nesting inside it goes a long way to making the point.

Driver and I are quickly able to get out of the pod and stretch our legs. We thank our rescuers, but they insist the real thanks are all due in the other direction.

A drink of water goes a long way, too. I settle in for the rest of our return journey feeling a restrained kind of accomplishment.

In objective terms, a cynic could argue that we're no safer

than we were a few hours ago. But we *are* further forward, and we *have* achieved a massive goal.

We've done what the aliens suggested. Now, I just hope they're paying attention.

57

We return to the Balena, which is the only destination large enough for this craft to dock.

It's also where most of our friends are, including the most important few right now: those actively looking and listening for a reply to our SOS call.

Driver and I are treated like returning heroes as soon as we step into the docking bay. I would never pretend it's not nice to feel appreciated for stepping up to take a massive risk, but neither of us did it for the thanks.

We did it because it had to be done, and our history of teamwork under pressure made me the perfect companion for Driver, our best and most reliable pilot by a country mile.

President Williams is most effusive in his praise for how we handled things.

Young Santino also offers me particular congratulations for hitting the button so close to the end of the countdown. He was the one who suggested waiting an extra half-second to make sure we didn't go too soon, and he seems proud and appreciative that I heeded his advice.

Even from here, the alien gateway looks truly incredible. As much as anything else, I can't believe how big it still looks. The team here assures me that it hasn't grown since the initial outwards expansion. Either way, it's one hell of sight.

The gateway really does defy description as well as belief, and I feel lucky to have seen it come into being at such close range.

I notice that I'm finding myself automatically thinking of it as a gateway. *Portal* could be just as accurate, as could *wormhole*.

The truth is that we don't know what it is, much less how it works. Everyone has their own take on the specifics.

What we all share is a common hope that help will soon come through it. We're hoping that comes in the form of further workable instructions, at the very least, but a few of us aren't giving up on the idea that the assistance could be more direct than that.

Inevitably, the Leak's acceleration is still a huge cause for concern. It actually feels more pressing now than it did a few hours ago, when I had a specific all-consuming goal to occupy my mind.

One of the first things I do when I get back on the Balena is find a quiet spot to call Eva.

She's awake, but the kids aren't. After an understandable outpouring of emotion — both ways — she tells me that the gateway is clearly visible from Earth.

From her perspective, it looks the same size as the Moon on an average night. She doesn't see any of the bizarre sparkling effect that's visible up here, and she says it looks like it's reflecting light.

It's all over the news, apparently. Ironically, Eva reports that the worst of the fear that consumed public discourse has now been replaced by wonder.

Nothing bad happened as soon as the gateway appeared, so the theory that a hostile and devious alien race were waiting for their first opportunity to strike has already fallen by the wayside.

I also learn from Eva that the team here, led by Chester,

have already shared with the media some footage of what Driver and I actually did. It's been received as an act of selfless heroism that has changed the way people were thinking of us. There's no more talk of dictatorial and reckless action. Now, it's all about our familiar duo taking another risk to try and save the world.

Again, we certainly didn't do this for the thanks. But there is a tangible benefit to people reacting like this, and that benefit is that future developments won't be subject to the same level of automatically negative assumptions as the initial alien message was.

We've changed the agenda through direct action, which has once again proven to be the only surefire way forward.

Laika is asleep during this call, too, and I can't wait to hear what the little guy makes of the gateway. The same is true of Joe. I'm hoping wonder will take over from fear in *his* mind, too.

I don't know how likely it is that the gateway will be visible during daylight on Earth, especially with the auroras choking the sky like they are. Beyond that, though, I'm hoping there's even more good news by the time Joe wakes up.

Harriet bursts into the room just as I'm getting ready to end my call and let Eva get to bed. She's briefly apologetic, but clearly itching to tell me something.

Given that *she's* the one bursting in, my heart dares to jump to a best-case scenario.

"A reply?" I ask.

"Already," she beams. "The signal is in the same format as last time, just with much less data. We're decoding it right now. It should take minutes now that we know what we're doing. Minutes at most."

I smile broadly. "You can hang on for *minutes at most,* right?" I ask Eva before getting ready to run to the computers.

She grins right back. "Oh, I wouldn't miss it..."

58

When we received the first alien signal, I could have had a million guesses at what the message contained and I never would have come close.

The same could be true here, but that doesn't mean my mind isn't trying.

Harriet leads me quickly to Sasha's office. Chester, Santino and Williams are already there, and we alert Driver on our way.

Everyone looks excited as they gaze up at us and then back to the screen.

I just wish Phil was still around to be part of this. His AI did the legwork of unlocking the decoding process, and that's what's making it so much faster this time. By the time I'm standing behind Sasha, she tells me it should be less than two minutes until everything is ready and the images are on her screen.

"It's definitely images again?" Driver asks.

"Looks like it, based on the structure," Sasha replies. "And that *is* the established common 'language' we've developed. I think they'll have stuck to the same way of laying things out, with the collages and the numbers. We did that in our SOS, to show that we understood when *they* did."

Everything sounds good and refreshingly straightforward.

I hold my phone towards the screen and flip to the back camera so Eva can see that rather than my face.

The short wait is one of feverish anticipation. It's long enough for a few negative thoughts to creep in, but I'm able to push them aside quite successfully.

The main one is that the aliens could be coming back with a message to say our Leak is already too far gone, and apologizing that we didn't get their warning earlier.

Another is that their new message will make no reference to ours, or that it might even be a partial repeat of the one we've already decoded and acted upon.

"One image," Sasha suddenly says, sounding surprised and — understandably — somewhat disappointed. "It'll surely be four pictures in one collage, but still. *One*?"

"Maybe it's something easy," Driver suggests, ever the optimist. "Last time they had to establish some concepts and then give us some pretty complicated instructions. This could be one simple thing. I think one image is *better* than if there had been another six or seven."

On the screen, I see what Sasha is relaying. Sure enough, the system tells us that it has detected and decoded one image.

With no hesitation or countdown, Sasha clicks Proceed.

Immediately, a four-panel collage fills the screen.

It's just too bad that the good news ends there.

"We didn't send that," Harriet immediately says, pointing to one of the images.

"They can see our broadcasts," Sasha replies, her voice already a hollow shell of itself. "Especially now, they're getting them right away."

My eyes don't move between the four images.

No.

They're locked on the third.

Although I flipped my phone to the back camera so Eva would see the message rather than me, that hasn't exactly worked out.

Because she *can* see me. In the third panel, standing next to Driver, she *can* see me.

"What the hell is going on?" Driver shrieks. "Ray, what is this?"

I take in every detail of the brain-melting third image. It's a group photo showing me and Driver with a team of workers before the Vita's initial relaunch from Colorado. Each of the faces in the picture, other than ours, are covered with black X-marks.

Scored out.

Unimportant.

Not wanted.

Belatedly, my eyes explore the other three images. Their meanings aren't as painfully obvious, but it doesn't take a genius to see what the aliens are telling us.

First there's a timescale, using the sun and moon as reference points. Terrifyingly, it's measured in days.

Next, there's the all-too-familiar image of human corpses that the aliens have previously used to signify mass death. Two-way arrows link the first two images to make the point clear: this will happen, very soon, unless the instructions below are followed.

And so I move to the instructions below.

Lastly, after the picture of us, comes the fourth image.

Like a few of the images they used to signify relatively complex ideas last time, today's fourth is a still from a movie. It shows a spacecraft flying through a portal that's passably similar to the one we just activated.

Minutes ago, we already knew that the urgency of our situation is so great that we have to do whatever it takes to stop the Leak.

We knew that believing these aliens and acting on their instructions would be our only chance, just like it was with the first message.

But a few minutes ago, *no one* expected this.

My stomach falls as the message sinks in.

"They want you two, and you two only, to cross the gateway," Santino says, as straightforward as he is intelligent. "For some reason, they're saying it's the only way."

I look down to my phone and flip the screen back to the front-facing camera. I see tears welling in Eva's eyes and feel them in my own.

Because there's no way around the truth. There's no way around the fact that Santino is right.

I still can't answer Driver's question of what the hell is going on, but the warning and the instruction could hardly be clearer.

We have to cross the gate.

To give *our* world any chance of surviving the next few days, we have to journey to *theirs*.

AUTHOR'S NOTES

Thank you for reading ***Reason To Fear***!

Ray's story continues in ***The Last Horizon,*** which is is available to order now.

To stay up to date with news on my future books, as well as promotions and other news, please visit my website:

www.craigafalconer.com

— *Craig A. Falconer,*
Scotland, July 2023

BOOKS BY CRAIG A. FALCONER

The Earthburst Saga

Last Man Standing

Into The Fire

Operation Starshot

The Anomaly

Reason To Fear

The Last Horizon

Not Alone

Not Alone: Second Contact

Not Alone: The Final Call

Not Alone: Fractured Union

Not Alone: Leap of Destiny

Not Alone: Revelations

Not Alone: The Awakening

Not Alone: Hidden Wonder

Not Alone: Endgame

Not Alone: Origins

Terradox

The Fall of Terradox

Terradox Reborn

Terradox Beyond

Cyber Seed

Sycamore

Sycamore 2

Sycamore X

Sycamore XL

Sci-Fi Sizzlers

Wanderlust

Pamela 2.0

Sunset Stays

Pumpkin Splice

Happy, Inc.

When Santa Slays

Arise With Us

Replica

Whence They Came

A Scent Of Man

Megaton Murphy

Yester Year

Too Good To Be True

Bound For Glory

Funscreen

Seedling

Empty Nesters

For more, visit **www.craigafalconer.com**